GONE

RUBY SPEECHLEY

Boldwood

First published in Great Britain in 2023 by Boldwood Books Ltd.

Copyright © Ruby Speechley, 2023

Cover Design by 12 Orchards Ltd

Cover Photography: Shutterstock

Every effort has been made to obtain the necessary permissions with reference to copyright material, both illustrative and quoted. We apologise for any omissions in this respect and will be pleased to make the appropriate acknowledgements in any future edition.

A CIP catalogue record for this book is available from the British Library.

Paperback ISBN 978-1-83751-380-2

Large Print ISBN 978-1-83751-376-5

Hardback ISBN 978-1-83751-375-8

Ebook ISBN 978-1-83751-373-4

Kindle ISBN 978-1-83751-374-1

Audio CD ISBN 978-1-83751-381-9

MP3 CD ISBN 978-1-83751-378-9

Digital audio download ISBN 978-1-83751-372-7

Boldwood Books Ltd
23 Bowerdean Street
London SW6 3TN
www.boldwoodbooks.com

For my dearest son Edward, with all my love.

PROLOGUE

His breath is a plume of white as he stumbles into the cold tunnel of darkness ahead of him, the tangle of spiky branches thick with leaves slowing him down. He checks over his shoulder; he can't see them, but he can hear them getting closer. His chest and throat are burning with exertion; the mossy earth is damp beneath his bare feet. He must reach the other side, where warm lights beckon him.

An arm reaches around his middle and bundles him to the ground. He falls on his face and lets out a pitiful groan. There's a taste of blood on his lips, his nose thick and wet and throbbing. The smell of damp mud and torn grass are the last thing he remembers.

When his eyes flutter open, he's lying on his back, on something as hard and cold as steel. He can't move, not even a finger. There's a stark white wall in front of him, grey ceiling tiles and right above him, a brown liquid stain. He blinks. *Am I dead, or dreaming?* A roaring pain tears down his side. His dry lips peel open but the scream in his throat is silenced by a hand pressing over his mouth. There is no face to this person, no words, only the milky skin of an arm, bleached by the bright light.

A woozy feeling washes over him, his vision blurs and his eyes fall shut.

1

DAY ONE

Rachel Gulliver wakes up on Monday morning with the headache she went to bed with. She thought she might sleep it off, but she's barely slept at all after yet another row with Shay. Somewhere under all that bravado and swearing is her sweet boy, her firstborn. She's absolutely certain of it.

She sits on her bed wrapped in a towel and checks her watch on the bedside table: 6.33 a.m. She thinks back to Friday night when Shay had joined their family movie night for the first time in ages. They'd watched *Beetlejuice* and devoured pizza followed by popcorn. She'd loved watching him laugh and be part of the family again; it seemed so rare these days.

David sits up in bed and kisses her cheek. She smiles at him, pleased at the occasional fizz of excitement at having a man in her life again. He gets up and goes straight into the en suite, shutting the door with a soft click. She dries herself, pulls on underwear and a pair of black tights. She takes one of her favourite wrap dresses she picked out the night before. She has several routines David finds amusing, such as checking all the doors are locked at night, making sure all the lights are off and the children are asleep in their beds before she can settle.

She adds a few soft curls to her blow-dried hair which emphasise the scattering of highlights. Opening the jewellery cabinet on the wall, she stands staring at the array of necklaces and bracelets she's accumulated over the years. There's no denying that Shay's behaviour has nosedived since David moved in five months ago, but the truth is, it had already started to change before that. It's too easy to blame it on her new relationship, her grasp at happiness. Mick blames it on her, of course he does. He blames everything on her to make himself feel better for being such a shit dad.

She sometimes secretly regrets asking David to move in so quickly. They'd had the perfect set up sharing their time in each other's houses, his Victorian town house only a few minutes' drive away in the centre of Pinner and her 1930s detached in Eastcote village. They'd each had their own space, their own rules. They'd been used to being on their own. In normal circumstances she would have waited, no doubt about it. Perhaps they would never have made that leap at all in the natural run of things. She certainly wouldn't have wanted to move herself or her boys out of their family home and she guesses David had been quite happy living alone too, but the fire that gutted the ground floor of his house changed everything.

Rachel picks out a tiny star necklace and peers closely in the mirror to fasten it. She slips on her watch and checks the time: 6.42 a.m. David has almost finished in the shower. Shay and Josh need to wash before school.

She arranges the pendant then stands back. Not looking too shabby for forty-two. Three clients today: two regular, one new. She prides herself on looking professional at all times, despite the unpredictable dramas two growing boys often bring.

Josh is fast asleep when she walks into his room. She draws

back the Minecraft curtains and calls his name. He yawns and stretches his arms out, sitting up like a cartoon zombie.

'Time to get up,' she says in her brightest morning voice.

'Do I have to?' He's croakier than usual. She hopes it isn't the beginning of a cold. Mondays are the always the hardest and they're only a few weeks into the new school year.

She trudges downstairs to put the filter coffee on and switch on her mobile. Various notifications pop up. She scans through but can't spot anything urgent. There's a light tap, tapping on the front door.

'Hello Raymond; how are you?' she says to her neighbour from across the road who is standing on her doorstep beaming at her. He's always smart in an ironed shirt and trousers. Today he's added a moss green cardigan and moccasin slippers.

'Good morning, Rachel. I got your kind note about my mending. Hope I'm not too early.' He waves the square of notepaper she posted through his door. 'I can't believe you've finished it already.'

'Not at all. They were only tiny fixes.' She reaches down to the cloth bag, full of neatly folded clothes. Holes in elbows, frayed hems, missing buttons. 'I hope they're all right for you.'

'I'm sure they're perfect. You are a treasure.' He takes the bag from her and holds out a twenty-pound note, fixing his small blue eyes on her.

'No, no.' She crosses her arms.

'Go on, just this once. Buy something nice for the boys.'

Rachel shakes her head, amused that they still go through this ritual every time, even though she's told him how much she loves sewing and mending clothes. Her mother's voice comes into her head: *Don't throw it away when you can make do and mend.*

'Let me know if there's anything I can do for you.' He stuffs the twenty back in his pocket.

'I will, thank you.'

'I mean it. Be sure you do.' He points at her before he thanks her again and turns to go. She shuts the door, smiling to herself at what a bright start to the day he's given her. He prides himself on looking smart, even at his age and she's more than happy to help him out.

Before she goes back upstairs, she knocks on Shay's door and waits a second before easing it open a crack, half expecting him to yell at her to go away. A year ago, she let him move his bedroom downstairs to her old office in the front room because he kept complaining that he should have the biggest room as he's the eldest and it was unfair that she'd made him swap with Josh. She's always tried to be fair with them, and thought it was Josh's turn to have more space. She'd bought him a kids'-sized pool table that Christmas and there was no chance of it fitting in his old bedroom. At the time, Shay was going through a phase of not wanting any of his old toys any more because at fifteen, he was 'too old for childish things' so they were either handed down to Josh or the charity shop. He was left with a single bed, a computer desk and a laptop which he had decked out in multi-coloured LED light strips, so it had made sense that he moved into the smaller room. But after a few weeks she'd caved into his nagging and decided that she didn't need the big office. She could quite easily see clients in the conservatory, which was a lighter and more inviting area. But since Shay moved down here, he's become more and more distant from the whole family.

Peering into the gloomy darkness, she's hit by the stinking fug first, then her heart thuds sharply – his bed is empty. A trickle of ice slithers down her spine. Not empty as in he's recently vacated it and the duvet's been thrown aside, but empty as in it hasn't been slept in at all. It's neatly made. Her throat tightens as her mind automatically slides to images of Shay crying, smears of blood on his face, in his hair, skid marks of mud up his ripped joggers. He could be lying in a ditch somewhere, beaten to a pulp again.

The rest of the room is tidy as usual; desk clear except the laptop which is shut. Everywhere is in its normal dusty state. Rings of coffee cup stains on the table. A half-drunk pint glass of orange squash is next to the bed. Above is a black and white *Call to Arms* poster. She opens his bedside table drawer. Cables and wires, a lighter, a single condom and cigarette tips. A brown paper bag at the back catches her eye. She eases it forwards and takes the package out. A wad of ten- and twenty-pound notes is wrapped up inside. She takes it out and counts it. Just shy of £600. Where's he got this amount of money from and what's it for?

'Do you know where Shay is?' she asks David as soon as the en-suite door opens. A cloud of steam swoops around his head; his dark brown hair is lightly peppered with grey and is short, spiky and sticking up, making him look younger than his forty-five years.

'What?' He rubs his head with a small towel, his face still scrunched up with sleep.

'Shay's not in his bed. Did he say anything to you about going out?' She pulls up his texts. The last one he sent was twelve hours ago, begging her to let him go to a party nearby in Bayhurst woods.

'No.' David shakes his head, as though it's an absurd idea. Pointless trying to get any sense out him until he's had his first coffee.

'He was in his room last night when I locked up at eleven.' She paces up and down, gesticulating wildly, mobile in hand. 'We argued about him going to that party. I told him he couldn't go because he was still grounded.'

David shrugs and dries himself.

'He didn't mention he was going anywhere, meeting anyone?'

'No. Why would he when he knew he wasn't allowed out?' He pulls on his boxers.

'Because you're not his parent? I thought he might have asked you to keep quiet about it?'

'I think he'd guess I'd tell you.' He sits on the bed and puts on a pair of *Star Wars* socks.

'Did you hear anything last night or early this morning? I didn't hear the front door go.'

'Maybe he snuck out of the window like last time?'

'I thought we'd locked them.'

David stands at the mirror and sighs. 'He needed some fresh air; it's been so warm these last few nights.'

'So you unlocked them without mentioning it to me?' A surge of heat rises through her body. Her fingers hover above her mouth. She taps her top lip to stay calm.

'Treating him like a prisoner in his own home is not helping the situation,' David says, palms up in surrender. His facial lines have been smoothed away with an expensive cream, hair tamed with balm rubbed in with his fingertips, mimicking his Italian barber's technique. He puts on a navy suit and looks at her with an expression that is ever so slightly mocking; perhaps he's amused at her concern over something seemingly so trivial.

She shakes the thought away. She has to remember that David doesn't have children, so he won't fully understand. She tries calling Shay's phone and sends him a text demanding to know where he is but there's no reply.

Downstairs, she lays out breakfast for Josh. A selection of fruit and yogurt, pain au chocolate and croissants, warmed for a few seconds in the air fryer. When he comes down, she pours a cold glass of milk and hands it to him.

'Do you know where Shay has gone?' she asks as calmly as she can, clinging onto the belief that there's a perfectly good reason that he's gone out all night without telling her. She hopes her words come across as matter of fact and Josh doesn't detect the slight waver. It's not cool to show panic or concern, apparently. Shay's voice comes to her loud and clear: *Mum, chill. I was at a mate's house. When are you going to start trusting me?*

Josh is staring at her blankly. Shit, she zoned out. She hasn't done that in ages. Did he answer her question?

'He's gone?' Josh puts his glass down heavy-handedly and wipes the white moustache of milk off his top lip.

'His bed's not been slept in. Did he tell you where he was going?'

His eyes glaze over for a moment. 'Nah.' He blinks a few times and swallows hard then he grabs a pain au chocolate and mumbles, 'Gotta go.'

Rachel follows him to the bottom of the stairs, hanging back slightly. He picks up his rucksack from the bench under the coat rack then stands in Shay's doorway, staring into the cavernous room.

'Can you think where he might be?' she says quietly. Josh spins round towards her with a look of alarm and shakes his head emphatically. It cannot be good if Josh doesn't have a clue either. Unless he's lying for him.

'Okay, don't worry, I'm sure he'll be back soon.' She tries to keep her tone light, but her chest is fluttering like a thousand pieces of paper tossed into the air. All the times Shay's threatened to pack his bag and move out. Is this it? Has he gone for good?

Josh pulls back the curtain and unlocks the front door; heavy metal bolts that can only be secured from the inside. She doesn't say what she's thinking.

'Have a good day at school.' She closes the door after him and stands still for a moment as different scenarios play out in her head. Taking a deep breath, she marches into Shay's room and yanks the cord to raise the Roman blind. The window is indeed unlocked, handle up. Her palm thuds against the double-glazed glass and sure enough, it swings open wide.

Wide enough for Shay to climb out.

2

Where are you?

She texts Shay again and waits for an answer. Wherever he's been, she hopes he's not been stupid enough to miss school. His rucksack has gone but there's a pile of exercise books on his desk. Maybe they're ones he didn't need today? She can't see his school blazer.

David comes down the stairs, flicking through his phone.

'Can you stay here today until we find out where Shay is?' she asks.

His mouth opens to protest, but she crosses her arms and strides back into Shay's room. He follows her in and she points to the wide-open window, which says it all.

'Are you blaming me for this?'

'I wish you'd told me, that's all.' *Does* she blame him? She's not sure what to think at the moment. He follows her into the kitchen and speaks on his mobile to his secretary, asking her to change his morning group meeting to an online Teams call; something's come up and he needs to work from home. He looks her way when he says this. It's one of the perks of having his own private clinic. He confirms that his first surgery of the day isn't until 1.30 p.m. and he's expecting to be in for that.

Rachel pours them both a coffee. His with loads of milk, hers without. He eats a pain au chocolate without using a plate then swallows his daily pill with a glug of coffee. She calls Shay's school and explains to Lorna, the receptionist, what's happened. Rachel has known Lorna since Shay and her daughter, Samantha, were at primary school together.

'Don't worry, Rachel, I'll check the year eleven registers as soon as they come in and get straight back to you.'

'That would be so helpful, thank you.' She ends the call and checks for any texts from Shay. Still nothing. Her breathing quickens. *He's okay, calm down.* He's punishing her for not letting him go out. He knows how much she worries about him. But if he's not at school, where's he gone?

Her first client, a new lady, is due to arrive at 10 a.m. She can't afford to lose new business but she'll have to cancel her other appointments today.

'Are you sure he didn't say anything to you at all?' She drinks a mouthful of coffee.

'Yeah.' David pauses. 'You know what he's like.' He looks at her sideways as if he's not sure it's his place to even say that.

'What do you mean?' She tips her head to one side, wondering how he sees her teenage son as he rarely passes comment. He stares back at her for a few moments before blinking, probably considering if he should say.

'The usual types turned up for him while you were at your yoga class last night. Hoodies up, joggers, expensive trainers with the laces undone, but they all looked like they hadn't washed for a week. The tall one grunted Shay's name and flicked his chin up at me like I was worth less than the dirt under his shoe. Some kids have no fucking respect.' He looks up at her, seemingly forgetting himself and how much she hates swearing. 'I'm sorry, but it incenses me. I was tempted to tell them he was out and shut the door, but a loud thud came from Shay's room, he must have dropped his phone or something, anyway they knew immediately he must be in. One of them even stepped onto the garden and tapped on his window. Honestly Rachel, I know it's not my place to say, but I think it was a bad move letting him have his bedroom downstairs, and at the front of the house too.'

'Could they be the same boys that beat him up?'

'Possibly. When I called Shay and knocked on his door, he took his time coming, then came out and just stood there looking at me like he'd rather I told them to go away, but the tall one called his name and Shay went to the door like a magnet. He didn't let them in thank God, but he pulled the door around him, so he was standing in the small gap. I couldn't hear what they were saying.'

'Shit. Maybe he's in trouble again.' Rachel stands up.

'I hope not.'

'Why didn't you tell me when I got in last night?'

'I don't know. By the time you got home it had completely slipped my mind.'

Rachel frowns, not sure how he could forget something important like this.

'I know which boys you mean but I don't know their names. I don't think they go to Shay's school. They seem older, maybe at college.'

'They certainly act older and didn't look like the type that bothered much with learning.'

'Perhaps they are the same ones. You said he seemed scared of them.' She walks round in a circle.

'That's probably why Shay's not told you their names. Have you spoken to Finlay and Aidan? They might know if he was planning to meet them.'

'No, but I'm hoping to.'

'But would they tell you anything? Probably sworn to secrecy.'

Rachel tops up their coffees. Her mobile flashes the name 'School'. She swipes to answer and Lorna speaks first.

'Hello Rachel. I've looked through the registers for year eleven and Shay has been marked down as absent. I double-checked with his teacher, went along to the classroom myself actually in case there'd been a mistake, but he's definitely not in today.'

'Oh no. Tell me I've forgotten about some school activity or away match.'

'No, sorry.'

'Are Aidan and Finlay in today? I was just wondering if it's possible to come in and speak to them? If anyone knows where Shay has gone, they surely will.'

'Yes, that will be okay.'

'Great, I'll come straight over now. Thank you, Lorna.'

Rachel tries to ignore the nagging voice in her head telling her it's a mistake to pin all her hopes on Shay's best friends knowing where he is or him answering his phone to them, because she doesn't know what to do if they don't.

3

Rachel parks in the school car park. Before she gets out, she texts Mick to ask if Shay said anything to him about where he was going. Is it possible he's at his dad's house? He may have contacted him after their row; he seems to confide in him more than her these days. Normally she puts her mobile on silent when she goes into the school, but not today.

Lorna is sitting in the small office behind a sliding glass window, talking with the phone tucked under her chin while stuffing envelopes. She nods at Rachel, passes the receiver to the older woman next to her and inches open the hatch.

'Are you okay?' Lorna frowns, her cherry lips pursed together. Rachel nods and takes a deep breath to try and shift the tightness in her chest.

'I'll come round and let you in,' Lorna says. A buzzer sounds and Rachel pushes the door open and meets Lorna on the other side. Rachel is always astounded by how helpful Lorna is. She's one of the kindest people Rachel knows.

'Actually, I was going to call you today about the costumes for the school play. We were wondering if you'd be able to help us out again this year.' Lorna leads the way down the corridor.

'Yes of course, just let me know what you need and when by. Do you want me to source the material?'

'If you could, that would be fantastic.' Lorna beams at her. 'I'd better stay with you when you talk to the boys in case one of them kicks off. I don't want them to think you're accusing them of anything.' She shows Rachel into an office half filled with boxes and racks of lost property. 'If you just wait here, I'll go and fish them out of class for you.'

A few minutes later, Aidan and Finlay come in with Lorna and sit on a low sofa in the far corner. Both boys have their legs stretched out in front of them. Aidan's curly mop hangs down across his eyes and Finlay has a cluster of zits on his chin.

'Hello, thanks for coming,' Rachel says. Lorna pulls up two plastic chairs and they sit opposite the boys. 'I was wondering if either of you have heard from Shay this morning.'

The boys look at each other and say no several times, shaking their heads for good measure.

'The thing is, he wasn't at home this morning, and he didn't sleep in his bed last night.'

Their eyes widen as they glance at each other again. She tries to work out if they're hiding something or if it's genuine surprise.

'Yet he was in his room at 11 p.m. I checked before I went up.'

Aidan shifts back in his seat and pulls his legs in. Finlay smooths his hands across his trousers.

'Come on, lads, do you have any idea where he might have gone? It looks like he climbed out of his window.'

They side-eye each other and shake their heads.

'I know there was a party at the woods last night. Did you both go?'

They shake their heads again.

'So if I check with your mum, Aidan, she'll confirm you were at home all evening, will she?'

He looks at the stained carpet tiles then up at her. 'I did go for a bit.'

'And you, Finlay?'

'Yeah, for a little while.'

'But neither of you saw Shay and you don't know where he went?'

'No,' they say together.

Rachel steps outside and Lorna follows her, shutting the door behind her.

'Talk about as thick as thieves. I'm sure they know more than they're letting on. I don't suppose Samantha went, did she?'

'No, I won't let her go to those things; there's always trouble, too much noise, too much drink and drugs. And last night was no exception according to the local Facebook page this morning.'

'Really? I haven't looked yet.'

'There's a rumour there was a bit of trouble,' Lorna says, lowering her voice.

'What sort of trouble?'

'Not entirely sure, but like I say, just a rumour. By all accounts the police were called to break the party up.'

'I just hope Shay was somewhere else.'

'He probably went to a friend's house. Give these teenagers an ounce of freedom and they think they're all grown up.'

'Do you think the local page will let me post a photo of Shay in case anyone remembers seeing him there?'

'I don't see why not. It's a good idea.'

'So how am I going to deal with those two?' Rachel and Lorna look through the window at the same time. The boys are both leaning forward, heads down.

'That's one of life's mysteries, isn't it? The teenage brain and what goes on inside it.'

Rachel normally finds jokes like that funny. Lorna pats her arm, and they go back in.

'Look,' Rachel says, standing in front of the two boys, 'I'm worried the people who beat Shay up before are causing him trouble again.'

Aiden and Finlay shift in their seats. Rachel presses her hand to her forehead and waits for one of them to speak. They keep looking at each other, probably to check what the other is thinking, but they stay silent.

'You could be doing him more harm by not speaking up,' Rachel says, her voice rising. She's had enough and moves towards the door to leave.

'Thing is, he... he's not really spoken to us lately,' Aiden says, looking at her and then Finlay as he speaks.

'Yeah, 'cause he hangs out with a new crowd now,' Finlay adds and hangs his head.

Rachel nods. She's more out of touch with her son's life than she realised.

'Thanks, boys. If you could let me know if you do hear anything from him, I'd really appreciate it. In fact, could I have your mobile numbers please so we can keep each other informed?' She hands them a piece of paper and they scribble their numbers down.

'Also, could you come up with a list of Shay's friends and their contact numbers, if you have them. It's okay to let them know that I asked and that I might be in touch to ask a couple of questions.'

'Yeah, except we don't know any of these new ones,' Aiden says.

'Okay, well one of the others might know some of their names.'

Both boys nod and seem to brighten up. Perhaps they thought she was accusing them of something.

'I knew all the parents when they were at primary school, but since I've been back at work, I've lost touch with so many of them,' Rachel says.

'It happens to us all. Well except me I suppose, being in this job. But I was going to say that the school could put out an appeal in an email to parents if you like? Obviously, I'd need to check first with Nigel, Mr Cross.'

'Oh gosh, could you? What a great idea. That would really speed things up, thank you.' Rachel turns back to the boys. 'I know I'm not Shay's favourite person at the moment, but if you do know anything or you remember something you think might be important, please, please call me.'

'We will, Mrs Gulliver,' Aidan says. Finlay nods his agreement. They slope out of the door back to their classes. She wonders how much Shay has told them about their disagreements at home, if they think she's a bad mum.

'Thanks for your help, Lorna.'

'No problem. I hope he turns up soon. But we'll aim to get that email out by the end of school today. I'll start drafting it now while I've got a minute and send it to you before it goes out. I'm sure Mr Cross will think it's fine. And I'll ask Samantha if she knows where Shay might have gone.'

'Thanks, I appreciate that.'

As they walk back to the foyer, Rachel's phone rings. She pulls it out of her pocket and raises a hand in goodbye.

'Hi Mick.' She walks across the car park, digging in her pocket for the keys.

'You left a message; what's up?'

Rachel explains the situation to him and asks if he's heard from Shay in the last twenty-four hours.

'Yeah, he phoned me last night as it goes; I wanted to talk to you about it. Said you two had another row and you locked him in?'

'I did not lock him in. What time was this?'

'About ten past eight. You need to give the boy some freedom, Rach, he's not a kid any more.'

'I'm aware of that, thanks for the advice. And where were you when he was being bullied last year?'

'Yeah, all right, I might not have been living there, but he knew he could call me whenever he needed to.'

'Hardly the same, is it?' She unlocks her car and jumps in. She doesn't mean to keep punishing Mick, but it just slips out. They'd still be together as a family if he hadn't been messing around with that woman. Maybe Shay wouldn't have gone off the rails if his home life had been more stable.

'Look, about last night. He sounded really agitated. I tried to calm him down but...' Mick goes quiet.

'But what?'

'...But he asked if he could come over here.'

'And is that where he is now?' A kernel of hope rises in her chest.

'No. I said he'd have to ask you first, but he went ape. Wanted me to come over and pick him up straight away.'

'For goodness' sake.'

'But that's not all. He said he wants to move in with me permanently.' The hint of victory in his voice is unmissable. Mick's been pushing for this for the last three years.

'And you said no, I hope.'

'I said I'd talk to you about it this morning. I didn't think it was urgent.'

'You know that's not possible. He's got important exams coming up next year. He doesn't need any more disruption.'

'Rach, you're not listening.'

'No, you're the one not listening. I have no idea where he is or where he slept last night. He's not at school today. You should have called me.'

'Shit. He warned me he couldn't stay at yours any longer. I thought he was exaggerating.'

'Why couldn't he stay there? I don't understand.'

'Because he was too scared.'

4

'Scared of what? What are you talking about?' Rachel asks.

'He wouldn't tell me. Said he'd explain when I picked him up.'

'But you didn't, did you? Is he there with you right now?' For once she wishes Mick had gone against her and driven here last night and taken their son to his flat, because right now she'd know he was safe.

'No, I already told you he's not. I said if he wanted to come and live with me, we had to keep you on side otherwise it wasn't going to work.'

'I appreciate that.' She puts the phone on loud-speaker and starts the car. 'Do you think this means he's run away?'

'Sounds like it could do.'

A dull pain thuds through her head as if someone has hit her: her son doesn't want to live with her any more. She has failed him. Perhaps it's to do with David moving in. She can't bring herself to ask Mick because he will wallow in such a possibility. He could quite easily hold it against her, not asking his opinion about her new boyfriend living with his sons, but thankfully he doesn't.

The fire at David's house was so devastating and left him technically homeless. She had to do something to help. Yes, he could have moved in with one of his friends or gone to a hotel, but it looked likely that it could take months before the insurance money came through and all the repairs were completed. Anyway, it had felt the right thing to do, inviting him to live with her. She'd longed to wake up next to him every morning. It had been ages since she'd been in love with a man and felt loved back. She couldn't bear to be parted from him. It was the most impulsive thing she'd done in years, and it had felt good. She'd hoped she was not going to regret it, but with everything that was going on with Shay, she couldn't help but wonder if she'd made the right choice for her sons.

'I'll keep trying his phone,' Mick says.

'I will too, and I'll let you know as soon as he turns up. Do you know anything about a party?'

Mick is quiet. She wonders if he's still on the line.

'Mick?'

'Yes, he mentioned it a couple of days ago. Said he wasn't allowed to go out because he was grounded.'

'And what did you say?'

'I told him that if he did some chores around the house, you might change your mind.'

Rachel pictures Shay's sudden burst of activity after school yesterday, vacuuming and going round the house, emptying all the bins. She thanked him for doing his chores without having to be prompted. But then he'd asked if he could go to the party as he'd been good and she'd told him it didn't work like that, he was still grounded but if he kept up his good behaviour maybe he could go out next weekend. He'd sworn at her and punched the door, leaving yet another dent.

'I'm guessing you didn't change your mind?'

'He needs to learn.'

'I think you're being too hard on him, Rach.'

'You weren't there when that boy's mother turned up. It was so...
humiliating.'

'You've got to stop making it all about you. Think about what
made him behave like that.'

'I've no idea what made him steal a bloody moped.'

Mick tuts. 'I don't think you realise how unhappy he is.'

'Don't make excuses for him and do not tell me how to deal
with my son.'

'Our son.'

'Whatever.' Rachel stabs the 'end call' button and slows down at
the traffic lights. Her face is burning. God, she's starting to sound
like a teenager. But is what Mick said true? Is Shay so unhappy that
he'd rather live with his dad? She has to admit she doesn't know
what's bothering him any more, except that he thinks life is so
unfair, she's unfair. He's told her he hates her. He barely talks civilly,
let alone confides in her.

She pulls onto the drive, imagining Shay running out of the
house to hug her, tell her how sorry he is for behaving so badly.

In the kitchen, she tops up the coffee maker then tidies her
appearance in the downstairs cloakroom. She can hear David
talking in the office upstairs on his Teams work call.

The sky has darkened, and a sudden crack of thunder followed
by a downpour brings the conservatory to life, like a million tiny
stones dropping onto the roof in a cacophony of sound. Rachel
plumps up the cushions on the two-seater sofa and highbacked
wicker chair. Usually, she'd have gone through her notes from the
initial phone enquiry in detail, but she's not had time. She picks up
her notepad and pours a fresh cup of coffee for David.

She scans through what she's written: *Alice Kirby, age forty-four,
TV and theatre actress. Looking to 'unblock', regain her confidence after a
long break away following a nervous breakdown. Has undergone months
of bereavement counselling but now needs to get her life and career back*

on track. Rachel will use the half-hour introductory session to find out more about Alice and see what she really wants and expects from life coaching. Sometimes people are under the illusion she can supply all the answers to their problems and she has to rein in their expectations and make it clear that it's what they put in, the hard work they do, that counts towards a successful outcome.

She carries the coffee up to the office for David and taps on the door before going in. His face is grey and heavy with stress. She leaves the mug on the table and glances out of the window. A red sports car, a Mazda or BMW, is pulling up outside the house. Is this her new client? She's ten minutes early. She turns to leave but David grabs her wrist.

'Wait a sec.'

'What is it? I think my new client has arrived.'

'Just wondered if you'd had any luck at the school?' He tugs the headphones off so they're resting around his neck.

'Nothing. If his friends know anything, they're not saying.'

'I was just speaking to Simon from work. Apparently quite a few kids from their school went to the party. He said Ethan stayed over at a friend's house and he thought Shay may have gone too. They're probably still sleeping it off. He's waiting for a call back.'

'I hope so. Can you let me know as soon as he's spoken to Ethan?'

'Will do.' David nods, clearly deep in thought. 'Makes sense that they're together.'

She pictures Ethan when he came to the door with Simon to pick Shay and David up for football. They'd decided to take one car to the train station to keep costs down. She'd said hello to Ethan when Shay climbed into the back seat next to him. Always a friendly boy with an open smiley face and good eye contact. Confident but not arrogant. Clean clothes and hair. The sort of boy she hoped Shay would become good friends with instead of the ones he'd been knocking about with in the village, the ones who hid their faces under hoodies and snoods. Shay texted her after the game to say Man City had slaughtered Watford 6-0. When they got home, David mentioned how well the boys got on with each other.

She checks her mobile. None of her messages to Shay on WhatsApp have been delivered. She wants to believe he's okay, but bile pushes up her throat.

She texts him yet again.

I promise I won't be mad at you, just let me know you're okay please. Love you, Mum xx

A car door slams. She looks out of the window again. A woman locks the red car then starts walking up the drive in a pair of beige high heels.

Rachel plants a kiss on David's lips. 'My client's here, so we'll talk later.'

5

The woman standing at the door looks older than she expected but extremely glamourous. Her perfume has a syrupy, expensive smell. A Liberty print scarf is arranged across her shoulders and hangs down perfectly over her front.

'Alice Kirby? Lovely to meet you; do come in.' She reaches out to shake her hand, to which Alice lamely shakes the ends of her fingers.

Rachel smiles and leads the way through the living room to the conservatory, Alice following at a slow pace, taking in her surroundings. She pauses by the fireplace and stares at a photo of Rachel and David smartly dressed at a friend's wedding, Shay and Josh standing reluctantly behind them. She had to bribe them to be in it with the promise of a glass of wine.

'Lovely family you have,' Alice says, but the wide smile she pulls has a sadness to it. Alice holds her with an intense look, and it takes a long moment before she looks away. Rachel feels strangely uncomfortable but smiles to cover it up. This woman clearly has some serious issues to deal with. Rachel hopes she can help her move forward in her life in a positive way.

'Do sit down and make yourself comfortable.' Rachel directs her to the two-seater sofa. 'Would you like a glass of water, or I have fresh coffee?'

'Water please.' Alice sits at the far end of the sofa and lifts her tan leather handbag up next to her. Rachel pours two small glasses of lemon water then closes the conservatory blinds to prevent them from being disturbed.

'So you said on the phone that you contacted me because you feel you need some help with your confidence and getting back to work. Can you explain a little further, if you feel comfortable doing so?'

'I've been an actress for twenty years, on the stage and screen; you may recognise me from the TV work I've done.' She pauses, her lips pressing together.

Rachel nods even though she doesn't recognise her from anything she's watched.

'But you see, I haven't been able to work for the last two years or so because of a family bereavement. I've been in the depths of despair. My doctor says I had a break down; I suppose that's what it was. I couldn't get out of bed for weeks except to go to the bathroom. I couldn't see the point in going on. But now I've had counselling to learn to cope with the loss and I've realised my life must continue. I heard about you from the noticeboard at the hospital and thought, that's what I need, someone to coach me back to my working life, someone who will be by my side every step of the way.'

'I'm so glad you contacted me. That's exactly what I'm here for. I hope you had time to read through some of the testimonials on my website. I mentioned them on the phone?'

'Oh yes, thank you, I read several. They all fill me with such confidence that you are the right life-coach to help me. It feels like the stars have aligned. It takes a special person to believe life can continue and still be fulfilling after a sudden death.'

'I'm pleased you think so. Do you feel you want to share with me who passed away?'

Alice nods, her eyes creased. 'My youngest child.' Tears drop onto her lap.

Rachel gently rests her hand on top of Alice's for a moment, taking in the enormity of such a loss. 'I'm so deeply sorry. I can only imagine how devastating losing a child must be, at any age.' She can feel her face drain to white. Her body is ice cold. She needs to stay focused, professional, give her new client as much space and time as she needs to speak while she listens. In feedback, her clients often tell her that this is one of the most valuable parts of coaching; being listened to, not having someone interrupt or give unwanted advice.

'Thank you. Our children are so precious to us, aren't they? As soon as they're born, our whole lives shift and what we thought was important before, isn't so much any more. We put them first, before ourselves, our husbands, friends, other members of the family. We would do anything to protect them, wouldn't we?'

Rachel nods, goosebumps rising all over her body. She rubs up and down her arms. Panic surges up her throat again. She's not sure David understands the lengths she'll go to, to protect her boys. She would die for them. All he sees is her curbing their need for fun and adventure.

'I'm still trying to come to terms with her not being there when I wake up in the morning. She had such a beautiful smile. Always smiling and laughing. The counsellor says bereavement is an ongoing process which has no definitive end.'

'Grief is invisible. It's a painful human emotion and manifests itself in so many different ways. My heart aches for your loss.' For a second, the urge to hug Alice overwhelms Rachel. In a matter of moments, this confident smart woman, this mother, has disintegrated in front of her eyes.

Alice clutches her hands together. 'Sometimes it's too much too bear. But I'm working through it. I've learnt how to let it flow through me.'

'I will do everything I can to help you move forward with small exercises and goals, nothing that will overwhelm you. It's important to allow space and time for your grief in every corner of your life.'

'Thank you. I can't tell you how much I appreciate this.'

Rachel pulls a cardigan from the back of her chair and drapes it around herself, but she can't seem to warm up. She wants to check her phone, see if Shay has replied, desperate for the comfort blanket of knowing her boy is safe. For the last few hours, she's been trying so hard not to let her mind wander to the worst possible scenario. And here is what it will be like, right in front of her. She shivers. She needs to stay positive. Shay is bound to be with Ethan. Wherever they are, her son is very much alive.

6

After Alice has gone, Rachel makes a fresh pot of coffee. David comes down, his briefcase packed.

'How'd it go with your new client?' He pours coffee into the ceramic England travel cup and presses on the rubber lid.

'Well, I think. I'd say she's still quite traumatised, maybe not ready to finish counselling in my opinion, but I'm happy to help her as much as I can.' Rachel is careful not to give away any personal details about her clients. She prides herself on her professionalism and says so on her website. She wants clients to know that every detail of their life, their problems and anything they share with her is strictly between them. Of course, David has sworn an oath to patient confidentiality too and would expect nothing less from her.

'I texted Simon. He hasn't heard from Ethan yet. Turns out he's not sure which friend he stayed with. You know what these teenagers are like, changing their plans at the last minute.'

'Oh great. Maybe he shouldn't be so free and easy with his parenting. How do we know if Shay is there too?'

David shrugs. 'Sounds to me as though they're likely to be together, wherever they are.'

'I wish he'd switch his phone on.' Rachel picks up her mobile. Her WhatsApp messages to him remain undelivered.

'He's a teenage boy; he probably wants some head space, that's all.'

Rachel grinds her teeth together to stop herself saying anything she can't take back. She opens the Facebook app. There are more than a dozen notifications from the local page, full of expletives about the party.

'Look at the state they left the woods in. There's rubbish everywhere.' She holds up her phone to show David a photo of bottles and cans strewn on the grass and remnants of a bonfire in the middle of the clearing.

'Shit. What if Shay and Ethan were involved?'

'I hope not. According to Lorna there was some sort of trouble. The police were called to break it up. Drugs were found too. The residents' group are asking for parents to go and help clear up. Quite a few items of clothing have been left behind. I think I might go up there, ask around to see if anyone saw Shay.'

'Good idea and hopefully he'll have phoned you by the time you get back.' David kisses her lips and leaves for work.

The car park by the woods is busier than usual for a Monday lunchtime. The air is crisp and a weak winter sun leaks through the cracks in the clouds. The darkness of the trees looms in the background, the leaves swishing in whispers carried by the wind. There are plenty of parents milling around in wellies and waterproof jackets. She waves to a few faces she recognises and thinks how they've all moved on. Glitter and glue on clothes or in hair is no longer their biggest crisis.

She follows the trail to the clearing. There's rubbish everywhere. She's never seen anything like it. It reminds her of the mess they show on the news after music festivals. There are even a few pop-up tents, presumably empty now, which gives her hope that after the police left some of the revellers came back and slept here. She'll be mortified if Shay is one of them, but as long as he's okay she'll forgive him.

A group of parents is gathered at one end of the clearing, a man in a high-vis tabard handing out black bin liners and litter pickers. As she heads in his direction, the high-pitched sound of police sirens fills the air. Everyone freezes, as though they've been caught doing something they shouldn't.

Moments later, two policemen and a policewoman are striding towards them waving their arms.

'Sorry, you can't touch anything; you'll have to leave. This is now officially a crime scene.'

'What?' Rachel runs up to them. 'I'm looking for my son; he's not come home.'

The policewoman turns to Rachel. 'Was your son here last night?' She takes out her notebook.

'I don't know, he was supposed to be grounded. I'm guessing he was, that's why I came here, to see if I could find out because he's not answering his phone.'

'Okay, can you give me your son's details? Name, date of birth, when you last saw him, what he was wearing etc.'

Rachel tells her as much as she knows, when she last saw him, what clothes she thinks he had on, although he could easily have changed if he was coming to a party.

'So why *are* you here?' Rachel asks.

'Because a girl was attacked in the woods last night.'

'Oh my God.' Rachel takes a step back. 'What girl?'

The policewoman lifts an eyebrow. 'I can't tell you; it's confidential.'

'Of course, sorry. Poor thing.' Her mind flicks through the few girls she knows and hopes it's none of them, although it's horrendous whoever it has happened to. Could Shay know something about this? He wouldn't do anything to hurt anyone. Maybe those older boys are involved. They might have been drunk or high on drugs. That could be the reason why Shay hasn't come home. Those boys could have hurt this girl and are blaming Shay, like they did with the moped. And now the police have his details. Has she just handed them their prime suspect?

7

Back in her car, Rachel checks her phone. It's already all over the local news and Facebook page.

GIRL, 16, ATTACKED AT ILLEGAL RAVE IN BAYHURST WOODS

She might be from Shay's year. A close friend or classmate? If she knew the name, it might give her a clue as to whether Shay was here or not and if he knows something about it.

She sends the news link to David, even though he won't be able to check his phone for a couple of hours. David will be in theatre by now, concentrating on fixing someone. Every time she thinks about what he does for a living, it puts everything else into perspective. She pictures a family huddled together waiting for news, waiting to see if David has improved or even saved the life of their loved one.

She sits silently for a few moments in the sanctuary of her car, watching the frantic activity around her. Parents on their mobiles or hurrying back into their cars and zooming off. More police arrive. She needs to check again when Mick last spoke to Shay. Could it have been after the party instead of before? Is this attack something to do with what Shay meant when he told Mick he was scared? Perhaps he knows who did it and is covering up for them even though he doesn't want to. There's only one obvious place Shay would hide and that's at his dad's. But Mick swore he didn't pick him up last night and take him home. She wants to believe he wouldn't lie to her, but she's trusted him before and look where that got her. Besides, if Shay begged him not to tell her something, he'd cover for him.

She drives to the small row of terraced houses on Barnes Road and pulls up a little way back, so as not to alert Mick or Shay, if he's there. She watches the ground floor flat for a few minutes. The curtains are half closed. They don't give her any indication as to whether anyone is in or not. Mick's old Škoda is parked outside.

She gets out of the car and walks up to the communal door and rings the bell marked with the initials MM.

'It's Rachel,' she says to his laconic voice asking who it is. The buzzer sounds and she pushes the door open.

It's like an ice box in the foyer and smells musty, maybe stale beer and mould. She knocks on number five and the door opens immediately.

'Hey, Rach, are you okay?' Mick steps forward and hugs her and she wishes he wouldn't be so nice to her, because it makes her forget all his lies and instead she remembers how much she once loved him.

He shows her into the living room and they sit down together while she tells Mick everything that's happened.

'Please tell me Shay is here safe and well?' A soft bang like the sound of a cupboard closing silences them. 'Seriously, Mick?' Rachel walks the few paces to the kitchen and opens the door. A skinny woman is standing there eating from a small pot of yogurt. Rachel looks back at Mick and he grins at her.

'This is Andie.' He jumps up and the next moment his arm is

around the woman's tiny waist. He doesn't say she's his girlfriend, but she must be. She's pretty and at least ten years younger than her.

'Hello,' Rachel says and wonders how much more awkward this is going to get. At least it's not the one she caught him with. 'So is Shay here then or not?'

'No, I told you. He wanted to come but I wouldn't let him. You can search the place if you don't believe me.'

'I will actually, because you never lie to me, do you?' She stomps into the small bedroom, annoyed that his latest girlfriend is witnessing this. The duvet is in a pile in the middle of the bed and Mick's clothes are stacked in a heap on a chair in one corner. There's only one bedroom so if Shay is there, he'd have to sleep on the small sofa. Through a sliding door to the right is a tiny bathroom, then the narrow galley kitchen with a half depth counter on one side. There are no other rooms. There's barely space for any privacy. And would Mick really want his son here when Andie is? She glances round the living room again and checks behind the faux leather sofa for signs that Shay has been there, maybe having left something behind. He could have gone to the shop minutes before she arrived and is on his way back. But from the look of worry on Mick's face, that isn't the case.

Shit, he's telling the truth. Their son is still missing.

'Where can he be?' she says, tapping her phone on.

'He's not texted me; you can check my phone if you like.' He hands it to her.

She scrolls through Mick's last few messages with Shay. 'Hang on, the text you sent him this morning has been read, look.' She shows him the two blue ticks. She checks her own phone and gives Mick his back. Sure enough, Shay's finally read her messages too. She checks again because she can hardly believe it. His mobile is linked to hers, so she opens the find phone app. 'Look, it shows me exactly where he is. It looks like he's about twenty minutes away at St Ann's Shopping Centre. Will you come with me to find him?'

'Course I will.' Mick grabs his keys then glances at Andie.

'You go.' She flaps her hand. 'I need to leave for work in five minutes anyway.' She kisses his cheek, then his lips. He presses her to him, his hand in the small of her back.

'We need to hurry.' Rachel turns away. It feels wrong to watch and it stirs up a sick feeling in the pit of her stomach. She opens the front door. 'I'll drive,' she calls over her shoulder. They need to focus on finding their son. Who knows what state they'll find him in? If he does know anything about the attack on that girl or is involved in any way, will she be able to hand her own son over to the police?

In the car, Rachel hands Mick her phone so they can follow the small dot as it moves on the map at the shopping centre in Harrow. Ethan may be with him but she hasn't got time to call David to speak to Simon about it. Anyway, he's bound to be too busy with a patient.

It's a clear run and only takes twenty minutes. Fortunately, the small dot hasn't moved very far. He's near Nationwide Building Society on Station Road. They park in St Ann's car park just off of College Road and follow the tracker on foot. Rachel holds the phone in front of her, Mick by her side.

'It looks like he's gone into Caffè Nero just up here.' They hurry towards the entrance, weaving in and out of shoppers, and go in. The queue is long and untidy. He could be right at the front. They dart around, trying to catch sight of him. 'Shit, he's not here; he's gone out,' she says, looking back at the screen.

They push their way out of the door and Rachel breaks into a trot, following the dot as it moves on again. Mick tries to keep up. She hopes to spot Shay on the pavement up ahead, but it's too crowded and they're not sure which jacket he's wearing.

'I think he's going towards the bus station,' Rachel says. They break into a run back towards College Road and finally their dot seems to be catching up with Shay's. He's so close now. She's going to give him the biggest hug.

They reach the bus station out of breath. Rachel's chest burns. She thought she was fitter than this. Almost every stop has a long queue of people, with lots of family and friends grouped together.

'Fuck,' Mick says, 'he could be in any of these. How are we going to find him?'

Two buses turn into the square and swing round to their stops, one just ahead of them. When they get there, the target on the map has stopped moving; their dots are side by side. Rachel can barely breathe, he's so close. She's temped to call out his name, but it might scare him and make him run off. People start boarding. Mick pushes his way on board, explaining to the driver he's searching for his son, and he'll only take two seconds.

Rachel scans the unruly queue, checking each of the faces as they climb aboard, mainly the boys and men in hoodies, or casual clothes. Would he have disguised himself? But why? She looks at anyone about his height, but most people's faces are clear to see and none of them are him. Shay isn't there. *Where are you?* She glances down at the screen again, the two dots together. He's right under her nose; why can't she see him? As she looks up, there's a boy with his back to her she didn't spot before, half hidden in a pack of chattering youths. His hair is the same sandy colour as Shay's and he's wearing the same brand of black puffa jacket. The boy seems to sense her behind him and pushes forward.

'Shay, Shay!' she shouts and grabs his elbow, but he yanks it away, almost ripping her nails out.

He turns to her and snarls, 'Get off, weirdo.'

Her heart drops. His nose and eyes are too big, his eyebrows dark and untidy; he's nothing like her boy. Even his arm didn't feel like Shay's.

She steps back, ignoring all the strangers' inquisitive faces. The queue trickles down to nothing. Mick barrels down the stairs, giving the driver a thumbs up as he jumps off. The doors close and the bus pulls away.

'He wasn't there.' He sighs.

'That's not possible. Are you sure you checked everyone?' She looks down at her phone tracker.

'Yes, every single person.' He leans against the bus shelter to get his breath back.

'But you can't have, look.' She shows him her phone screen and the dot indicating Shay's phone is moving away from them, and when they look up, the back of the bus is disappearing into the distance, in the same direction as the tracker.

8

Rachel tries to call Shay's mobile, but it goes straight to answer phone. She sends him another message on WhatsApp instead.

Please, please call me. Dad and I were trying to find you on that bus just now. Why are you hiding from us? If you've done something bad, I'm not going to be angry with you, I promise. I know I said if there was any more trouble, you'd have to move out, but I didn't mean it. I just want to know you're safe. Your dad and I are here for you, and we want to help. Whatever it is. Please call. Love you. xx

A few moments later a WhatsApp message arrives.

I'm fine, leave me alone. I need to sort things out my way.

'Look, he's replied.' Rachel's voice wavers. She presses her fingers to her lips and shows the message to Mick.

'He's okay, he's actually okay.' Mick touches his forehead. 'I was getting really worried there.' He hugs her and she buries her face in his musty smelling coat and it feels like the best moment of her life.

Her phone rings and they pull apart. It's Lorna from the school.

'Where are you, are you free?' Lorna asks.

'Yes, I am now.' Rachel mouths the word 'school' to Mick and he nods.

'The police are coming in to speak to the parents and older children about the party last night. They've found some items of clothing and need to find out who they belong to. Sorry for the short notice but it's at 2 p.m. Can I count you in?'

'Yes, of course. Should Shay's dad be there too?' She glances at Mick, his familiar smell lingering in her nostrils.

'It might be an idea. Oh, and the other thing, I started getting the email about Shay ready to go out, but to be honest this has taken up most of the morning, calling parents etc.'

'That's okay. I was going to call you in a minute anyway. I've just had a text from him. He says he's fine, wants to be left alone for a while.'

'Oh, that is good. One less thing for me to do.' Lorna's voice is flat.

'Are you okay? Is there something else?'

Lorna sighs deeply. 'Honestly, it's one thing after another today. You'll never believe it, but the cash collected for Zach's special wheelchair has gone missing.'

'Oh no, you're joking.' Rachel's stomach flips. She shakes her head at Mick.

'I wish I was. I haven't told his mum yet. Six hundred bloody pounds. I mean who would do that?'

'I... I've no idea. It's despicable.'

'I don't even know what to say to her. She'll be devastated.'

Rachel pictures the paper bag of money stuffed in the back of Shay's drawer. She can't bring herself to tell Lorna about it, not that she can believe he would take it. He loves Zach like a brother. They've known each other since pre-school. But where else would

Shay get so much cash from? He's not had a Saturday job for months.

'I'll see you at two then.' Lorna sighs again, and the line goes dead.

'What's despicable?' Mick frowns at her.

'The cash raised for Zach's wheelchair has been stolen.'

'Shit.'

Rachel forwards Shay's message to David. Simon has probably heard from Ethan by now too. She tells Mick about the police asking for parents to go in to identify the belongings. They walk back to her car.

'I really need your support on this one, Mick. Money going missing from the school and now this girl being attacked, I'm worried they might start pointing the finger at Shay because he's gone AWOL.'

'They can't accuse him without evidence.'

'It doesn't look good though, does it? I found a bag stuffed with cash in his room. Do you know where he got almost six hundred pounds from?'

'He hasn't told me anything about that.'

'All in ten- and twenty-pound notes. The same amount that's gone missing from Zach's charity collection.' They climb into her car and she drives to the school.

'Message Shay back, ask him about it,' Mick says.

'I think if I do, it will push him further away.'

'If it was him, he must know he'll be in serious trouble.'

'He said he needs to "sort things out his way", but what does that mean exactly?' She hands Mick her phone. 'Perhaps it would be better coming from you.'

'If he did steal it, what's it for? Why didn't he take it with him?' He starts tapping in a message.

'Hopefully it will give him a reason to come back.'

Mick reads it to her before pressing send.

Hey mate, Dad here. We're worried about you. Are you in some sort of trouble? Do you know anything about the money missing from school? We won't be mad at you. Please give us a call. I searched everyone's face on that bus, but you outwitted your old man! Love you lots. xxx

As Rachel pulls into the school car park, her phone beeps. She glances across at Mick who shows her the screen as the alert flashes up then folds away.

A single heart emoji from Shay.

9

There are two police vehicles near the school entrance. Rachel parks the car and takes her phone from Mick, dropping it into her bag. She leads him in through the main door to the hall where Lorna is helping unstack chairs and set them up in rows. A few other parents are early and sitting waiting with their teenagers. Mick immediately starts helping with the chairs, while Rachel gravitates towards the policewoman she spoke to at the woods.

'Hi again, I'm glad you're here because I wanted to let you know that my son messaged me to say he's okay.' Rachel shows her the message.

'That's good, thanks for that. I find they don't usually come back for a few hours especially if there's been a disagreement in the family.' She smiles knowingly while Rachel recalibrates in her mind how old she thought she was. She guessed she was much younger but it sounds like she's speaking from experience.

'Did you find out if he was at the rave?' The policewoman is pinning up a row of large blown-up photographs showing the clothing and items which were left behind. There's one of a black hoodie scattered with grass and twigs. It has a small shark logo on the left-hand side which catches Rachel's eye. The photo is slightly pixelated but the initials SG in faded ink are visible on the collar label. So he was there, but she hasn't a clue if he's done anything wrong. Running away implies that he has. If only he'd call and actually speak to her or come home so they can talk about it. Maybe Aidan and Finlay were lying, covering up for him. Has he done something which makes it impossible for him to come home? For a moment she forgets the policewoman's question.

'Erm, I'm not sure he was there because I've not actually spoken to him yet. We've been out trying to find him. I spoke to a couple of his friends here at the school this morning, but they claim not to have seen him at the party. We only got the text from him a short while ago.' Rachel glances round as the double doors squeak open. Parents and year elevens and twelves trickle in and fill the seats. Rachel recognises some of the parents from the PTA and waves.

'Any of these items look familiar?' the policewoman asks her.

'Nothing leaps out at me, no.' The words are out of her mouth before she realises what she's doing, but she won't get away with pretending the hoodie isn't Shay's. One of the other children or parents are bound to point out they're his initials. If he's involved in something bad again, is she capable of covering up for him? She guesses she must be. She gave those parents the money for the moped Shay stole so they wouldn't report it to the police, didn't she? Except everyone in the neighbourhood knew it was him. The kids who filmed it recognised his face. But Shay had insisted a boy made him do it and she'd given him the benefit of the doubt.

Mick calls her over. She's glad to get away from the awkward questions. He's saved a seat for her in the front row. Great. She'd feel happier at the back so she wouldn't have to try to avoid the police officer's gaze.

'The police have found his hoodie,' she whispers in Mick's ear.

He whips his head round to look at her, an expression of horror frozen on his face.

'You don't think he's capable of hurting that girl, do you?'

'No, of course not.' She keeps her eyes forward. Even though she hasn't done anything wrong, she feels like she's being watched. It was only a few weeks ago that the police were knocking on their door to speak to Shay about some damage at the playground park and she can't help wondering if the policewoman has already looked up his name and knows he's been on their radar recently.

The policewoman and her colleague begin their presentation. A map of the woods and the surrounding area is shown on the large computer screen at the back of the stage. They run through what they know, when the party started and which way through the woods to the clearing most of the teenagers came. It seems the bonfire had been prepared in advance because it was carefully constructed with collected branches and twigs.

'There is evidence of heavy alcohol consumption and drug taking.' She points to another screen with zoomed in photos of empty bottles of vodka, cans of beer, remnants of MDMA tablets and cannabis smoking paraphernalia. Murmurs of shock ripple around the room.

One of the policemen stands up. 'We believe the rave went on until around 12.30 a.m., when the police were called by local residents. The party was broken up and several children were in a rather bad state, shall we say. After the attending officers left the site, we understand that some of the teenagers who'd hidden in the woods, returned to the clearing with the intention of camping on the site in pop-up tents. The assault victim was found this morning. We think she was attacked by blunt force trauma to the back of the head around 1.10 a.m.'

'We need all of the teenagers who stayed on after the party was broken up to come forward and give a fingerprint and DNA sample to help eliminate you from our investigation. Could those who stayed on also please come forward and speak to one of us, as you may have vital information which could help identify and catch the attacker.' The policewoman surveys the silent room and takes a sip of water. 'The assailant may be known to you, and you may have been pressured not to reveal their identity, but let me be clear, this was a brutal attack on a vulnerable girl, and you wouldn't want to be responsible for this person having the chance to hurt someone else. Of course, if you do not come forward, you would more than likely be charged with withholding information.'

Rachel slides her hands together and grips hard.

'This is where the attack took place.' The policeman points with a stick to an area a few metres into the woods. 'If any of you were near there and heard or saw anything unusual or suspicious, you need to speak to me or my colleagues this afternoon. We're here for the next hour at least. Around the walls you'll see we've put up large-scale copies of photographs taken of all the clothing and items found in the clearing, which is where the main party took place. Look at each item closely and if you recognise it as yours, your child's or anyone else's, again, let us know straight away so we can hopefully eliminate that person from our enquiries.'

'The clothing and items are being kept by us in evidence bags to preserve the DNA until the belongings are matched to the owner.'

Rachel and Mick stare at each other. They both know they're going to have to say the hoodie is Shay's and hope that in doing so they don't drop him in it. If Rachel had been asked a few months ago if her kind, thoughtful son could be capable of any sort of misdemeanour, she'd have said with absolutely certainty that he wasn't. Unfortunately, she's already been proved wrong more than once. It still smarts now, the thought of what he did. But this is another level entirely. She will not believe her little boy who used to love toy trucks and cartoons, has turned into a violent monster.

10

Everyone gets up and gravitates towards the queue, examining each photo before moving onto the next, speaking to each other in hushed voices. Every photo is numbered and at the end, after the last photo, which is of Shay's hoodie, a couple of policemen have clipboards with lists, on which Rachel guesses they're scribbling down names next to the corresponding numbers.

Rachel and Mick don't recognise any of the other items: a plain white T-shirt, one torn flip-flop, hairband, a faux strand of rainbow coloured hair with a clip attached, a broken friendship bracelet, a pair of knickers with Betty Boop on the front, a bikini top, a grey sock, the list goes on. The embarrassment levels in the room are palpable.

If Shay was here, he'd probably have had one of his tantrums by now and stormed off. He's been angry about everything for months and he seems to blame it all on her. She can't do or say anything to appease him. It's hard to pinpoint when it started, but it was around the time Ethan introduced him to that online game, *Call to Arms*. It seems to make lots of children angry and frustrated. Only last week there was a phone-in on Radio 2 about how addictive it is. One child wet themselves because they wouldn't leave the game to go to the toilet. Why hadn't she known this before he started playing it? Do all these other parents know this? She tries so hard to be a good mum and cut down the hours he plays after school, but lately he's so tired in the mornings that he must be playing through the night. He knows it's the only time she can't monitor him.

They approach the last photo and stare up at it as though they've made some mistake and the initial S written in pen on the label isn't really an S, but more like a worn-out B. But there's a smaller photo next to it of the back of the hoodie and the unmistakable big white lettering: F–CK YOU. She's embarrassed by the slogan and wishes she could explain that it's just another thing he's bought himself online and had delivered before she can approve or not.

She is about to speak when the boy in front of them says to one of the policemen, 'That's Shay's hoodie.'

'Shay who?' the policeman asks, pen poised over his list.

'It's our son, Shay Gulliver,' Rachel says before the boy can say any more. Everyone turns to look at them.

'So he was at the party, was he?' Rachel asks the boy.

'Yeah.'

'And your name is?' the policeman asks him.

'I'm Jordan Walsh.'

'And where was Shay exactly when you saw him wearing the hoodie?'

'He wasn't wearing it, she was.'

'She, meaning who?'

'You know, that girl, Bella.' Jordan looks down at his spotless white trainers.

The policeman writes something down. 'And you were where?'

'We were all sitting around the fire. She was feeling cold.' Jordan glances at his mum. She pats his arm. 'I guess you could say they were together.'

'Why'd you say that?'

'He had his arm around her.'

'In what kind of way?' The policeman looks at him pointedly.

Jordan glances at his mum again and she nods for him to carry on. 'I guess because he liked her a lot.'

'And how was she reacting?'

'Her head was leaning on his shoulder,' Jordan says.

'Sorry, who is Bella?' Rachel butts in.

'The girl who was attacked,' the policeman says quietly. 'She's still in hospital.'

'Oh goodness.' Rachel blinks rapidly and turns to Mick. His face is pale, lips pinched tight. They go back to their seats and sit in silence. Gradually the hall empties. The policewoman comes over.

'We'll hopefully be interviewing Bella later this afternoon if she's up to it. See what she remembers about the attack and what her connection is to Shay and his hoodie.'

'Is she in a... very bad way?' Rachel asks.

'It's a serious head injury; she's not been able to speak yet.' The policewoman scribbles something in her notebook.

'Oh, God, really?' Rachel thinks of Shay's message saying he had things to sort out.

'Is Shay a suspect?' Mick asks. Rachel wants to kick him, as though saying it aloud will plant the idea in their heads.

'We're just making enquiries at this stage, sir.'

In her heart Rachel knows Shay's not capable of attacking a girl. It sounded like he's really keen on her. But maybe that's the old Shay she's thinking of. What about his behaviour recently? Swearing at her and answering back. Losing his temper and throwing things across the room. Those boys who came to the door last night could have made him do something terrible. Why else has he gone off if he has nothing to hide?

11

David is late home from work. Today of all days, Rachel hoped he'd be able to get away early, but his job doesn't work like that. She let him know Shay messaged her, so he knew he was okay. She's hoping Shay will make an appearance this evening, but so far, he's not contacted her again.

She calls Josh down for dinner and dishes up generous portions of lasagne and salad. She covers the rest in foil and puts it back in the oven.

'Do you want some water?' Rachel asks, taking two glasses down from the cupboard.

'Yeah, please.' Josh tucks into his food with gusto. He's always been a good eater and often has seconds, unlike Shay who is picky about each ingredient she puts on his plate. He wants to know where everything has come from, if the meat is local and grass fed. Sometimes he doesn't eat at all; he says he's fasting and that it's a perfectly natural thing for humans to do but she's terrified he'll become anorexic. Even though it's rare in boys compared with girls, it can be a problem amongst teenagers.

'Has Shay messaged you? He messaged me earlier.'

'Nah.' Josh doesn't even look up.

'Do you have any ideas where he might have gone?'

Josh pulls a face, glances up at her and shakes his head, mouth stuffed like a hamster.

'Has he said much to you, about anything that's bothering him?'

He shakes his head again, staring at his plate.

'What about those boys he's been hanging around with; you know, the ones who beat him up?'

He takes a gulp of water. 'He's dumb hanging out with them. They're always causing trouble round here. They pulled up someone's for-sale sign and chucked it through their window.'

'What? Today? How do you know that?'

'On the way home from school, a guy was boarding up his window and my mate asked him what happened. I think he's put it on the local Facebook page with a vid from his security camera of them doing it.'

'Do you know if Shay was involved?'

'Can't really see their faces; they're wearing snoods over their noses and hoodies over their foreheads.'

'Have they been arrested?'

He shrugs.

Rachel eats a small mouthful of food. Her boys chat all the time, but she's not sure how much they confide in each other. She's not been paying them as much attention as she normally would, since setting up her life-coaching business has taken up every spare moment. Dealing with Shay's bad behaviour has used up what little energy she's had to spare.

'I don't suppose you know anything about a large amount of cash in Shay's room do you? Where he got it from?'

Josh stuffs a loaded fork of salad into his mouth. Rachel waits for him to finish.

'How much money?' He speaks while he's still chewing.

'A lot. Please don't speak with your mouth full. Some money has gone missing from Zach's fund at school. I want to know if it's anything to do with that. That's why I'm asking. I thought you might know.'

Josh looks at her as though she's mad if she thinks he's going to squeal on his own brother.

'I'm concerned he's in trouble, that's all.'

'I don't know about any money. All I know is he's a cheapskate. Promised to give me five pounds after school for wiping and buffing his trainers.'

'What? When did you do that?'

'Last night. Took me ages, said he'd give me the money this afternoon.'

'Why did he ask you? Was he going somewhere special?'

'I dunno, do I?' His fork clatters onto his plate. He picks it up again and twirls it in a circle.

Rachel examines his expression and isn't convinced he doesn't know anything about it. Shay's not normally mean to Josh. Is it possible Shay wanted to come home last night but couldn't for some reason?

David's car finally pulls up on the drive as she finishes putting the plates in the dishwasher. She takes the lasagne out of the oven and slices a generous portion onto a warm plate. She uncovers the remains of the salad and pours David a glass of water. He's much quieter than usual. She hopes he's not upset that she and Josh ate their dinner early. In the light over the dining table she notices his face is sallow, creased with stress and exhaustion. On days like this she doesn't like to ask him how his day has gone, partly because he can't say too much about what sort of cases he's been treating, but also because she's not sure she wants to know if there were any complications or if he had to deliver bad news. She can only imagine the toll of having other people's lives in his hands, day in, day out, their hope riding on his decisions and actions. If she and David weren't living together, would he even bother feeding himself after a long stressful day?

'So you think Shay's okay then?' he asks, picking up his fork and using the side of it to cut a corner off the lasagne. The sweet-smelling meat and bechamel sauce ooze out of the layered sheets of pasta.

'Seems so.' Rachel explains how she searched Mick's place before realising Shay's phone was back on, and how they had gone into town together, tracking the phone to the bus station and to one particular bus.

'Mick swears he looked at every single face on that bus, but Shay must have been hiding under the seats or something because he didn't see him. As soon as the bus left, the tracker confirmed he was still on it. I messaged Shay again and that's when he replied, thank goodness.' Rachel shows David the message even though she sent it to him earlier. She wants to know what his take on it is.

'Makes me wonder what he means – sorting what out himself?' David forks a large mouthful of lasagne into his mouth.

'I don't know.'

'Where do you think he's gone?'

'I'm hoping you're right about him staying at a friend of Ethan's, and that he'll come back tonight and talk to us about what happened in the woods.'

'Have you tried calling him since he texted?' David rips a piece of ciabatta and wipes it across his plate.

'His phone is off again. Did Simon speak to Ethan?'

'When you told me Shay had got in touch, I spoke to Simon, and he said he received a similar message from Ethan around the same time.'

'So did Ethan say they were together, or where they were going?'

'I don't think so, just said he was okay and had stuff to sort out.'

'The longer this goes on, the more I'm worried Shay is running away from something to do with the attack on that girl.'

12

'What girl?' David puts his plate in the sink and stands there staring out of the window.

Rachel takes the key lime pie out of the fridge. 'Didn't I tell you? A girl called Bella was attacked in the woods at the party. She was seen with Shay, wearing his hoodie.'

'Shit, really?'

She cuts a piece of pie and hands it to him while she tells him about the police turning up at the woods, stopping the parents from clearing up the party mess. 'They said they didn't want any evidence disturbed.'

'Do they know what time it happened?'

'Late, just after one I think.' She tries to read his expression, wondering why the time matters. 'The police called everyone into the school this afternoon and showed photos of all the things that were left behind and surprise, surprise' – her throat catches – 'Shay's hoodie was there.'

David stops chewing and shoots a surprised look at her.

She folds her arms.

He swallows then picks up the pie crust and stuffs it into his mouth in one go, leaving it open so she can hear every slurp and crunch of him chewing. He hurriedly swallows, choking and coughing into the back of his hand, crumbs and spit flying everywhere.

'Are you all right?'

He nods. Much as she loves him, it makes her cringe. He grabs his glass of water and drinks it back. She's seen all sorts of unsavoury sides to him since he's moved in. He was all set to stay in a hotel; perhaps she should have let him instead of doing her usual thing of trying to save someone at her own expense. She'd only have seen the smart polished side of him, not the toilet habits or the nail clipping over the bin that makes her shudder at the thought.

'We spoke to one of the other kids who saw this girl wearing Shay's hoodie at the party.'

'Sorry, you mean the girl who was attacked?' His voice is croaky.

'Yes, in the woods.'

'I see. Shit. Do you know if she's okay, if she's said anything?'

'She's in hospital with a bad head injury. She can't speak.'

'And you think Shay could be involved?'

'No, he wouldn't hurt anyone, especially a girl. But this boy thinks Shay and Bella were together, as a couple.'

'Oh, did you know about that?'

'He's not mentioned her to me. The problem is, it's not the only thing pointing at Shay.'

'Why, what else has happened?'

'Lorna at the school told me the cash they collected for Zach's new wheelchair has been stolen. Six hundred pounds. When I checked Shay's room this morning, there was around the same amount at the back of his drawer.'

'I thought he'd learnt his lesson about stealing.'

'I don't know if he took the cash but part of me knows he's certainly capable. I mean, after the moped incident anything is possible. Then I thought, why would he? If he needed the money for running away, why didn't he take it all with him?'

David is silent for a moment. His head hangs forwards, hand pressed to his forehead as though she's told him someone has died.

'There's something I should tell you.' He looks up, his tone solemn. He puts his fork down on the plate.

'Oh, okay.' She rests her chin awkwardly on the back of her hand, trying to look calm, but her pulse is racing as she wonders what's coming.

'Please don't be mad at me.' He presses his palms together.

Rachel's heart pounds in her ears. David pushes his plate into the middle of the table and looks away as though he already wishes he'd kept quiet. The vein in his temple is pulsing. He stares back at the floor.

'You're making me nervous. Please tell me what it is.' Nausea pushes up her throat.

'I knew Shay was going to the party.'

'What? How?'

David sweeps his hand across the melamine table, then brings his hands back together.

'Because I was the one who told him he could go.'

13

'Why did you do that?' Rachel stands up, her chair grating against the flagstone tiles. Suddenly she's unsure of this man sitting opposite her. This man she's allowed into her life, into her bed when she was vulnerable, lonely.

'I'm so, so sorry.' David rubs his head.

'What made you do it?'

'I don't know, I felt sorry for him I suppose. I remember being that age, being impulsive, sensitive, getting in trouble for making stupid decisions. He's a good kid who's just got caught up with the wrong crowd. I wanted to give him a break.'

'So you left the window open for him to climb out, not because he was too hot.'

'I'm sorry.' He drags his hand through his hair.

'After I explicitly told him he couldn't go. And with no thought to those scumbags who were after him before? What if one of them had climbed in and attacked him? Attacked us while we were asleep in our bed?'

'I know, I admit I didn't think of that, what danger we could be in.'

Rachel turns away, tears pricking her eyes. 'You didn't see him when he came home that day, clothes torn, blood everywhere. He was shaking and could barely speak he was so scared they'd come back for him.'

'I don't know what I was thinking. I was tired I suppose. It was a moment of weakness.'

'What hurts the most is you lying to me, going behind my back.'

'I'm so sorry. I thought I was helping in a way. We had a chat and cut a deal. He was allowed to go for about an hour as long as he was back by midnight. I thought he'd appreciate it and it would be the start of him behaving more responsibly.'

'It wasn't for you to decide.' She thumps the table with her fist.

'I know that now, but he promised he'd be back on time.'

'And you believed him.' Rachel throws her hands up.

'I trusted him. I thought we had an understanding.'

'He was grounded. Have you forgotten that?'

'We'd talked a bit while you were out with Josh last week, and he confided in me, said there were things he'd done that he was ashamed of, but he couldn't share them with you because you were always so...'

'Yes?'

'Judgemental about everything.'

'I see. What sort of things?'

'Drugs, stealing.'

'So how long have you two been having these cosy chats?' She leans down, pressing her fingers into the table.

'It's not like that. It was you who asked me to take him go-karting, remember? Try and bring him out of this mood he's always in.'

'I didn't expect you to become chums and work against me.'

'I'm sorry, I didn't mean it to be like that.' He reaches across the table, but she snatches her hands away.

'Did you find out what he's been up to, what's bothering him?'

'No, he wouldn't say. He seemed too scared to tell me.'

'So how do you know he didn't come back at midnight?' She crosses her arms again and strides around the kitchen.

'I stayed up, checked his room, messaged him but there was no reply.'

'Why didn't you wake me?'

David is quiet for a long moment. 'Because I went out looking for him.'

'You did what?' Rachel's face burns at what she's hearing.

'I drove to the woods.'

'What on earth? You should have woken me up.' She slaps the table with her palm.

'I suppose I wanted to put it right first, by myself. I realised what a big mistake I'd made by trusting him. He let me down. I honestly thought he'd grown up a bit, stopped getting in trouble.'

'So what about that girl...?'

'What about her?' David frowns.

'Did you see them together? Was she wearing Shay's hoodie?' She tries to read his face but he's giving nothing away.

'I don't even know what she looks like.'

'What *did* you see then?' She steps back from him and leans against the counter, hands behind her back.

'Some kids milling around a few pop-up tents. It looked like the party was over, but the bonfire was still alight. I asked a couple of people if they'd seen Shay and no one had, or they were too out of it to remember.'

'So, what did you do?'

'I walked round the clearing calling his name. I tried texting and phoning, but his phone was off.' He lays his arms on the table, palms up.

'You should have told me straight away.' She paces up and down the kitchen. If only she'd heard him go out. 'We could have gone up there together and maybe we'd have found him.'

'I can see that now. I'm so sorry.' David shakes his head slowly.

'You know what this means, don't you?' She stops dead and spins round to face him.

'What?'

'You have to tell the police you were there. Explain that you tried to find Shay, that you didn't find him or see Bella.'

'Okay... if you really want me to.' David frowns.

She leans across the table and presses her hands down again.

'Because if you don't, someone else will and they might start pointing the finger at you.'

14

'But if I go to the police and say that, they'll put me straight on their list of suspects.'

'You didn't do anything wrong though, did you? You can't lie to the police. They'll find out. They may already know.' Rachel sits on the sofa in the adjoining living room.

'Do you think Shay was playing me? That he never intended to come home last night?'

'Possibly, but why do you say that?'

'His bad behaviour seemed to start soon after I moved in here. I've been wondering if I somehow caused it, because he didn't agree with you moving your new partner in.'

'I must admit I've been pondering the same thing. He was upset from the moment I told him about you. I think he was holding out hope that Mick and I would get back together.' She fluffs a cushion and hugs it to her body.

'Remember that first time you brought the boys to my house? It was the most awkward evening, wasn't it?' He gives a half-hearted laugh.

'I was so embarrassed.' Neither of her boys spoke to David until

Josh was desperate for the toilet. It was as though they'd made a pact with each other to be as awkward as possible. David had been so welcoming, although his house was very grand, furnished with antiques and family heirlooms. He's not once complained about losing all those valuable items in the fire.

David rubs his palms together. 'As I'm in so much trouble with you already, I'm going to say something that you're not going to like, but frankly it's been playing on my mind, and I'd rather come out with it.'

'This sound ominous.' She hugs the cushion tighter.

'Do you think it's possible that Shay had something to do with the fire at my house?'

'Woah, that's a biggie.' Her nails dig into the soft fabric. 'You're accusing my son of arson?' Her voice rising as she shoves the cushion away.

'I'm sorry, I know it's a wild accusation but given everything that's gone on and the people he was hanging out with, I thought maybe he was involved because he's angry I'm dating you, but the fire got out of hand.'

'I honestly cannot believe you think he'd do that.'

'I wasn't going to say anything, but the assessor's report from the insurers came back. They confirmed it was arson. Started in the hall by the front door. Accelerant was found.' He rubs his forehead with the heel of his hand.

'Bloody hell, David. I don't know what to say except you can't really think Shay has something to do with this, no matter how he feels about us being a couple.' She shifts forwards to the edge of the sofa rubbing her palms together, hoping David will see sense.

'Knowing someone wants to hurt me has rather shaken me up.'

He's not exaggerating. He'd been living there alone for years, so it's only him that could be the target.

'I don't believe for a second Shay would do that.'

'It was just something he said; I'm probably wrong.' He looks away.

'What on earth did he say to make you think it could be him?' She wrings her hands together.

'He joked just after the fire, that I must have an arch enemy, someone who's out to get me.'

'Why would he say that?'

David shrugs. 'Maybe he knows who did it.'

'I doubt that.'

'Those boys who were after him threatened to burn his house down, didn't they?'

'They did but it doesn't mean Shay had something to do with the fire at your house.'

He bows his head. 'I didn't know anyone hated me that much.'

'Oh David.' Part of her wants to put her arm around him and comfort him, but after his accusation and lying, she doesn't feel compelled to go anywhere near him.

'I might go to bed early,' he says, as though reading her thoughts. 'It's been a strange day. I'm so sorry, I seem to have made things worse between you and Shay. I'm not much good at this step-parenting lark, am I?'

'I know you were only trying to do the right thing. He took advantage of your good nature. I honestly don't know what's going on with him, but I'm sure he wouldn't do anything like that to you or your property. If you're going to bed, I'm going to try and call him again.'

David slopes off out of the room and up the stairs. It's only 8.30 p.m. Rachel's mind is darting around in all directions. She checks her phone but there are no more messages from Shay. The tracker confirms his phone is off again. Her heart sinks. All she can do is hope he's somewhere safe like at a friend's house. He's old enough to look after himself but she can't help thinking if he was safe, he'd have called her by now, even if he was still angry with her.

The floorboards creak overhead. She stares up at the ceiling. Why didn't she hear David going out last night or coming back in? She usually stirs at the slightest sound. He really should have woken her. It's so disappointing that he sneaked off like that, no matter what he said about trying to connect with Shay and give him some slack. There's something about it that doesn't feel right but she can't pinpoint what it is. Did he really not see Shay or Bella at the woods? It's hard not to doubt his word after he's lied to her. The police will not look favourably on David being there and not coming forward about it straight away.

And thinking Shay started the fire at his house is just crazy. Yes, he's done some stupid things, but he'd never destroy someone's property or potentially harm them. It must be really stressing David out to be thinking that. Maybe someone *is* out to get him. She shivers. There could be some truth in his theory that Shay was trying to put him off dating her though. Perhaps that's why he's been playing up. Boys can be so protective of their mums.

But what keeps popping into her mind is, what else is David hiding from her? She didn't think he was the type to go behind her back. But he's lied about helping Shay disobey her, gone to the woods in the middle of the night, and not told her Shay had gone missing. He could be keeping other secrets from her.

How well does she really know the man she loves?

15

The doorbell rings. For a split-second Rachel freezes. Is it Shay? Or maybe it's those friends of his David told her about. She checks the doorbell camera and is surprised to see the policewoman who was at the woods standing on her doorstep.

'Mrs Rachel Gulliver? I'm Detective Sergeant Diane Groom. We met at the school yesterday.'

'Oh my God, have you found him? Is he all right?' Rachel's face is burning.

'Could I come in?' DS Groom isn't giving anything away.

'Yes, of course.' Rachel steps aside.

DS Groom has a stout build and is a little heavy-footed as she steps over the threshold in her black regulation boots.

They stand facing each other in the hall. Rachel indicates the living room. Her legs are shaking as she follows DS Groom in and sits near her on the sofa.

'Has something happened to him?' Rachel's voice wavers. She twists her hands together in her lap.

'We don't have any news about Shay but Bella, the girl who was attacked, has remembered a little of what happened to her on the night of the party.'

'Oh, that's good; how is she?'

'She's still in hospital but the doctors say she's improving slowly and she's beginning to remember things and piece together what happened.'

Rachel nods and laces her fingers together, unsure of where this is going.

'Bella was hit with something from behind and fell forwards onto her face, hitting her head on a rock half buried in the ground. She must have blacked out and it was some time before she was found.'

'Poor girl. Did she see who did that to her?'

'No, she didn't, but she does remember one thing that's significant in our investigation.' Her eyes flicker over Rachel's face as if she doesn't want to miss one twitch of her reaction.

Rachel tips her head to the side.

'She remembers very distinctly that she was with Shay at the time of the attack. In fact, she was wearing his hoodie earlier in the evening. As you know, this has been confirmed by one of the other pupils at the high school. And this was before Bella went into the woods with Shay.'

'Oh, I see.' Rachel's eyes widen. She doesn't know what to make of this and resists the urge to swallow hard, not wanting to show how alarmed she is.

'Bella says she took the hoodie off because she became too hot sitting near the bonfire. Both of them had had quite a bit to drink by this point, and she admits they shared a joint.'

'So, what are you saying here? You think my Shay attacked her?'

'I'm not suggesting anything. But the fact that he was there when it happened *is* significant.'

'If you want to speak to my son, how about trying to help me find him and see what he has to say about it?' Rachel immediately regrets her snarky tone, but all she wants to do is bring her son home.

'That's what we'd like to do, hear his side of things. You said he messaged you?' She refers to her notebook. 'Did he say when he'll be back?'

'No and I don't know where he's gone. I was going to contact you again because he's not answering my calls and I'm really worried about him. He's not been himself lately, and not telling me where he's going is so unlike him. I'm sure he wouldn't hurt anyone, especially a girl.'

'Bella doesn't believe for a moment that Shay is the one who attacked her. She said they are... close. And as far as she knows, they care for each other. He was looking after her, consoling her in fact, because her mum and dad recently split up.'

Rachel nods and takes that as a small apology. That's more like the son she knows and loves.

'The thing is, when she regained consciousness in the woods, Shay wasn't there.'

'He wouldn't go off and leave her; he'd have gone to get help.'

The sergeant nods. 'So you've definitely not heard anything at all from Shay since that one message, and you've checked with his friends and don't know where he is?'

'That's right.' She should tell her that David was there looking for Shay. Or call him down so he can do it himself. But she can't bring herself to. She's still trying to process why he lied to her. She isn't sure if she believes he didn't see them.

'Please let us know as soon as he makes contact. We need to speak to him to find out if he knows what happened to Bella.'

Rachel sees her out. She can't shake off the thought that David might know something too.

16

Rachel can't sleep. Her body is rigid because she's lying next to a stranger. He even smells different tonight. He's making strange snoring noises that she's not heard before. She thought she was growing into him, becoming familiar and comfortable, but her mind lists every little thing she doesn't know about him. How does he behave when he's red-rage angry? What is he like if he falls out with someone? What was his nickname at school? Does he prefer chocolate or strawberry ice cream? She's never asked these things and she realises she's only seen the side of him he wants to show her. With her clients, it usually takes several sessions to glimpse the real person as she chips away at the many masks they hold up to protect themselves. David is proving even harder to unravel because there are parts of his life he's not willing or able to share with her.

She was dazzled when she first met David, by his steady, calm but powerful demeanour, and when he showed an interest in her, she was a pushover. She admits that. They met at her friend Sarah's New Year's Eve dinner party. And Sarah being Sarah sat them together. The two singletons among all the loved-up couples. At first she thought he was aloof because he was quiet and hadn't seemed to notice her. But she later found out he was trying not to come across as too keen. Trying to keep a semblance of decorum.

She sits up and checks her phone. Even though it's on, she wonders if she's missed hearing the ping of a message arriving from Shay. Nothing. Worry grips her again. Her jaw clicks. What if he's not all right after all? What if he's harmed himself? She shivers involuntarily. David is fast asleep next to her, wrapped in the duvet. How can he sleep so soundly when they've no idea if Shay is safe? He should feel some responsibility.

She reaches for her satin dressing grown from the chair and slips it on, sliding her phone into the pocket. Padding across the landing, she checks on Josh before creeping downstairs to Shay's room. She opens the Roman blind a few inches to avoid putting the light on and slides open the bedside cabinet drawer. Carefully, she eases out the brown paper bag of money and sits with it on the bed. There are two bundles of tens and twenties. She still doesn't want to believe he stole the money collected for Zach. He could be caught up with selling drugs or petty crime. But if there was something he needed, why didn't he ask her for it? He'd go mad at her prying in his drawers. But she's his mother, not his best friend. He's barely sixteen and still her responsibility. A child in the eyes of the law. The cash could be to do with the youths who came to the door. If it *is* Zach's money, then what is clear is that she cannot tell the school about it until she's spoken to Shay and found out exactly how he came to have it in his possession.

She puts the money back and notices his laptop light on. She decides to look through his email and web history to see if she can find out where he's gone, but she doesn't know the password. The light makes her squint in the darkness as she opens it. She remembers his old password and tries that. Two other guesses fail before it locks down. She's tempted to slam the lid. Instead, she tugs hard at the blind and lowers it. Shay is really testing her this time. He knows how much she'll worry. He wouldn't do this to her deliberately. But his message was abrupt, harsh. If she's upset him about something other than the party, she wishes she could think what it is.

In the kitchen she pours a glass of apple juice and drinks it down. She takes her phone out of her dressing gown pocket. There's a message on the home screen from Alice Kirby, her newest client.

Thanks for today's taster session, Rachel. Would love to book a full slot in a couple of days if you have anything available? I'm keen to get started. Regards, Alice

Rachel will reply in the morning when she has her diary in front of her. She's not sure she's going to be up to working at all until she knows Shay is safe and well, but she can't afford to lose a new client, especially one who will need quite a lot of guidance. She thinks about the bereavement Alice has suffered. Losing a child must be the hardest loss of all. If she can help her get her confidence and work life back on track, it will have a huge knock-on effect with everything else.

She refills her glass and takes it up to her bedroom. As she's going to the en-suite bathroom, David's phone lights up on his bedside table. The name flashing up is Julie. Someone from work, she guesses. It's 9.15 p.m. She's tempted to ignore it. He's not on call as far as she's aware, but what if it's urgent? David is snoring. She hates to wake him, but he might be annoyed if she doesn't tell him.

'David, your phone is ringing,' she whispers close to his ear.

It takes a couple of seconds for him to stir.

'It's someone called Julie. Do you want to take it?'

He grunts something and opens one eye. She passes the phone

to him. Normally she'd leave him to it, but she's curious to hear what this is about. If he's not on call, why is she ringing him this late?

'Are you okay?' His voice is croaky. He opens the other eye, sits up and plants his feet on the sheepskin rug. There's a look of alarm on his face as he walks onto the landing, pulling the door closed behind him. Rachel tries to listen, but she can't hear anything concrete. Whatever it is, it seems serious.

When he comes back in, David's face is pale and drawn in the dim lamp light.

'Who's Julie?' she asks.

'She's one of our nurses. Her son Olly goes to the same after-school football practice as Shay.'

'So why is she calling so late?' Rachel crosses her arms.

'Olly hasn't come home. He's missing.'

17

'What do you mean?' Rachel sits on the bed.

'Olly went to an outdoor concert with some friends after school. He was supposed to be home by now. Julie heard about Shay going missing so called me first to see if he'd come back, if there was a possibility they were out together. I've offered to go over there.' He pulls his socks on.

'Do you think they're out somewhere together?' She's desperate for reassurance.

He goes to speak then pauses. 'It doesn't sound likely as Shay's been gone a while now. Might be an idea to check his laptop, see if you can find any clues, because I've got a bad feeling he's not coming home anytime soon.'

'How can you say that?' Her voice jumps up.

'I thought he'd be back by now, didn't you?' He stops and tilts his head at her. He's more perceptive than she thought.

She nods. Her chest aches with worry. Shay has never gone anywhere this long without letting her know where he is. Even through the worst patch of him going off with those boys, he always told her what time he'd be home and where he was, if he was hanging out in the village or round a friend's house.

'Don't you want me to come with you?' she asks, wanting to hear what Julie has to say, trying to convince herself that their situation is different.

'What about Josh?' He puts on an old pair of jeans and a sweatshirt.

'I'll wake him, bring him with us. I mean, this is beginning to freak me out.'

'I think you should stay here. There's no point alarming him and he has school in the morning.'

'I suppose there's a slim chance Shay could still turn up tonight, and someone ought to be here.' She follows him downstairs. 'Do you know if Simon has heard from Ethan yet?'

'No. But I'm going to call him. I think we'll have to inform the police about Shay.' He kisses her cheek.

'I've already told them. A policewoman came over while you were asleep. Bella, the girl who was attacked, remembers Shay being with her.'

'Is that all she remembers?' He looks her in the eye.

'She knows it wasn't him who attacked her. Sounds as though they're fond of each other.'

'That's something. But there was nothing else?'

'You really need to tell them you were there.'

'I will, I promise.' He gives her a bear hug. For a moment she melts into his reassuring embrace and part of her trusts him again.

'Please keep your phone on and let me know if there's any news.'

'Will do. See you later.'

His mobile pings in his pocket. As he takes it out, Rachel glances at the name on the screen. George. That's Nate's dad.

Another boy from school. David reads the message then frowns at her, mouth open. For a second he doesn't speak.

'George says Nate didn't come home from school this afternoon. Left for the bus at the usual time but apparently didn't catch it. Not answering his phone. Thinks he might have dropped it again, so maybe his phone's stopped working. He's checking round all his friends. Wonders if Shay is back and if he might have heard from him.'

'This can't be a coincidence, can it?'

He shakes his head.

'Do you think they all know what happened to Bella? Maybe they witnessed the attack and are worried about coming forward.'

'I don't know.' He texts George back.

'Mick said Shay told him he was scared.'

He looks up. 'Of what?'

'We don't know, but maybe Olly and Nate felt like that too.'

After he's gone, she bolts the door and checks the live doorbell webcam on her phone. As he gets into his car, David takes another call. Is he speaking to Julie again, or is it one of the other parents? She hopes he lets her know as soon as one of the children turns up safe and sound.

She creeps up the stairs so as not to wake Josh. He is tucked up in bed, she can cling to that at least. His door is slightly ajar and he's shifting under the sheets. Has he been listening to their conversation? If he heard what they were saying, he'll be terrified. She sits in his computer chair facing his bed.

'Mum,' comes his little voice from under the duvet.

'Why aren't you asleep?' she says gently, moving closer.

'I can't.' He sits up and she leans forward, wrapping her arms around him and the bed clothes in one big hug, realising she needs it as much as he does. 'Is Shay home yet?'

'Not yet, but soon, I'm sure. Just not today.'

'Why?'

'I'm sorry, I don't know. Can you think where he might be?'

Josh shrugs.

'Do you think he's gone somewhere with Ethan, maybe Olly and Nate as well?'

'How would I know?' He sounds annoyed with her now. She doesn't want to push him, but he could know something, a tiny thing that could help them work out where Shay is and maybe the others too.

'I thought you might know if they had a special place they go to meet up, like a secret den.'

Josh shakes his head, hair flicking out in all directions.

'It's okay.' She hugs him again and he tries to resist her, but she strokes his head and the back of his neck and gradually he calms down. For a few moments he's quiet and then he cries into her shoulder, his whole body shaking with the effort.

'Everything is going to be okay, I promise,' she tells him, and tries her hardest to believe it herself.

18

When Josh is asleep, she goes back downstairs and switches the TV on, but she can't take in anything the news presenter is saying.

She ought to start getting ready for bed, but how can she until she hears some good news? She checks Facebook. On the local page, one of the mums she knows posted two hours ago, asking if anyone has seen her daughter. Maybe they're all being teenagers, not coming home when they're supposed to and her and the other parents are worrying too much. But she can't help it. Something in her gut is telling her this is different.

There are no new messages from Shay or David. She thought there would be something. Surely one of the boys has contacted home by now. Perhaps she should call David and ask. What has he been doing all this time at Julie's house? She pictures him with his arm around her, consoling her. They move closer into a kiss like in a TV drama. *Stop it!* She trusts him. This is not his fault. Except, he lied to her.

Her phone lights up and buzzes. She snatches it up from the sofa hoping it's Shay or David. It's Suki, the parent who posted on Facebook.

'Everything all right, Suki?'

'So sorry to call you this late, Rachel, but I'm just ringing round all Kim's friends.' She pauses and seems to catch her breath. 'I wondered if by any chance Kim was there with you or Shay? I'm sorry I should have checked, but has he come home yet?'

'I saw your post on Facebook. No, no, he's not come home, and Kim isn't here either. I'm sorry, I've not seen her.' Rachel doesn't know what else to say. It's been over a year since Kim and Shay dated. She must be at the end of a long list of Suki's contacts.

'My husband called me at work this evening to say Kim wasn't home yet. She had violin practice so wasn't leaving school until about 4 p.m. and then she was going to walk to a friend's house, but the friend said Kim texted to cancel because she was getting a migraine and was going home instead. We didn't know about this. And she certainly never arrived home. Trouble is, we weren't expecting her until about 7 p.m. when in fact it's been hours since anyone's seen her. No one seems to know where she is.'

Rachel swallows hard, taking in the rising panic in Suki's voice. How can she begin to offer help when her son is missing too? Four children missing is too big to comprehend.

'Where can she be? It's as though she's vanished.'

Suki's desperation stabs Rachel's heart. 'I'm so sorry. Have you told the police? Two more of Shay's football friends didn't go home either: Nate and Olly. George messaged David earlier, and Julie called before that. He's gone over to see her. I think all our children must be together. Is it possible they've gone to another one of these parties without telling us?' Rachel is aware that she's rambling now, trying to fill the silence because the other possibilities are too frightening to take in. She stands up and paces around the room.

'But our Kim doesn't like parties.'

The deafening silence that follows balloons. Rachel has no response. No other explanation as to where they could have gone.

'We'll have to call the police,' Suki says at last.

'I'm sorry I can't help. I'll get David to call you; he's spoken to the other parents.' As soon as the call ends, Rachel lets out a long breath. What is going on? She texts David to tell him Kim didn't arrive home this evening and to call Suki if he can. She sends him her number.

It's a few minutes before he replies saying he'll call Suki.

Any news on Olly or Nate?

Nothing. Ethan is still not answering Simon's calls. They're going to report him missing.

19

Five children missing. They must be somewhere together, surely. Now she's reported Shay missing, will the police take it seriously? The message from him shows he's alive and well but like Ethan, why haven't they heard from him again?

In the kitchen she props her phone up sideways, so she can see the whole screen. She decides to make herself a hot chocolate and switches Talk Radio on low. The chatter about mundane subjects – the pros and cons of online shopping – is soothing and normal. She boils the kettle and spoons three heaps of the brown powder into a mug and adds a large splash of milk. She stirs until long after it has dissolved and then tops it up with boiled water. The chocolaty aroma is delicious and calming. She carries it into the living room with her phone in the other hand.

As she's about to sit down, a banging noise outside makes her jump. Hot chocolate splashes over the rim of her mug, burning her hand. She hurriedly licks it off and clicks open the door camera app on her phone.

Someone in a hoodie is standing at the front door. It's not Shay, even though she can't make out their face, which is half covered in a snood. Shay doesn't walk with a swagger. This person's eyebrows are thick and dark. She thinks it's a man, older than Shay by a couple of years, but a similar height. He turns to the right and taps on Shay's bedroom window then looks around, shifty, checking to see if anyone is watching him. Another man in a dark red hoodie stops at the end of the path, smoking and jigging about on the spot, scanning around in all directions. The first man tap-taps again on the window. Rachel marches down the hallway and yanks open the door.

'Where's Shay?' she asks loudly, making him jump.

'Fuck's sake man, you wanna give me a heart attack?' He wipes his mouth on the back of his hand.

It takes her a moment to decipher his mumble.

'Where is my son?' she says again.

'I don't know, do I man. In there I guess?' He aims a punch at the window but stops short of touching it.

'No, he's not. He didn't come home last night.'

His puzzlement mirrors her own. It seems he really believed Shay was at home. 'Shit, man. He owes me big time, innit.'

'What do you mean? What does he owe you?' She frowns, wondering if he's armed. She wishes he would stand still for two seconds.

'You tell me where he is, like, and I give you no trouble.' He twirls his hand in front of his face then grabs his groin and jerks his hand upwards.

'I don't know where he is. He's gone missing.' She's annoyed at her trembling words and coughs before she continues with a steadier voice. 'Are you sure you haven't seen him? You need to tell me if you know something.'

'Better not have run off with my cash.' He tuts and looks at the other man then back again at her, ending with an exaggerated shrug. It's probably a tick he's developed to make himself look cool.

Does Shay normally open the window to speak to them or invite them in? Perhaps these men have something to do with where that money has come from. But how can her sixteen-year-old schoolboy son owe this man hundreds of pounds? If it was possible to have a decent conversation with him, maybe she'd ask, but she's shaking all over. The man at the end of the path whistles and walks towards where the man is standing in front of her. She flinches, wondering what they're going to do to her, if they're going to push her into the house and follow her in. But he passes something to the first man who puts it in his pocket and turns to go. Was it a knife? Could he be here to give something to Shay to look after? A blade, drugs, drink, as well as to collect that money?

They stroll away as if they've just left their own house. They could go to any lengths to get that money back. But she couldn't just hand it to them without speaking to Shay first.

She shuts and locks the front door then staggers into the living room, where she picks up the hot chocolate with shaking hands. A thin wrinkly skin has formed on the top. She takes a sip. It's cooled down and doesn't taste as good as it usually does.

She has no intention of going to bed until David comes home. For now, she watches the door camera on her phone again, hoping the man doesn't come back with more than one friend.

What has Shay been up to right under her nose?

20

DAY TWO

It's gone midnight and Rachel is still waiting for David to come home. She unplugs Shay's laptop and sits with it in the living room, determined to get into it this time. She switches it on and thankfully enough time has passed since it locked her out. It asks for a password. She tries his date of birth and the month. Too obvious. She tries Josh's. No luck. She goes back into his bedroom and looks around. She spots an old photo of Shay and Josh on the beach in Corfu propped up dog-eared on a shelf. She remembers it well. They're walking backwards into the sea, a competition between them to try to stay standing the longest. Of course, being older, Shay won. Josh was only about five. Shay was eight. He'd been a quirky child, always wanting to do things differently and he'd gone through a phase of doing everything backwards. He'd even tried to talk backwards.

Parenting seemed so simple then. Their lives were uncomplicated. She and Mick were content. They were focused on the kids. The children's needs were manageable. If either of the children hurt themselves, she could place a plaster or a bandage over the injury and give them a cuddle. Shay was a cheeky, smiley child who laughed a lot. She's almost forgotten he was like that, and her heart tugs; she misses it so much. Guilt gnaws at her bones. Whatever is bothering Shay, whatever trouble he's in, he didn't feel he could turn to her for help like he used to, like he should be able to.

That photo must have been taken in 2011, or was it 2010? She picks it up and turns it over. It's not that long ago really, yet for him it's half his life. She's written 29 July 2011 on the back. Could that be it? She takes it into the living room and types in 290711. The screen miraculously opens up to her.

His background is a photo of their old dog, Prince, who died four months ago. The boys pestered her to buy a puppy after his death, but she couldn't bring herself to and then David had moved in, so getting another dog seemed too much to deal with. Was it that, or was it more because David might not approve? Although she didn't ask him, she knew he wasn't used to living with pets. Maybe she's been trying to please David too much, putting him above her children's needs.

She clicks on Outlook and when it loads up, his emails scroll down in front of her. She doesn't recognise many of the names. It's mostly spam and sales pitches from sports companies. It downloads yesterday's and today's emails. She scans through them, but nothing jumps out, so she checks the deleted folder which is full. That could take a whole afternoon to go through. There are two emails in the drafts folder, both with the same words in the subject box: *Please read this*. Her stomach drops. She opens the first file written at 10.37 p.m. last night:

Mum, please be careful, David

It's the beginning of an email that Shay decided not to send. She knows this because she never received it. He's obviously not realised that Outlook saved it to the drafts folder. She clicks on the next one, dated a few minutes later at 10.41 p.m. It looks like he's started it again.

Mum, you can't trust him, whatever he says, he's not telling you

Is it to do with David going behind her back and letting him go to the party? Why didn't Shay finish the message and send it to her if he wanted to tell her something important?

She clicks on the start menu and opens Word as a recently used programme. The last document saved is one named Red. She opens it and at first she doesn't know what she's seeing. There's a list of numbers on one side and a list subtracted on the other side. The total at the bottom is minus £15,000. Is this to do with the game he plays? This can't be real money. There's a list of hyperlinks underneath but none of them work, except the last one at the bottom. It opens Outlook and an email from someone called Red.

PAY ME £3,000 BY THE END OF THE WEEK OR THAT PHOTO OF YOU WILL BE SENT ROUND THE INTERNET AND TO ALL YOUR FAMILY AND FRIENDS.

She can't believe what she's reading. Why hasn't he told her about this? She glances through the list again. It looks like this is the sixth email Shay has received from this person. Why are they blackmailing him?

Next, she goes through his browsing history. It's all been wiped except yesterday's searches: 'Bayhurst woods', 'how to get help' and 'Suicide Club USA'. She freezes. Shit. Is this what he's been planning? Are all the kids in this together? He's been so unhappy lately and she's felt powerless to help him. What if he's gone off to harm himself? *I need to sort things out my way.* His last words to her are haunting. Is this what he meant? What if all the children who've gone missing are in this club and are planning on doing the same? A sound escapes her lips. She presses her fingers over her mouth and opens the website of the suicide club. On the homepage is a crude graphic of the Grim Reaper holding up a clock, which is counting down the time. There are two days, three hours, forty-six minutes and thirty-eight seconds remaining. She gasps into her hand; hot tears burn behind her eyes as she reads:

Fed up with your life? Why put up with all the shit that's coming your way? Join us on Freedom Day – click on the link and add your pledge.

She shivers. She cannot read any more. This is utterly sick. The thought of Shay being influenced by this brings bile to her throat. Who encourages people to take their own lives as a solution to life's problems? This should not be allowed to be up here, for vulnerable, impressionable children and young adults to read. Perhaps his email to her was meant to be his final one, a cry for help. She swallows back the lump in her throat. There's even an RIP page for people who 'took part' on previous dates. It's sickening to think people really go through with this. Why isn't it in the news, these mass suicides? It has to be some kind of virtual game surely; it cannot be real.

Feel togetherness at last, in this life and the next, with all those taking part.

Does Shay really want to end it all? How can he have been this unhappy without her realising?

After Shay came home beaten up, Finlay managed to persuade him to go to boxing club with him on Tuesday evenings. She hoped it would give him confidence to fight back plus give him a new focus away from the screen, but after a few weeks, he admitted it was harder than he expected, and he gave it up and reverted to staying in his room in the dark playing *Call to Arms*. She should have made more of an effort to speak to him. He might have told her he was being blackmailed. Aiden and Finlay hardly come round any more, so they probably aren't aware. He goes out in the evenings, and she knows he hangs out with older kids at the park because she's seen them. But it's hard to distinguish them in their hoodies, so she can't know whether they're the same ones as earlier.

She remembers one of Shay's rages after having lost a game of *Call to Arms* a week ago, how he started hitting walls and doors, crying and shouting. She tried to persuade him to go for a walk to calm down, but it had made him worse. He blamed her for his dad not being there and for not letting them get a puppy. She suggested he played the game less, take up a hobby or try boxing again and he'd said, *What's the point, what's the point in anything? I just want it all to end.* She didn't think that much of it at the time, but now seeing this website, it makes her wonder whether he was already looking into this suicide club.

Already planning to end his life and persuade his friends to do it with him.

21

It's almost 1 a.m. by the time she hears from David. He tells her there's been no message or call from Olly, and Julie is distraught. Luckily a neighbour went over to stay with her, so David is on his way home.

She checks on Josh who is fast asleep then tiptoes down the stairs and unbolts the front door. She opens the door camera app on her phone and sits on the bottom stair to wait for David.

When his car pulls up on the drive, she opens the door before he rings the bell. He's slow coming in, as though he's walked all the way back.

She shuts the door quietly behind him.

He shakes his head and yawns. 'Olly's still not answering his phone. Julie's left countless messages. She told the police. They might be able to trace his mobile signal if it's still switched on but other than that, as far as they're concerned, it's another case of a runaway teenager.'

'What about all the children put together? Five missing teenagers is too strange to ignore surely?'

'The police are looking into it by all accounts.'

'Two of those boys in hoodies came by earlier and scared me to death. They were older than Shay, at least eighteen.'

'Sounds like the same ones.'

'They knocked on Shay's window expecting him to be there. I asked if they knew where he was, but they didn't have a clue.'

'Did they say anything about calling round the other night?'

'No, but one of them said Shay owes him money.'

'What for?'

'He wouldn't say. Come and sit down. I've got something to show you.' She leads him into the living room where the laptop is open on the sofa.

'Can't it wait till morning?' He yawns again and follows her.

'Not really. I had a look on Shay's laptop and found some very disturbing things. I don't want to alarm the other parents, which is why I think you should see it first.' She isn't going to show him the half-written emails until she's certain what Shay was trying to tell her.

'All right, what is it?' He sinks down into the sofa.

'It's something that could confirm the children have gone off together in some kind of pact.'

'What do you mean?'

She clicks on Shay's internet history and slides the laptop across to him. He frowns, then clicks open the website.

'Fuck this.' He half closes the lid and looks at her.

'Exactly. It scared the shit out of me too.'

'This can't be real, can it? It must be illegal.'

'I thought that, but you hear about these cults in America, don't you? Did Julie say anything at all to you that would flag up self-harm?'

'Not at all. Olly is a happy normal teenager. He misses his dad, of course.'

'He's never suffered with anxiety or depression?'

'I don't think so. As far as I know this behaviour is completely out of character. He doesn't go out and not come home, ever. In fact, as far as I know, they're all A students.' He opens the lid again and scrolls down the page. 'I don't know how to tell if this is a real-life planned event or not.'

'I think we should email this website to the other parents and see what they make of it.'

'We'll have to because if something happens to the children in precisely two days' time... I don't think I could live with myself.' He meets her eyes and looks as though he's going to cry. 'What on earth can have driven them to this?'

'Shay was being blackmailed, so I think it's a fair guess to assume the same was happening to all five children.' Rachel swings the laptop back her way and clicks open the Word document and email from the blackmailer.

'Who is this, what photos?' David squints at the list of emails.

'I can only assume they've taken photos of themselves and sent them to someone they trusted who is now maliciously threatening to spread them around.'

'Not of each other?'

'Could be.'

He takes his phone out and jots down the web address then sends an email to all the other parents, suggesting they check their child's computer history and emails.

Fifteen minutes later, David's phone rings. He speaks for several minutes then hangs up.

'That was George. He's checked Nate's computer and found a couple of those blackmail emails in a folder. There's all sorts in his history including the suicide club. He says it seems to be connected to an online game.'

'I hope that means the suicide club is not real.'

'No, I think it means it *is* real. Nate's been targeted in the game he's been playing. George logged into Nate's computer, went into the game app, because it's already running in the background, and looked in Nate's profile. He clicked on a message notification icon, which took him into the inbox where he found loads of generic in-game messages about the suicide club. Looks like he's been bombarded with them.'

'What game is it?'

'*Call to Arms*. I think it could be one they all play.'

'Oh, shit.'

'George said there was a tagline on the game's homepage: *If you think you're a loser, then you probably are one.*'

'Jesus. Then I don't understand why Shay didn't delete all of this. Every other day's searches have been cleared from his history, including most of yesterday right up to when he pretended to go to bed before the party.'

'Maybe he forgot, or he did intend to come home.'

'Did he say or hint at anything at all to you?'

'Nothing specific, but he did seem down in the mouth considering he was sneaking off to a party.'

'Maybe he wanted me to find that website.' She's not sure yet if she'll be able to forgive David for helping Shay go out. If anything has happened to her son, it's his fault as well as hers. What if those draft emails were to show how scared he was of something? What was it he was trying to tell her about David? She examines the side of his face. If the fire at his house was intended to hurt him, who's to say that person won't try again, except this time he's in her house with her sons. Maybe Shay was right, and David can't be trusted.

Maybe everything left on his laptop was a cry for help. What if Shay did expect to come home last night, but someone stopped him?

22

They wake early the next morning to messages from Suki, George, Simon and Julie. David suggested it was easier to add them all to a WhatsApp group which he's offered to look after as she's under enough strain without having to reply to everyone's comments. All the other parents confirm that their children also had the website for Suicide Club USA in their computers' history. And they all have emails from the blackmailer, threatening to share photos of them if they didn't pay up. George offers to hold a meeting at his house at midday to discuss what to do next.

Rachel checks her diary and emails Alice Kirby with a few dates for her next session. She thought about postponing it, but she can't bring herself to let her down. Besides, it's better to be distracted by work than pacing up and down waiting for Shay to call her. Anyway, Alice seems particularly in need of her help since she's living with the loss of a child. With some clients she's found that it's best to get their sessions under way as soon as possible after the initial taster session in case they get cold feet and decide they don't need a life coach after all, thinking they could easily do it themselves. They sometimes come back a few weeks later telling her they couldn't stick to their self-imposed plan of improvement, and they desperately need her guidance. That's when they realise the true benefit of how a coach can gently ease them along with encouragement and small steps towards their goals.

Alice emails her straight back saying she was hoping for a slot this morning. Rachel wasn't planning on having any sessions today but she says she'll fit her in at 10.45. She wants to be as accommodating as possible, and she feels they made a real connection, but it will be a bit of a rush to get to George's in time for a meeting with the parents of the other missing children.

Rachel makes some fresh coffee and sits at her desk. She should update her diary and check her schedule for the week, but she can't stop worrying about Shay.

The doorbell rings. It's Sergeant Groom. Rachel's heart pounds.

'Hello again. Any news about Shay?' Rachel stands aside and the DS steps inside. Rachel leads her into the kitchen. The DS glances around the tidy room then faces Rachel square on.

'I'm afraid not, Rachel. Can I call you Rachel?'

She nods, eager to hear DS Groom's update.

'Yesterday we combed the woods and found signs of a scuffle not far from where Bella was found. There were tyre tracks that probably belong to a transit van from the housing estate side. We're trying to find a match and check out any CCTV along that road.'

'What do you think happened?' Rachel's neck flushes with a sudden heat that rises to the top of her head.

'We're trying to piece together what occurred after Bella was attacked. What I'm beginning to wonder is, whoever attacked her may well have hurt Shay too.'

'Oh my God,' she murmurs and stares into space.

'Is there anything you can tell us that you think might help?'

'I thought he would have phoned me again by now or come home.' Tears fill Rachel's eyes. She tries to swallow them away, but she's no longer able to cover up how upset she is. 'He's been having a hard time lately after some trouble he got in over a moped and a bunch of layabouts he was hanging around with, so I told him he couldn't go to the party. He sneaked out of his bedroom window.' She tells the DS about the suicide club website she found on Shay's computer. Rachel covers her mouth to try to stop a sob escaping but fails.

'Do you want to show me?' Sergeant Groom's voice is softer.

Rachel picks up the laptop from the living room and opens the lid. DS Groom has a close look at the page filling the screen.

'I think it's because he's being blackmailed.' Rachel shows her the messages demanding £3,000 and the list of other defunct emails.

'I see, yes. It certainly looks like it.'

'The thing is, four of his friends went missing yesterday too. They all have messages like this and the website in their history, and they all play that *Call to Arms* game together online. What if they're all meeting up to go through with this together?'

'I'd like to take this laptop with me and have a look at what's been going on. It might give us some clues as to where they all are and possibly who attacked Bella, if it's linked.'

Rachel takes out her phone and shows the DS Shay's mobile number. 'Maybe you could try and get through to him or work out why it says his phone is switched off.'

DS Groom makes a note of it. 'We may be able to find out where he was when he sent that last message to you.'

'We think he was on a bus leaving Harrow.' She explains how they followed the signal.

'Then if the phone was still on, we should be able to find out where he went from there.'

'Thank you.'

'If you could also give me a list of all the other children who've gone missing, then I can contact their parents and build up a picture of what's going on.'

Rachel opens the WhatsApp group and shows her all the phone numbers, which DS Groom writes down. 'We're having a meeting with the other parents later today to discuss it.'

'Okay, keep me informed please.' She hands Rachel her card.

'I will, thanks.'

She's tempted to tell the DS about David going to the woods to look for Shay, but she'll give him a bit longer to tell them himself. If he knows more than he's saying, they'll find out. She can't protect him. Finding Shay is more important to her than anything.

23

As Rachel is letting the sergeant out of the front door, Alice Kirby is walking up the path. Her red sports car is nowhere in sight. She must have walked or got a taxi. According to the details she gave Rachel, she doesn't live nearby.

'Should I come back?' Alice calls as she approaches.

'You're all right, I'm just leaving.' DS Groom replies. 'I'll be in touch,' she says to Rachel.

DS Groom and Alice pass each other and exchange a pleasant smile. Having a visit from the police is not the image Rachel wants to give to a new client, but the reason is too important and anyway, she'll explain. They're hardly criminals.

'Lovely to see you again, Alice. Do come in.'

'And you. I hope I wasn't interrupting.' When she speaks, her smile doesn't quite reach her eyes. Can a person ever really be happy again once they've lost a child?

'I'm so sorry about that.' She takes Alice's coat and hangs it up.

'Not to worry.'

'Do go through to the conservatory. I'll make some fresh coffee.'

'That would be lovely, thank you.'

In the kitchen, Rachel checks her phone for any messages on WhatsApp from Shay or any developments from David. But there's nothing. If just one of the children turned up, she could believe that they were all fine, but it doesn't feel like that will ever happen.

When Rachel walks back into the living room with a tray of coffee and chocolate biscuits, Alice is standing in front of the fireplace, looking closely at one of her family photos again. She jumps back slightly at being caught out.

'Such handsome boys, but I think they look more like you than their dad. Am I right?'

'That's not their dad, that's my new partner, David.'

'Oh, I see. That explains it then.' She turns towards Rachel and the tight little smile is there again. This time a note of laughter trips off her tongue but Rachel's not sure what's so funny. Maybe she's trying to work out why the police were here.

'Is he not at home today?'

'Sorry, who?' Rachel rests the tray on the conservatory table.

'Your partner... David.'

'Er no, he's working.' Rachel frowns. They've not talked about Alice's partner or husband, if they're still together. Sometimes relationships don't survive long after a child has died.

'What does he do?' Alice follows her in and sits down.

'He's a surgeon.'

'You're here on your own then?'

Rachel's back stiffens. 'Actually, we've had a family crisis.' Something she'll relate to and Rachel hopes it will stop her prying and alleviate any fears she may have about how professional she is.

'I'm sorry, would you rather I came back another time?' Alice moves to pick her bag up from the arm of the sofa.

'No need to be sorry. It's better for me to keep working.' The practiced words fall out of her mouth, but right now she would rather be ringing round all Shay's friends again.

'Are you sure you're okay? You seem a bit... unsettled.'

'I'm coping, thank you. It's just my eldest son.' Rachel sighs. The last thing she wants to do is overshare but saying it out loud might ease the tension in the air and in her head. 'We're not sure where he is. He didn't come home after a party at the weekend.'

'Oh dear, teenager trouble.' She glances back at the family photo.

'You could say that.' She's tempted to tell Alice more, how four other children didn't come home either, but she resists the urge, not wanting to seem unprofessional. This session needs to begin, or she will be late for the meeting at George's house.

'I hope he's back soon.' Alice's lips lift in a bigger smile which pulls at her eyes and Rachel thinks she really does understand the weight of worry that having children brings from the moment they are born. And how no one tells you it gets worse not better as they get older.

By the end of the hour, Rachel is exhausted with the effort and is desperate to get away to George's to find out if there's any good news. She's given Alice a task to come up with five small ways she could reward herself and after two, Alice is struggling. More than once she has to stop herself sighing out loud because she can't wait for the session to end. How rude she would seem if she did that! And how unlike her to feel that way. Her eyes keep flitting to the clock above Alice's head. It was a colossal mistake to work today when she's struggling to concentrate. God, it was unbelievably unprofessional of her to tell a new client about her own family problems. What was she thinking? And this woman has stopped sharing anything; she's being such hard work, resisting all the opportunities Rachel's giving her to open up about herself and get to the root of her lack of confidence. The mask she wears is of someone so full of confidence it comes across as arrogance, which she knows she's not underneath it all. She's just a mother grieving her child with this heavy defence mechanism in place. Wouldn't she be the same? But if Rachel could just see a chink in that façade, perhaps find out what her home life is like, she could find a way through to help her.

'We'll have to leave it there for today,' Rachel says and almost sighs with relief. 'Would you be able to finish this task at home and bring it with you next time?'

'I'll try. Can next time be tomorrow?'

'I usually recommend once a week to give you time to process what's come up in the session.'

'But that seems too far away. I feel I'm making progress already. It's like I've found a lifeline in you Rachel and I don't want to let go.'

Rachel's never sure how to take compliments from clients. Alice could become too dependent on her. But maybe it would be okay for the first few sessions. It would just be so much easier if she knew Shay had been found safe and well.

'Okay, let's book in your next two sessions and aim to make a real breakthrough, shall we? Then we can move on to weekly.' Rachel opens her desk diary. 'I can do tomorrow at midday; how about that?' She grits her teeth and smiles. She hopes it's worth the effort in the long run.

'That would suit very well, thank you.' Alice's whole demeanour changes, as though they've just booked to have a cream tea together. She's gone from desperate woman not wanting to 'let go' of Rachel a few moments ago, to the smug face of the cat that got the cream. Rachel can't help feeling completely unnerved by her.

She shows Alice to the door, then remembers she didn't spot her car.

'You're not driving today?'

'No, my son offered to drop me off and pick me up.'

'Oh. That's lovely. He's grown up then?' A forest green Mercedes is parked across from the drive. It's too far away for Rachel to see him clearly, but she can make out he's wearing a baseball cap.

'He turned twenty a couple of months ago.'

'I never would have imagined you with grown up children.' Rachel wonders if that's come out as a backhanded compliment.

'Just the one.' Alice's jollity vanishes.

'Of course, I'm sorry, my mistake.' Rachel's not sure what made her use the plural. 'I'll see you tomorrow at midday then.' She stands on the doorstep, arms crossed, and watches Alice stride off down the drive. As she gets in the passenger side, Alice's son turns to look at Rachel. She raises a hand in goodbye. He doesn't wave back but faces the front and drives away.

Rachel checks her watch. Two minutes past midday. They've gone way over time and now she's already late. Whizzing round, she grabs her keys, handbag, coat and phone and glances at the screen. Shay's name is there. Her heart skips. At last, he's messaged her. Joy floods her veins. She presses the phone to her chest then swipes it open and taps on WhatsApp. Strange, it's from a different number.

IF YOU WANT TO SEE YOUR SON ALIVE AGAIN, PAY £50,000 BY 9PM TONIGHT. UNDER NO CIRCUMSTANCES TELL THE POLICE. DROP OFF DETAILS WILL FOLLOW.

Rachel stares at the words, trying to make sense of who this has come from. She sits at the bottom of the stairs and drops the phone into her lap. Nine hours? She cradles her face in her trembling hands. How can she possibly raise so much money in less than a day?

What if they've already hurt him?

24

Rachel's phone rings loudly, making her jump.

'Are you coming over? We're all waiting for you. There's been… a message.' David's tone is solemn, flat.

Rachel tries to speak but a sob escapes her lips. She catches her breath, tears running down her cheeks.

'You've got it too, haven't you?'

'Yes,' she whispers.

'All the parents. Fifty thousand pounds.'

'I don't have that kind of money. What the hell is going on?' she screams.

'I don't know.' His voice is small and distant.

'Who's doing this? I don't understand who would take Shay. Why him and the other children?'

'I wish I knew.'

'Do you think it's genuine?' She pulls a tissue out of her bag and wipes her eyes.

'If it's a prank by one of the losers he's been hanging out with, then it's really sick.'

'Maybe it's to do with the fire at your house? What if whoever started it is out to get you, and now they're after us too because you're living here?'

David is silent. Rachel hopes she's not offended him, but she needs to put her child's safety first. She needs to find out who is behind this.

'If that's the case it doesn't account for the other children going missing.'

'I suppose so. Look, I'm coming over.' She wipes the tear tracks on her cheeks and picks up her keys.

'Are you sure you're all right to drive?' David sounds concerned.

'I'll be fine. I need to come and speak to the other parents. We have to decide what to do together.' She ends the call and blots her face with another tissue. She's very tempted to get straight on the phone to DS Groom and tell her everything, but what if the threat is real? The message said not to tell the police. She could be putting Shay's life in danger. No. She can't risk it. She climbs into her car and drives off. She needs to tell Mick about this. It'll break him.

As soon as she arrives at George's she wonders how she got there because she doesn't remember the journey at all. Perhaps she shouldn't have driven, being in such a state of shock. Her mind is so preoccupied, sifting through all her recent conversations with Shay, hunting for something he said or did that would indicate where he could be now, who could have taken him. Was his abductor a stranger to him or someone he knew and trusted? His words echo around her head: *What's the point, what's the point in anything?* It's as though he knew something bad was coming. Is that possible? Had someone threatened him before the emails about the photos? She hopes the police find clues on his laptop to help find him. Part of her wishes she still had it so she could look herself.

David comes out of the double fronted Victorian house before she's got out of the car. He takes her hand and gently pulls her into his arms.

'Where are we going to find fifty thousand pounds from?' She starts crying again, her face planted against the warmth of his shirt.

'I don't know. Try not to worry about that right now; we'll sort it out somehow.'

'How can I not worry? We've got less than nine hours. I don't have anywhere near that amount of money.'

'Look, come and meet everyone. They're in the same predicament.' He links his arm through hers and takes her inside. The hall is lit by half-moon wall lights and would be completely dark without them as there are no windows in this part of the house. David pushes open a wood panel door into a sitting room where two plump sofas are arranged around a roaring fireplace. Several worried and tearful faces look up to greet her. It's as though she's walked into a wake, but she barely knows any of the relatives.

'This is Rachel, my partner and of course Shay's mum. I don't think you've all met each other.'

'Hello everyone. Sorry we're meeting under such awful circumstances,' Rachel says, unable to raise a smile. They all seem to be drinking, which is hardly surprising but she'd rather stay clear headed. She smiles at Suki, petite, pretty and mother of Kim, whom she remembers as a bright, sporty girl with long dark hair, and Simon, Ethan's dad, is sitting next to her nearest the fire. Ethan is the one who Shay hit it off with in the summer. A stocky woman with rosy cheeks she doesn't recognise, jumps up and shakes her hand.

'I'm Julie, Olly's mum. Good to meet you. I take it you've had this demand for money too?' She flashes Rachel her phone screen as if she hasn't already seen the message.

'That's the wording in mine, in shouty capital letters.'

'Same then,' she says, turning to the rest of the room. 'Seems we all received it simultaneously.'

'Is the message from Olly's mobile?' Rachel asks.

'No but it came up with his name as though it was. It's a different number.'

Rachel nods. 'When I saw his name, I thought it was Shay's phone. I'd been so convinced he was okay because he sent me a message to say he was fine. Now I wonder if that was from whoever sent this too.'

'That's what we've been trying to work out.' A man with slicked back greying hair stands up.

'This is George, Nate's dad,' David says. George reaches out to shake her hand.

'I think the messages purporting to tell us our children were fine, were simply to put us off the scent, delay the moment we realised they've been kidnapped and not run away from home.'

Rachel isn't the only one who takes in a sharp breath at the word kidnapped. Suki presses her palms to her face in a pained expression.

'We had some cash go missing at home about a week ago,' Julie says. 'Of course, Olly denied any knowledge of it but now I suspect it's to do with these emails.'

George crosses his arms and nods. 'Come to think of it, Nate received money from all the family for his birthday and he said he was going to put it in his savings account, but when I checked, it hadn't been paid in.'

'I found almost six hundred pounds in cash in Shay's bedroom.'

'Whatever these photos are of, your children were trying to stop the blackmailers from sending them around the internet,' David says. 'And now I'm guessing they're coming to you for more money, this time in exchange for your children's lives.'

'What we need to decide is: do we take a chance and tell the police about the ransom, or do we try and sort this out ourselves?' George asks.

'I can tell you, the police are already on to it,' Rachel says.

'They've found car tracks in the woods near the party and signs of a scuffle. The DS was already theorising about the possibility of Shay being taken.' A murmur runs through the room. 'I think you're all aware that a girl, Bella, who was with him at the party, was attacked? She's still in hospital but at the moment can't remember exactly what happened. Though she does recall she was with Shay. The police have taken his laptop to try and find clues. They know about the emails and suicide club website and are looking into it.'

'It doesn't seem to be to do with the suicide club though does it, which is a small blessing,' Julie says.

'It might be an option they considered if they were scared of the blackmailer,' Suki says.

'I hope the police being aware isn't going to jeopardise our children's safety. Whoever has taken our children might not take too kindly to the police sniffing around,' says George.

'How are you suggesting we pay this ransom then?' Julie asks, incredulous. 'Some of us aren't in a position to magic up fifty thousand pounds out of nowhere.'

'We're not paying it and we're not telling the police yet,' David says and folds his arms. He's been listening intently.

'You can't be serious?' Rachel asks.

'Who's to say they won't ask for more?' He frowns.

'And if we tell the police, they'll be all over it and could scupper our chances of getting our children back,' Simon says, catching David's eye. Rachel assumes they've already discussed this and worked out a plan.

'These are our children we're talking about; I can't believe you're considering this option,' Rachel says. Everyone gawps at her. She doesn't really know these people. She doesn't have to do as they say.

'Whether we like it or not, we're all in this together, and we have to come to a consensus.'

Rachel grips her phone tighter. Suki's on the verge of tears.

'I say we take a vote, first on whether we involve the police. Hands up if you agree,' George says. A murmur ripples around the room. Not one hand goes up.

'Good. Now who's in favour of paying the ransom?'

Rachel and Julie are the only ones who raise their hands. Rachel's not sure how she's going to find such a large amount of money. She glances at David, incredulous that he's agreeing not to pay. She half hoped he would consider lending it to her. It's clear it's a risk, but how else are they going to get their children back?

George stands up. 'That's it then. For the moment we've voted not to give in to whoever these criminals are, and not to tell the police.'

'And you'll happily put your children's lives at risk?' Rachel asks.

'Not happily. But I'd rather try and find out who's behind this first. Who it is playing games with us.' George drains his glass of red wine.

'It could even be the kids themselves for all we know. They're an intelligent bunch. Who's to say they've not hatched up this whole plan to see if they can squeeze some money out of us.' David lets out a half note of laughter, looking to George then Simon who both nod their approval. It's feeling more and more like a boys' club, which Rachel does not feel a part of.

'Are you being serious? They're playing games, is that what you think? Whoever attacked Bella was not mucking about.' Rachel glares at each of them in turn.

'Like David says, who's to say they won't ask for more if we pay the first amount?' Suki says.

'I can't believe this.' Rachel shakes her head. 'David, I want to go home. I'd rather deal with this on my own.'

'That's up to you, of course it is. None of us are bound by this decision.' Simon helps himself to some more red wine. No one has even offered Rachel a drink, not that she wants one. She looks round at them all. Apart from Julie, they're all well decked out in expensive clothes and from the cars she's seen parked on the drive, are more than capable of raising a large amount of money quickly, yet they don't want to pay it. She's not sure she wants to mix with people who put money before their children. It feels as if she's gate-crashed an exclusive club and doesn't understand the rules.

'Have any of you thought about who, other than our children, could be behind this?' she asks.

'Of course we have,' George snaps.

'And David, could there be a link between you, Simon and Julie and where you work?' Rachel waits for an answer, but their faces are blank. 'What I mean is, maybe check your records for disgruntled patients?'

The atmosphere drops to a sub-zero temperature with her suggestion. Everyone stays silent, glancing at each other.

'That's a long shot and how does that apply to the other kids who've been taken?' Simon asks.

She can't answer that, and no one is even looking at her. She's had enough and turns to go. David doesn't move. He's staring into space like the others. Was he even listening to her?

'David?'

'I'll see you at home,' he says, snapping out of his trance. 'I need to drive my own car back, don't I,' he adds, seeing the incredulous look on her face. Is he really more likely to side with these people than her? The feeling of disappointment and betrayal pulls heavily in her stomach. It certainly seems that way.

'Of course.' She nods at Suki and Julie, puts her head down and leaves without saying goodbye to any of them.

25

Rachel drives home slowly, going over everything that was said. And the strange atmosphere she'd sensed in the room. It didn't hit her properly until she was outside. When she'd first walked in it was as though she'd caught them red-handed. But caught them doing what? Talking about her and Shay? But David had been there. Surely he wouldn't say anything against them. Maybe she's just too upset to think clearly and the emotion is playing tricks on her mind.

What bothers her the most, is David. His lack of loyalty towards her and her children has caught her by surprise. After she's gone out of her way to welcome him into her home. Is she wrong to expect him to be on her side? She thought their relationship was growing stronger, that he'd do anything for her and the boys. She couldn't have been more wrong. There's a sick taste in her mouth again. She's been too trusting and let a stranger into her home. If the fire at his house was arson, it seems unlikely it would have been a random attack, which means someone is trying to hurt David, but why? The police must be looking into who could have done it. Does he have an idea who it was, but isn't telling her?

And now this; her family is the target, potentially caught up in whatever David's involved in. Her son has been kidnapped and is being held to ransom.

Shay didn't text her. He wasn't on that bus. The message can't have been from him or he'd have contacted her again by now. The truth is, he's been missing almost two whole days. The enormity of it envelops her and she swerves over to the side of the road. She shoves the car door open and dashes to the grass verge. She falls on her knees retching, a pain pulsing through her head. When she thinks there's no more to throw up, she sits back on her heels and digs in her pockets for a tissue. She cleans herself up as she sobs.

When she first met David, she thought he looked like George Clooney as the handsome Dr Doug Ross. She used to watch the show with her mum who adored him. She remembers when David first told her he was a surgeon, she glanced down at his strong hands, the long capable fingers, and tried not to imagine them covered in blood, cutting into people's flesh. Instead, she tried to think of them as healing hands, capable of doing good.

At Sarah's New Year's Eve party, he was reserved, some might say cold in nature, but she assumed it was because in his job he needed a certain amount of emotional distance. Once she got chatting to David and they'd shared a few glasses of wine, he'd opened up a bit more about his passion for helping people. It was more than a job to him, it was a vocation. His purpose in life was saving lives.

Rachel climbs back into the car, the sour taste of sick in her mouth. She drives on and turns into her road, wondering what was said after she left and when David will leave the meeting. She needs to discuss with him how to raise such a large amount of money. Whether he agrees or not, she hopes he will help her pay the ransom and hopefully get Shay home as quickly as possible. If he refuses, she will have to ask him to leave. How can she possibly continue their relationship if he won't support her?

As she turns into her drive, a parcel on her doorstep catches her eye. There isn't anything she ordered she can think of. Maybe it's David's or even for Shay.

She locks her car and walks up to the front door. The parcel is quite big. A plain brown box with a typed label addressed to her, only by name, no address. It must mean it's been hand delivered. It could be something of Shay's from the school perhaps. She's not sure what though. She lifts it up. It's not that heavy. Something shifts inside. She unlocks the door and takes it in, resting it on the hallway console table while she takes her coat off. She checks the time. Josh will be home from school soon. What will she say to him? She can't lie and pretend Shay is safe. She'll need to explain someone has taken him. It's possible Josh knows more than he's saying.

There are no hints on the box as to where it has come from. Her stomach flutters. What is she worried about? It's probably some plant cuttings from Tod the school caretaker. But would he seal them in a box? Wouldn't he have stabbed some holes in the lid to give them some air? Clear tape has been used to secure the flaps. She picks at one corner with her nail and it comes up easily. She swipes it away, like ripping off a plaster.

Slowly she opens it up and looks inside. Her heart thuds hard. She gasps as she stares down at the familiar pair of white trainers. The overpowering smell of sweat, mud and grass hit the back of her throat and make her nose tingle. She reaches in and lifts them out. Shay's trainers with the red laces, absolutely caked in muck. His newest most prized pair. She's never been sure where he got them from. He turned up with them one day a couple of months ago and wouldn't say who'd given them to him. He's never without them and he'd never let them get in this state. And didn't Josh say Shay paid him to clean them before the party?

Nausea fills her throat again. What the hell have they done with Shay that he doesn't have anything on his feet?

Whoever has kidnapped him must have sent these as a warning to pay up, or else she will never see her son again.

26

Rachel wishes she could rewind the video camera to see who left the box here. The front porch and down the drive should be visible when she opens the app, but the screen is black.

She opens the front door and stands in front of the camera, facing it full on. It doesn't look broken. She peers closer at the shiny lens, staring at it for a whole minute. Then she sees it. A dark disc. She touches it. Whatever it is it's stuck. She gently picks at it with her thumb nail and a tiny round black sticker comes off. She examines it on the end of her finger. This has been put there deliberately, but when? It must have been before the delivery. It could have been like this since yesterday. Was it one of those boys last night? Anyone could have done it.

She rushes outside to her next-door neighbour, Mr Andrews' house, and bangs on the door. No one answers. She calls out to Mr Andrews and a few moments later the side gate to the garden rattles open.

'Hi, sorry to bother you, but did you see who left a box on my doorstep?'

Mr Andrews is about eighty and his body leans forwards and over to one side. He looks up at her over his half-moon glasses and down at the muddy trainers in her hand.

'When was this?' he asks.

'I'm not sure, maybe in the last hour or so. Shay has been abducted and someone has left his trainers in a box.' A sob follows the last word from her lips. Saying it aloud makes it real.

'Abducted?' He wrinkles his nose as if she must be exaggerating or has been watching too much TV.

'Yes, and I'm going to have to tell the police about this.' She tries to catch her breath but she's frantically trying to work out in her mind where Shay can be without his trainers, what the person who has taken him is trying to tell her by sending them. She has to try to raise the ransom money as soon as possible; there's no question now, no matter what the others say.

'I'm very sorry to hear that, Mrs Gulliver. If I'd known, I'd have taken more notice.' His jaw grinds together and he scratches his stubbly chin with an arthritic hand. 'Come to think of it, a car pulled up over there about forty minutes ago. A man in a hoodie got out. I was in the front bedroom at the time so glanced out to see whose car it was. I thought it was the usual delivery man for the neighbour on the other side of you because he didn't park near your drive or mine.'

'Oh. Did you see his face at all?'

'I only caught a glimpse. He was wearing sunglasses and the black hoodie was up. I think he had a bit of hair on his chin, you know like they have nowadays.'

'And was he tall, short, thin, fat?'

'I'd say he was tall, maybe six foot and lean. Youngish, not your Shay's age, a bit older. Then I looked away. I didn't realise he was going to walk up to your house.'

'Okay, thank you for your help. If the police come knocking, you'll tell them everything you've remembered, won't you?'

'Oh yes, of course.' He nods and bows slightly and Rachel realises he's trying to turn around.

'Thank you, that's good of you.'

'I hope you find him.' He raises his hand in goodbye and turns back through his gate into his garden.

Rachel takes the trainers back indoors and sits at the bottom of the stairs. She thinks of the boys with hoodies coming to the door yesterday, knocking on the window for Shay. It'll be one of them who's left these on the doorstep. Shay must have let one of them borrow his trainers and that's why they're messed up. He'll be wearing a pair of theirs. He quite often swaps tops or hoodies with friends and occasionally sliders or trainers. That will be it. Although she's surprised he's swapped these ones.

She walks round to the neighbours on the other side and knocks on the door. There is no answer and neither of the cars are there. They must have just gone out. She'll try later. Raymond opposite is always keen to help her, like a second dad. He's out in his front garden pruning. He and his partner have been together for forty years and finally married six years ago. It had been such a beautiful wedding. It was the last big event she and the boys had gone to with Mick before they split up.

'Hi Raymond, I wonder if you can help me?' She marches over and stops at the low hedge.

'How are you, Rachel?'

'Not great actually. Shay's gone missing and now we think he's been taken. Someone left a box on my doorstep with his trainers inside. It's so odd because they're caked in mud, and he keeps them so clean normally.'

'Goodness, how strange. It's like something out of a horror film.' But he's not smiling. He's known her boys since they were babies.

'I don't suppose you saw someone put it on my doorstep?'

'There was a car that pulled up about half an hour ago. An old Datsun I think. I wasn't watching but I saw a tall, young-looking man jog back to the car and jump in. He could have been coming from your house.'

'Can you check your security cameras for me, please?' She presses her palms together, pleading with him.

'We can do that for you. I'll get Frank onto it right now.'

'Thank you so much. I'll see you later.'

'Hope you find him safe and well. Goodbye.' He waves and turns towards the house.

Rachel goes back inside and shuts the door. She climbs the stairs and pushes Josh's bedroom door open and stands staring at the mess. A pile of dirty clothes on the floor by the basket, more on the end of the bed. Sweet wrappers, empty crisp packets and fizzy drinks bottles. What is she even looking for? She trudges back downstairs and goes into Shay's bedroom. There must be a clue here somewhere.

Her head is heavy with worry. She's taken her eye off the ball, been too caught up with her new business and failed to protect her son. Shay could be locked up somewhere having God knows what done to him. She holds her fingers to her lips and swallows hard. Tears well in her eyes and threaten to spill over. She hates it when the house is so quiet. She's never felt so alone. Where is David? She thought he'd be home by now. Has he gone back to work? He seems to be drifting away from her. He isn't as invested in her and the children as she hoped he was.

Her phone buzzes, sending a surge of adrenaline through her body. But it's a text from DS Groom wanting to come over to speak to her.

We've found some significant information on Shay's laptop.

A chill runs through her as she wonders what they've found. She desperately wants to tell DS Groom about the ransom demand and the trainers but cannot risk putting her son's life in danger.

27

Rachel sits in the conservatory, trying to calm herself. Her phone rings, startling her. It's Mick.

'What's going on? You haven't contacted me all day.'

She fills him in on Kim not arriving home, as well as Nate and Olly. Ethan is still not contacting Simon and the demand from the kidnappers, sent to her and the parents of the five missing children.

'Why didn't you tell me as soon as you got it?'

'I... I don't know. Maybe because I know neither of us has that kind of money and I haven't a clue what to do.'

'Can't your rich boyfriend lend it to you?' Mick is not usually the jealous type, but he's taken a dislike to David. They are polar opposites in every way.

'He refuses to give in to blackmail.'

'Why doesn't that surprise me?' He lets out a long sigh.

'None of them intend to pay except me and one of the other mums, because we feel like we have no choice.'

'How can money be more important than the safety of your child?'

'They look like they could afford it too. It's a no-brainer to me. They seem to think it could be a hoax, but personally, I'd rather not take the gamble.'

'Me neither. They're all the same those rich types, putting their money ahead of their loved ones.'

'I'm hoping David will be back soon and then we can talk about it. I'd like to think he'll change his mind once he's away from the others. Time is running out.'

'I don't even know what to suggest. The only asset we have is the house and it's not something we can sell overnight.' If they sold up, Rachel's not sure where they'd go. As Mick was the unfaithful one, as part of the divorce settlement, he agreed to allow her to live in the house with the boys until Josh turns eighteen, then it will be sold up and split down the middle.

'Maybe David will lend me the money against it. Otherwise, we could go to the bank for a loan, but I don't hold out much hope now I'm self-employed.'

'What would we say, we need fifty grand to rescue our son from kidnappers?'

'All right, it's just an idea.' She takes a breath. 'Maybe we should tell the police.'

'You can't do that.'

'Why not? They could help us. It might be our only option.'

'It could put our son's life in danger. We don't know who we're dealing with here.'

'If we can't raise the money, I don't see what choice we have. The police might be able to catch them.'

'Have you told Josh any of this?'

'He's not back from school yet but he's due any minute. What am I supposed to tell him?'

'We have to be honest.'

'I know. I want to ask him again if there's anything he can think of that might help.'

'Good idea. We can speak to him together.'

She tells him about finding the box with Shay's trainers on her doorstep.

'He would never let them get like that.'

'That's what I thought. But isn't it odd addressing the box to me?'

'Not if it's a warning to pay the ransom. Christ, what have they done to him?'

'God no, don't say that.' She shakes her head and pushes her knuckles to her lips suppressing a whimper.

Mick sniffs then blows his nose. She pictures him wiping his tears away on the back of his sleeve. 'The detective is on her way over. You should be here.'

'What's she found out?' His voice is suddenly small and distant. He must be thinking the worst.

'Some things on his laptop they think might be significant.'

'Right. I'll see if I can knock off early and come over. Won't your boyfriend mind?'

'You're Shay's father,' she says indignantly.

There's a noise at the door. She looks up. Josh is letting himself in.

'Josh's here. Shall we speak to him now before anyone else arrives?'

'Yeah, put me on FaceTime.'

Mick tells Josh everything they know so far, including the message Rachel received from the kidnappers and Shay's muddy trainers. Josh peers in the box and opens his mouth, clearly shocked, but he doesn't say anything. He looks like he's going to cry.

'I knew; I'm sorry,' he blurts out and follows it up with a sob. He sniffs, looking at them with fear in his eyes. A fat tear rolls down his cheek and then another.

'Knew what, darling?' Rachel asks, glancing sideways at Mick on the screen.

'That he was going to that party. He planned everything, right down to what trainers he was going to wear. These trainers.' He speaks quickly, tripping up on his words and flicking his hand towards the box. 'I cleaned them for him for five pounds. I made sure they were spotless. He doesn't like a dot of dirt getting on them, never mind lumps of mud and bloody shit.'

Rachel puts her arm around his shoulders. Her heart aches at how deeply upset he is. Swearing is not normally allowed, but she lets it go.

'Who's doing all this, Mum? What's happened to him?' He looks up at her and his lips wobble. Rachel flashes a look of alarm at Mick.

'We don't know yet darling, but if there's anything else you know that you think might help, now is the best time to tell us.' She pauses, trying to assess if he does or not, searching for the tiniest indication on his face. 'Even if it's something he asked you not to tell us, because he could be in danger right now; you understand that, don't you?'

Josh nods slowly. She gently squeezes the top of his arm.

'Because someone is holding him against his will and is trying to get us to pay them a lot of money before they'll let him go.'

'Why though?' Josh's voice is whiney, making him sound like he's five years old and it reminds Rachel of how young he still is. Thirteen is no age. Especially to be dealing with something as frightening as this.

'That's what the police are trying to find out from his laptop,' Mick says. 'They're coming over soon to tell us about something they've found.'

Josh nods again.

'Do you think you know anything that might help them work out where he is?'

Josh stares at the floor and purses his lips, scrunching them from side to side.

'Josh?' Mick asks.

'Someone was making him do things he didn't want to do.' Josh glances up at them for a second before looking back at the floor.

'On his computer?'

He nods once.

'Do you know what sort of things?' Mick says.

'Photos, stuff like that.'

'Do you know if he had his clothes on?' she asks quietly, trying not to frighten him or push him too far.

'Sometimes I think.'

'And were these people friends of his?'

'I don't think so.'

'Why don't you think they were?'

Josh looks at her then away and flicks his thick fringe from his face. His eyes are red rimmed and wet. 'Because he was scared, and they were asking him for a lot of money.'

Rachel and Mick exchange a look.

'Do you know why?' Mick asks.

Josh shifts his weight from one leg to the other. He wants to be loyal to his brother.

'I know you don't want to squeal on him, but right now you can help Shay more by telling us everything.' Rachel kneels in front of him and takes his hands.

'It was to stop them showing the photos to anyone,' he says at last.

Rachel stands up, tears forming in her eyes as she wraps her arms tightly around him. He cries into her shoulder. She shivers at the thought of Shay dealing with this on his own. She wishes he could have confided in her. Her heart aches that he didn't feel he could. All this time she believed she was being a good mum, but the truth is, she's failed her son completely.

28

Rachel ends the call with Mick. He's coming straight over. It's 3.40 p.m., only five hours and twenty minutes until the deadline. She leads Josh into the kitchen and pours him a glass of cold milk.

'When the police get here, will you tell them everything you told us?'

He nods and wipes his nose on his sleeve, just like his dad, something she's asked him not to do about a thousand times, but now she wonders whether she should. Was it her constant nagging that drove Shay to lie to her, push her away and hide so many secrets? She can't lose Josh too. She pulls a tissue out of the box on the table and hands it to him with a smile. He half smiles back, takes it and wipes his nose.

'Did you know that David helped Shay go out by leaving his window unlocked?'

'No!' Josh growls, his face screwing up into a grimace. 'Tosser,' he adds.

'Josh, don't say that! Don't you like him?'

Josh shrugs and drinks a mouthful of milk.

'I thought you did.'

He shrugs again but doesn't look at her.

'Is there a reason? Please tell me.' She touches his arm with her fingertips. There was a time when he and Shay would run at her with arms wide for a hug. Back when they both needed her. Now she can't remember the last time they embraced without it feeling a bit awkward or forced. All this time she's been telling herself what a great mum she is, almost smug about it comparing herself to some of the others at the school, but all along she's been the one who's lost touch with her boys. Who do they turn to now for comfort or advice? She dreads to think what else they've been doing on their laptops. Not so long ago when they went upstairs to play or when she tucked them up at night they were safe in their bedrooms. Now when she shuts the door, they're exposed to the whole world looking in at what ought to be their safe space, their sanctuary. Presumably it's strangers behind all this, posing as kids their age, asking for private photos of them. She grimaces at the thought of it, yet is grateful in a way that she doesn't have daughters, but is it really any different or any worse? It seems not if Kim has got into the same predicament as the boys.

'It's because you and Dad can't get back together with David hanging around.'

Rachel turns away and smiles to herself at how sweet Josh is, but he's still so naïve, which terrifies her.

The front door rattles open and David steps in. He stands for a moment looking puzzled at them, then he hangs his coat up.

'How was it after I left?' Rachel asks.

He drags his hand through his hair, leaving some of it standing up on his head. He glances at Josh then back at Rachel. 'Heated, shall we say. I'm glad you didn't stay to see it.'

She wonders how much worse it could have become without her there. She felt completely outside of their close little group. She's probably being over-sensitive because parents normally gravitate towards her for help or advice, but she supposes she feels left out partly because it's boys and dads and football.

'Are you okay, Josh?' David asks, frowning.

Josh is glaring at him.

'Mick and I have told him about the... ransom, and then these turned up on the doorstep.'

'What are they?' He stares into the box.

'Shay's trainers.' Her words come out with a little yelp. 'They were left in this box on the doorstep, addressed to me.'

'How very odd.' He blinks a few times as though he can't process what he's seeing.

'David, will you be able to help me pay the ransom? I really need to know.'

'I thought we discussed this at George's.' He speaks behind his balled-up fist, as though he's not comfortable discussing this in front of Josh.

'I know you don't agree with me, but I need to pay it and can't afford to; I'll have to borrow the money. Please can you help me?' She stares at him with pleading eyes.

'All right, I'll think about it.' He turns away towards the kitchen.

Rachel blinks, astonished that the answer doesn't have any urgency to it.

'You know I only have a few hours left?' She can feel her blood pressure rising.

'Why did you help him go to the party?' Josh snarls at David. '*I* tried to talk him out of it.'

David turns around and regards him in his school uniform before he answers. 'Because he's sixteen and a boy likes to have some freedom now and again, spread his wings so to speak. You'll understand when you're older.' David fakes a smile.

Rachel raises her eyebrows at his childish dig. David knows how much Josh hates not being old enough to do all the things Shay is allowed to do.

'Do *you* know where he is or who's taken him?' Josh points at David. She's never seen him act like this before. Normally he's so quiet and polite.

'Of course not. If I did, I'd tell your mum.' He strides into the kitchen and runs himself a glass of water from the tap.

Rachel crosses her arms and considers their spiky exchange, recalling Shay's half-written emails to her. What was he afraid of? She needs to find out why he didn't think she should trust David. Was it because, like his brother, he too was resentful of her moving on from his dad? Or is there something Shay knows about him that she doesn't? The more she thinks about it, the more she wonders what has been going on between David and her sons.

29

When DS Groom knocks at the door, Rachel answers.

'Hello again. How are you?' DS Groom asks.

'Not great.' Rachel shows her and another policeman into the living room. Mick's still not here yet.

'This is DI Connor, head of our cyber-crime unit.' The sergeant always has this way of looking intensely into her eyes. It's difficult to hide the truth about the ransom from her.

'Thanks for coming,' Rachel says and sits next to them on the sofa. David lingers in the conservatory. He probably feels awkward because he's not Shay's father, but she's not letting him duck out of this when he's been so involved so far. 'Are you joining us?' Rachel calls to him, immediately turning back to DS Groom and DI Connor.

'Shay's dad Mick will be here any minute. Can we get you both a drink?'

'Coffee please, black no sugar,' DS Groom says.

'Same for me. White, one sugar thanks,' DI Connor says.

Rachel gives a brief smile and nod to David and he hotfoots it out to the kitchen. While they're waiting for Mick, Rachel considers showing them the trainers, but it will lead to too many questions, and she'll find it hard not mentioning the demand for money. Much as she hates lying to the police and wants them to help her, she can't bring herself to risk something bad happening to Shay.

'How is Bella?' she asks instead.

'Much better, thanks. She's remembered a lot more of what happened that night. More about Shay.' DS Groom is staring at her again.

'That's good to hear.' But is it? A whoosh of adrenaline shoots through her body. Her forehead is pounding. Is it possible Shay knows who hurt Bella? Or could he have been coerced into being involved in some way, like with stealing the moped? Maybe Shay saw it happen. But what about the other teenagers; that wouldn't make sense. Unless they were all there too and they witnessed it together and someone is trying to silence them.

David comes in with the coffees and puts them on the glass table. The doorbell rings, the sound repeating on Rachel's phone. She glances at the screen.

'It's Mick. I'll go,' she says, not expecting that David would want to answer the door to her ex.

She lets Mick in, and they hug. She breathes in his familiar smell of soap and tobacco. In a split second she's back with him at the seaside when the boys were little. That time they hugged after finding Shay hiding behind the sofa in the B&B lounge. He'd gone missing from the breakfast table, and she had become hysterical, convinced he'd been abducted. As soon as they'd found him, smiling and giggling and oblivious to their distress, they'd never felt so relieved and grateful. With the familiar scent and the memory, she relaxes a little.

'We're in here,' she says, leading the way.

'Hello, I'm Mick, Shay's dad.' He leans forward and shakes hands with DS Groom and DI Connor.

'Thanks for coming,' DS Groom says, looking him over.

'Pleased to meet you.' Mick nods at David who hesitates for a nano-second then nods back.

'Right, we've got a lot to get through,' DS Groom begins.

Mick blinks hard and sits close to Rachel. David pulls up a chair from the conservatory but keeps his distance.

'Firstly, I'm afraid we've found some disturbing images on Shay's laptop. Have you noticed any unusual behaviour from him in recent weeks?'

Rachel shifts round and faces Mick then speaks first. 'He's been quieter than usual and tense. He's lost his temper a few times. He's been hanging around with some unsavoury types we don't like.'

'And there was an incident recently, but he wouldn't let us report it.' Mick glances at Rachel when he says this, probably unsure of whether she'll approve of him bringing it up.

'Why, what happened?' DS Groom looks from Rachel to him.

'We honestly don't know,' Rachel tells her. 'He came home badly beaten up, clothes scuffed and torn where he'd scraped his skin, blood everywhere. His glasses were so badly damaged, I had to buy him a new pair.'

'Whoever they were, they really scared him, he was terrified they'd come back and... set fire to the house.'

Mick swallows hard. Rachel curbs her instinct to put her hand on his leg to let him know she feels anxious too. Those days are long gone.

'I was shocked and angry that his so-called friends would do that to him. I told him straight: they are not your friends, keep away from them, but he said it wasn't that simple and they were like family to him. More than we were. That really hurt. We just couldn't get through to him.'

Rachel and Mick exchange a glance, recalling the impact of his words, the barrier Shay put up between them.

'He said his *friends* did this to him?' DI Connor doesn't sound surprised.

Rachel and Mick nod at the same time. DI Connor writes something in his notebook.

'And did I hear correctly that you didn't report any of this?'

'I filled in a form online and a policewoman called us back, but he refused to speak to her. He was shaking and crying and wouldn't give any names. He was always checking out of my bedroom window upstairs, at the front of the house, to see as far as he could up and down the street in case they were hanging around, planning to cause more trouble.' Rachel looks to the floor then up at DS Groom's concerned expression. 'I think he must be involved with a gang. These men, boys, whatever, are controlling him.'

DS Groom makes a note on a small pad but doesn't reply.

'What sort of photos have you found?' Mick asks, picking at the cuff of his leather jacket.

'Very personal ones I'm afraid. Of Shay, in his bedroom.'

Rachel presses her palms to her face, bracing herself for how bad they are.

'You don't seem all that surprised,' DI Connor says.

'I am. Of course, I am.' There's no way Shay would have been able to pay £15,000 to stop these photos from being sent to everyone. Whoever was blackmailing Shay over email must be the same person who's holding him for ransom.

'It seems he's been groomed by someone he's been chatting to in an online forum on the game *Call to Arms*, and whoever it is has managed to gain access to Shay's life.'

'What do you mean?' Rachel asks.

'They know everything about him. His name, age, where he goes to school, where he lives. And all about you, his family.'

'Shit. He knows not to share information about himself online; we've talked about it several times, haven't we?' Rachel looks desperately at Mick to back her up. They must seem like the worst parents in the world. David remains silent, his fingers squeezing his chin hard as he listens to every word. He probably doesn't feel it's his place to contribute.

'Yeah, we've spoken to both boys about these kinds of things; separately and together,' Mick says.

'Well, I'm sorry to confirm that Shay was indeed being blackmailed.'

'Do you know who by?' Rachel tries to keep her voice calm when she really wants to scream at them to help her save Shay. How can this be happening to them?

'We don't yet, but whoever it is has managed to obtain several photos of Shay in his bedroom, getting undressed, on the bed with a girlfriend and at his computer... watching porn.'

'Oh God.' Rachel covers her face with her hands, her skin hot with embarrassment and shame for herself and her son. How could she not know this was happening to him under her roof?

'Fuck. How did they manage that?' Mick asks.

'There's someone who plays *Call to Arms* online going by the name of RED99. He's probably not the teenager that he's pretending to be.'

'Who is he then?' Rachel's blood turns cold as she pictures some middle-aged paedophile stalking children, making out he's their age.

'We've found in cases like this, he's more than likely much older than them. We have evidence to suggest he's been grooming Shay over several months via the game's chat room, befriending him.'

'Bloody hell.' Mick cups his mouth.

'Shay's confided in him, told him things that he wouldn't even tell you. He appears to have grown to trust this person completely.'

Rachel stares at DI Connor. There is sweat on his top lip. Does he have children too?

'You hear about these things happening but never imagine it's going to happen to your child, to your family,' she says.

30

'We've managed to retrieve all their conversations and we're still working through them,' DI Connor says, 'but like I say, it started a few months ago with Shay playing *Call to Arms* online with RED99 and inviting others to join them, probably the other missing children. We need to confirm this once we have the info from their devices.'

'We know from their parents that they all played it online,' David says.

'I'd like to know if they were invited by Shay or RED99. It can't be a coincidence that they all knew each other before going missing.'

'And when you say grooming, what do you mean exactly? What has this person been saying and doing to Shay?' Mick asks.

'All sorts. We can see from their chat they talk a lot about the game, obviously that was RED99's way in to gaining his trust, then they move on to talking about Shay and his girlfriend. What they get up to, what Shay likes her to do, that kind of boy talk.'

'What girlfriend?' Rachel asks.

'Bella.' DI Connor cups his hands together.

'I didn't know they were seeing each other until I was told at the park. He has different friends come round, girls and boys. I don't always see who comes in because they go straight into his room which is right by the front door, and he doesn't like me poking my head in to check up on him too much.' She probably sounds like a terrible mother not knowing who her son's friends are, who his girl-friend is. But she respects his privacy and she's been trying to trust him again.

'They had a conversation early on about their pets,' DI Connor continues. 'RED99 asked Shay to send him a seemingly innocent photo of his dog.'

'Oh no, you mean Prince?'

'That's right,' says DI Connor. 'Shay was confiding in his new friend about how sad he was that his dear old dog was dying, and sure enough RED99 empathised with him and furthered that bond by saying he too had recently lost his dog. Shay would have believed RED99, probably not even questioned who he said he was because they'd been friends for a while already, through the game. As far as Shay was concerned, RED99 was the eighteen-year-old gamer from Stoke he said he was, living at home just like him. By this point they'd played *Call to Arms* together for the last couple of months or so, several times a week. But as soon as Shay sent him that photo, it meant now RED99 could use the image's tagged data to pinpoint Shay's exact location on Google Maps.'

'What the hell?' Mick leans forward in his seat, hand to his neck.

'This is too much; it's frightening.' Rachel presses her palm to her forehead.

'That's how these people reel them in. They find out their exact location and use that against them.'

'Is this what has happened to the other missing children too?' David leans forward.

'More than likely. Those children's computers are being investigated too.'

'So what did this person do with this information?'

'From the messages we've managed to retrieve, the person targeting Shay told him he was going to Highgrove Park on a particular day and time if he wanted to meet him and have a smoke.'

'That's just down the road here.' Rachel points in the vague direction.

'Well, this is exactly it. It's somewhere he knew Shay would recognise as his local park. Reading his comments, Shay was astounded that the parents of the person he'd been chatting to and playing *Call to Arms* with online were divorced too, and RED99's father lived right round the corner from Shay. In fact, all RED99 had done was find the park nearest Shay's house and make out to him that his dad lived nearby, and when he was at his dad's every week, this was his local park too. He then suggested to Shay they meet up there. In reality, RED99 will have travelled miles from wherever he was based to be there and make it look like he'd just strolled around the corner from his dad's house.'

'I'm still not getting what's gone on here, how this leads to indecent photos being taken and our son going missing?' Rachel says.

DI Connor rubs his palms together and glances at DS Groom before continuing. 'It's quite simple really. Shockingly so. Like I said, RED99 groomed Shay, chatted with him via this game and gained his trust bit by bit, then using malware, he gained access to the webcam on Shay's laptop and was able to take photos of him without him being aware.'

'How exactly does this happen? I'm sorry I don't get it, I'm not a techie person,' Mick says, shifting to the edge of the sofa.

'Through the game's chat forum, RED99 sent Shay a link telling him to check out a site for some cool free skins. Kids love them, they're customisations for the game, so Shay must have thought, great, and clicked on the link which then not only downloaded the skins but unbeknown to him, also installed a trojan which is what allowed the malware to be installed on his laptop. This is what enabled RED99 to control the camera on Shay's laptop at any time he wanted, even when Shay was asleep.'

'That's disgusting. Why didn't we know about any of this?' Rachel cries, looking to Mick then David.

'Didn't the school run a cyber security evening recently? I'm sure there was one advertised in the newsletter?' Mick asks.

'Oh God, if there was, I didn't see it, I've been so busy with work.'

'You could have learnt all about this, possibly stopped it happening if we'd been more aware,' Mick snaps.

'*You* could have gone,' Rachel says.

'Okay. Let's not turn on each other. Shay needs you to work together to find him.' DS Groom nods to DI Connor to continue.

'RED99 then sent Shay one of these images he'd taken of him partially dressed and demanded three thousand pounds or he'd send the compromising photo to everyone in his address book, including you, his parents.'

'Bloody hell.' Mick shakes his head.

'He must have been worried out of his mind,' Rachel cries.

'Why didn't he come to us? We could have helped him,' Mick says to her.

Rachel wonders whether Shay felt he couldn't confide in her with David around. There must be a good reason why he wanted to warn her not to trust him. Is it possible David knew someone was blackmailing Shay?

'What do you think, David? You've been very quiet,' she says. She watches for his reaction, but he shows no emotion. She guesses that's his default at work too, not allowing himself to become emotionally involved even if there's a crisis. She's still trying to fathom why he was getting friendly with Shay behind her back, letting him go to a party she specifically forbade him to go to.

'Can you imagine the shame a sixteen-year-old boy feels when it comes to his developing body, his girlfriend and private things he's done in his room? Sharing that with anyone, let alone his parents and friends, could be enough to push him over the edge.'

Rachel nods at his considered answer.

'He's got a good point,' Mick says.

'He's right,' says DI Connor. 'Boys tend to bottle things up. He was trapped in a cycle by then too. RED99 had too much power over him. Shay couldn't escape what he owed, so to "help" him pay off his debt, RED99 got him doing some drug runs for him, which could be why Shay seemed to have a new bunch of older friends. Something must have gone wrong when he was delivering drugs to them, which is why we think they beat him up. Anyway, just as Shay thought he was coming to the end of paying off his debt, bam, he was sent another image of himself. Again, he got another blackmail message saying he owed RED99 another three thousand pounds.'

'What a nightmare. How long has this been going on?' Rachel stands up and walks in a circle, hand to her head in a daze. The humiliation must have been overwhelming for him. Especially knowing these photos can never be deleted. Once they're out there, they exist forever, floating around in the ether.

'We've trawled through messages starting around four and a half months ago and we're trying to find clues to RED99's identity.'

'That was just before Prince died.' Mick leans forwards, his elbows on his legs.

'Your house fire was a few weeks before, and you'd not long moved in,' Rachel says to David, hoping he'll elaborate.

'Did you report the fire?' DS Groom asks.

'Yes, there was extensive damage and it's unsafe to live in.'

'Where's your house?'

'Pinner.'

'Not far at all. What's that: fifteen minutes' drive? And how did the fire start?'

'They're saying it was arson.' David rubs his palms together.

'Anyone been arrested? Any clue who did it?'

'There aren't any clear images on the drive CCTV or in the surrounding area. Whoever it was made sure their face was covered.'

'Do you know if there's anyone who has a grudge against you? What do you do for a living?'

'I'm a surgeon. I do my best, but I expect there are a few people I've hurt in one way or another.' He opens his palms wide then closes them again. 'Unfortunately, in our business, the patient isn't always satisfied with the outcome.'

'It is strange that both these events have happened relatively close together. I'll contact my colleagues in Pinner and see if there's anything to link the fire to Shay's disappearance,' DS Groom says. 'Have the children all met in real life?'

'I... I don't know. Some of them go to the same football practice and school...' David's words trail away. There's a slight tick in one eye, a sign of when he's tired or nervous.

'The children were more than likely all targeted by RED99 because they played the same game together. Probably a coincidence some of them go to the same school.'

'And what about this suicide club? Does that have something to do with this? Do you think Shay and the others were seriously contemplated joining?' Rachel asks.

'They were probably considering several options. I expect one of them came across this website in a desperate moment and proposed it to the others. Unfortunately, we can't know for sure yet that that's not what they're planning right now, which is why we need to find them as quickly as possible.'

Rachel's hand flies to her mouth.

'We're doing all we can,' DS Groom adds quickly. 'I'm sad to say there have been several suicides of young people across the country in cases such as this. The embarrassment and shame they feel cannot be underestimated. Having your personal and intimate moments shared around the world can be too much for an adult to cope with, let alone a teenager. Even children who come from a loving stable family often don't feel they can share their feelings with their loved ones. The shame, fear, embarrassment, or self-loathing becomes too much. Shay and his friends may have been discussing a pact such as this for some time, but we don't have any evidence so far except the fact that they have all viewed the website. We think he and his friends were probably meeting up in person to discuss it, as there is no record.'

'Did you find out how much Shay owes RED99 in total?' Mick asks.

'Fifteen thousand at least. We're not sure how much he was able to pay off.'

'In the Word document I found it said fifteen thousand. It had a list of all the times Shay paid some off but as it kept increasing, I believe he still owed about that amount.' Rachel presses a pain creeping across her forehead at the thought of how frightened Shay must have been.

'What do you think has happened to him?' Mick throws a look at Rachel as if to say sorry.

'What we do know is that the debt became so high for Shay that RED99 offered him another way out. The last message from him on the forum said, *Want to pay it off in one go?* And Shay replied, *Yes.*'

'By doing what for goodness' sake?' Rachel asks.

'This is what we need to work out.' DI Connor turns to DS Groom who continues.

'We know this is a lot to take in, but if you have anything further you think may help our investigation, please say.'

Rachel glances at Mick's shell-shocked face. David is silent, his skin grey. She's a breath away from telling DS Groom about the ransom demand. But she cannot risk her son getting hurt. She checks her watch again. Time is slipping away.

'We've spoken to Bella.' DS Groom checks her notebook.

'Who happens to be Shay's girlfriend that I had no idea about,' Rachel says, still embarrassed that she's the last to know. She tries to catch David's eye but he's gazing at the carpet. No doubt something else he knew about her son that she didn't. Did he see them somewhere together before the party? She's not aware of Bella ever coming to the house.

'She says she remembers hearing someone approaching them in the woods from behind. They were sitting together on a blanket, "making out", as she put it. Shay turned to see who it was, and two men went for him. She cried out and tried to pull one of them away and that's when she was hit over the head. She doesn't remember anything after that. At first we thought Bella was the target, but from what she's told us, it looks like it was Shay they were after. So whoever hurt Bella very likely hurt him too and took him away.' DS Groom refers back to finding signs of a scuffle in the woods together with tyre marks from a van.

Rachel feels her face drain of colour. Inside she is screaming at herself to tell DS Groom about the muddy trainers and the ransom demand. But how can she put Shay's life in jeopardy when the kidnappers have specifically said no police? They could be watching the house right now and know the police have been here all this time, talking to them. It might give them enough reason to hurt Shay. She covers her face in her hands and groans.

'We're thinking at this stage that it's more than likely that Shay has been abducted as we haven't found... a body.'

Rachel doubles over, holding herself around her middle. *A body. Christ.*

'It's possible the person or people who have taken him may get in contact with you as they're probably still after the money they believe is owed to them.'

Rachel nods, lips pursed tight. She swallows hard to keep the nausea down. Thoughts of the consequences if she tells them everything swirl around in her head. Chances are he's still okay. As long as they pay the ransom and keep the police out of it, hopefully they'll let Shay come home. She stares hard at David. He must know he's her only hope of paying it. She'll do anything to persuade him. She can't concern herself with what the others decide to do.

'There's one more thing,' DI Connor says. 'We've found Shay's phone.' It was left under a table on a ferry in the port of Calais.

'He's in France?'

'Possibly.'

'What do you think that means?' Rachel asks.

'I'm afraid there's a real possibility that Shay has been shipped across to Europe by traffickers.'

31

'Jesus, what kind of traffickers?' Mick asks as he thumps a cushion.

'Teenage boys are becoming more sought after in the sex trade. They're being sold on to eastern Europe or even Asia,' says DI Connor.

Rachel runs out of the room, vomit rising in her throat. David goes after her, but she shuts the toilet door on him.

'Rachel, let me in. Are you okay?' He knocks gently. She stands over the bowl and retches while tears wet her cheeks. The thought of Shay being taken abroad for that... She shudders, goosebumps rising all over her body. How can this be happening to her boy? They're good people who don't break the rules, don't harm anyone. They live in a quiet respectable road. This isn't fair. She wipes her mouth and sits on the toilet lid, not flushing yet as she knows David will be calling again for her to come out.

Why couldn't Shay talk to her? He's her boy and he always used to tell her what happened at nursery every day, then at primary school. A right little chatterbox, Mrs Miles had called him.

She pulls the handle to flush then splashes cold water on her face and dabs at her cheeks with the towel. When she opens the door slowly, David is slumped against the wall. He stands up as soon as she exits and wraps his arms around her.

'What can I do to help? Please tell me,' he whispers in her hair.

'If you really want to help me you know what I need and I know it's asking a lot.'

He pulls back and cups her chin, searching her eyes, and nods once. She buries her head in his chest, holding him as tightly as she can. They pull apart abruptly as Josh stomps down the stairs. David heads back to the living room and Rachel waits for Josh to reach the bottom. She hugs him then walks him in to meet the two officers. DS Groom asks Josh a few questions and he tells her exactly what he told Rachel. Then he starts to cry and Rachel folds him back into her arms.

'I think you've had enough for one day; we'll leave you in peace,' says DS Groom. 'We'll be in touch again as soon as we have any more information. We're hoping to have some CCTV footage of the van. There was none directly around the woods nearest the housing estate, but there's a pub further up on the corner and there's a strong chance they have security cameras in their car park. We're really hoping they've caught the van passing by, and with any luck, a number plate.'

Rachel thanks them both and David leads them out.

'I don't know, Rach,' Mick says. Josh lets go of Rachel and moves into his dad's arms. 'Maybe we should have mentioned the ransom message. The police could help us get Shay back.'

'I know. It feels wrong withholding it from them, but the instructions are clear. I don't want to risk the kidnappers thinking we've gone to the police. We could be putting Shay in danger. We cannot risk him being trafficked abroad or worse.'

'What if they're right and he's already been taken out of the UK?' Mick asks.

'Without his passport?'

Rachel runs into Shay's bedroom and searches his bookcase. She's seen it there, she's sure of it.

'We can't tell them,' David says, standing in the doorway, 'especially if you want me to pay it for you.' He comes in and shuts the door.

'I really do, I'll be so grateful, and of course I'll do my best to pay you back, even though it may take a while.' She moves towards him, and David takes her into his arms. She tells him she's looking for Shay's passport.

'There it is,' he says, pointing to the top shelf behind her. He lets go and reaches up. She takes it from him and opens it. Shay's photo was taken five years ago, just before he started secondary school. The freckles on his nose were more noticeable then. He's not smiling but she remembers it took a while for his giggles to die down so they could get one with a straight face. This was just before he started to change and grow up, become more serious.

David follows her back into the living room. She waves the passport and Mick gives a sigh of relief.

'Hopefully this means he's still in the UK,' Mick says.

'Perhaps that will change if we don't pay the ransom.' She doesn't want to think what could happen if they don't. 'But David has agreed to lend us the money.' She turns to him and touches his arm.

'Honestly if you can do that, you're a top bloke.' Mick puts his hand out to David who shakes it once then lets go.

'You know you're the only parents paying it though, don't you?' David says.

'I'm sorry but at this point I'm really not bothered what the others do,' Rachel says.

'If they don't want to pay it, that's up to them,' Mick adds.

'We have less than four and a half hours left to pay,' Rachel says, looking at her watch. 'I can't lose my son.'

'I'll go and get the cash out.'

'Can you get this amount out just like that?'

'Don't worry, I've already arranged it. When they send you details about where to drop it, I'll do it for you.'

'That's good of you, but I'd like to come with you to make sure Shay is there.' Rachel opens the original ransom message and shows Mick.

'Can't this number be traced?' Mick asks.

'Chances are it's a burner phone,' David says.

'I can stay here with Josh when you go or take him back to mine?' Mick says.

'I don't feel safe here,' Josh says, pulling himself out of Mick's embrace.

'That's okay, we can go and hang out at mine.' He pats his son's arm and hugs him again.

'Right, I'd better go and get to the bank before it shuts,' David says, looking at his watch. It's already 4.37 p.m. He plods upstairs and shuts the bathroom door.

'Can we get a takeaway, Dad?' Josh pleads.

Rachel nods to let Mick knows he's welcome to eat it here.

'I'd better call my girlfriend not to come over tonight,' Mick says, taking out his mobile. He walks out of the front door and leaves it ajar. Rachel hands Josh her Monzo card she keeps for take-aways only. Josh smiles and takes it, then runs upstairs to order pizza on his phone. She sits in the conservatory and lets out a long breath and tries to centre herself. There are so many calming tech-niques she shares with her clients that she knows she needs to employ herself if she's to get through this and be there for Shay. It's hard to believe the other parents won't pay up. What could happen to their children doesn't bear thinking about.

She opens her diary. She'll have to cancel the three appoint-ments she has booked in for tomorrow, including Alice Kirby, even though she promised her. She closes it again. She cannot concentrate. And as for staying friendly and upbeat, it's not going to come easily. She could end up trying too hard and not come across as authentic. She doesn't know what state Shay will be in when they get him home tonight. She'll rebook when she's sure he's safe and well. Surely better to be honest with clients and let them know she's having a family crisis. They have worksheets in the meantime, something to prepare them for their next sessions.

She messages the three of them. Her two regulars reply straight away, sending their good wishes and telling her not to worry, to take as much time as she needs. Alice Kirby doesn't reply. In fact, the message remains unread.

Her phone beeps.

'It's a message from the kidnapper,' she calls loudly, striding into the living room.

Mick shuts the front door and comes in smelling of tobacco. David joins them from the hall, pulling his coat on. She reads the message out loud.

Come to Bayhurst woods alone at 9 p.m. and leave the money in a bag by the road, behind the big tree stump. Your son will be in the clearing. If you are not alone, the deal is off.

32

'Shit, I was going to do it. I should still come with you,' David says as he drags his fingers through his hair.

'You can't go to the woods at night on your own,' Mick says. 'What if I come with you? I'm his father.'

'Did either of you take in what they said? I'm to go alone. I have to do what they say. I don't have any choice. I need to bring Shay home which means sticking to the rules, much as that galls me. I won't have anything go wrong.' She reads the message again, to make sure she read it correctly. Shay will be in the clearing. She presses her phone to her chest, to where the anxiety is lodged there.

'What if I drop you off and wait nearby, just in case?' David asks.

Rachel circles the room, hand to her head. 'No! What if they see you? For all they know you could be undercover police.'

'They might hurt you; look what they did to that girl. You'll be out there all alone,' Mick says, fiddling with his collar.

'He's right, it could be a trap. I'd be much happier if I was nearby, even in the next street so you can text if you need back up.'

'Nothing is going to go wrong. You go and sort the money out please,' Rachel says and checks her watch.

'Okay.' He kisses her on the cheek and walks out the front door.

Josh runs downstairs. 'Pizza will be here in about twenty minutes. Everything okay?' His face drops when he sees their serious expressions.

'Everything will be fine.' Rachel puts her arm around Josh and gives him a reassuring hug.

'Mum's got to go and drop the money in the woods tonight and hopefully bring Shay home,' Mick says.

'Can't you go with her?' Josh asks him.

Rachel shakes her head.

'The kidnapper wants her to go alone, and she won't accept any help,' Mick says.

'Mum, what if they double-cross you?'

'You've been playing too many of those games online.' Mick laughs.

'Then I'll call for help.' She ruffles Josh's hair and pulls him in for another hug. She's never been more grateful for him not completely losing that need to show affection. He's still her baby. Maybe she's not been a completely useless parent after all.

David returns just as they're finishing their pizza. They've left a medium-sized one for him in the kitchen, with the weird toppings he likes: anchovies and capers. He opens a Sainsbury's bag for life and shows her the bundles of fifty-pound notes nestled at the bottom.

'Is that really fifty thousand pounds? Doesn't look that much, does it?' She looks up at him, but he turns away.

'It's all there.'

'Oh no, I wasn't questioning whether it was or not.' She didn't mean to offend him; she just expected the bundle to look more substantial.

'I'll put it in an old rucksack, so it doesn't spill out. Don't want any passing dog walkers getting suspicious.' Rachel rummages through a box of junk in the understairs cupboard and drags out an old bag she'd planned to send to the charity shop.

David takes his coat off and hangs it at the bottom of the stairs then helps Rachel transfer the money from bag to bag. Mick and Josh are sprawled on the sofa watching an episode of *Doctor Who*, oblivious to what they're doing. The theme tune kicks in marking the end of an episode. Rachel wonders what David makes of having Mick around.

'I think we'll get off back to mine,' Mick says to Rachel, coming into the hall.

'You're welcome to stay here,' she says, zipping up the rucksack. She doesn't show him the money because Josh's there and it suddenly feels dirty and seedy dropping money off in a bag in exchange for her son.

'It's okay. If Josh says he would rather be at mine, I think it's best we go.' He glances sideways at David. 'And if you do need any help, David is here for you, aren't you, mate?' Mick slaps him on the arm.

David jolts at the unexpected touch. His smile is fixed in place. He hates being called *mate*. Rachel finds it vaguely amusing that the two men are so different, but they have to co-operate for Shay's sake.

'Good luck.' Mick hugs her, then Josh does too.

'Bring Shay home, won't you, Mum?' There are tears in his eyes and her heart rips in two. He's relying on her. She can't let him down. She will do whatever it takes.

'Of course I will. I'll do my best, I promise.' She cups his face and kisses his cheeks, hoping he doesn't detect the tiny waver of nerves in her voice. There's no point telling any of them how scared she really is. 'Wobbly tummy scared' Shay would call it. She hates rollercoasters but it's like when you're at the highest peak and it pauses for a few seconds before plunging down into oblivion.

She has to find the courage to do this and save her darling boy.

33

At 8.40 p.m., Rachel zips up her black waterproof coat and slips into her wellies. David hands her a high-pitch whistle and a torch from the emergency supplies he keeps in the boot of his car in case of severe snow days.

'Don't forget, if you need help, press the buttons either side of your phone for the SOS signal or call me if you're able to. Do you want me to add a GPS location tracker so I can see where you are?'

'It's okay, you know where I'm going.' She frowns at him.

'Can't have you disappearing as well though, can we?' He gives a wry smile, and she slaps her phone into his palm, very much hoping he's joking because that's not an outcome she's thought of. She pulls on Josh's beanie hat, which he told her would bring her luck. All her senses and instincts are tingling, on high alert. She catches sight of herself in the mirror and David says what she's thinking.

'You look like a cat burglar.' He smiles at her reflection and hands back her phone then checks his own mobile. 'Right, it's synched with mine, so if anything untoward happens, I'll know where to find you.'

A shiver runs through her even though she's boiling hot under all the thermal layers.

'Good luck.' David gently squeezes her shoulders, gazing into her eyes. He can't hide the worry he's clearly feeling, and she's touched by his concern. She wasn't always the soft mumsy creature she is now. There was a time before she met Mick when she had to fend for herself on a council estate.

'No following me, promise? I don't want this handover messed up. Shay needs to be back home and tucked up in bed well before 10 p.m.' Handover. She makes it sound like an innocuous exchange. She picks up the rucksack. Fifty thousand pounds is heavy. David seemed to have no trouble at all in finding such a large amount of money. She can't help wondering if he has more. Years as a bachelor in a top-flight job must mean he's minted. She smiles to herself at her old way of speaking. Fifty pounds was a fortune when she had her first job doing a paper round.

David kisses her cheek. She hitches the rucksack over her shoulder and picks up her keys. She pauses, looking back at him one last time and catches a serious look on his face. A thoughtful look. She walks out of the door, her heart thumping.

All the way to the woods in the car, she keeps checking the time on her phone and for any new messages. What if they change the plan at the last minute? Can she trust they'll bring Shay with them? She'd not considered either of these questions and there's no way of knowing the answers. Not having any level of control is hard for her. What if they take the money and run? How will she ever find him? She takes some deep breaths to try to control the rising panic, the need to scream and lash out because the pain of not knowing if Shay is okay is unbearable.

She winds down the window and welcomes the chill in the air and the sound of the tyres splashing through the rain. The roads are clear. In the rear-view mirror, every few metres the orange streetlights illuminate the dark mound of the rucksack. At first glance it could be mistaken for a small child asleep on the back seat, like the time Shay was about five and he lifted his seatbelt, so it crossed under his arm rather than over his shoulder. For the rest of the journey, he'd slept on his side, head on a cushion. She'd been so worried he wouldn't be safe if she had to stop suddenly, it had been almost impossible to take her eyes off him.

It only takes twelve minutes and she's at the perimeter of the woods on the housing estate side. She'd rather be early if there's the faintest possibility of being reunited with Shay sooner. She parks several metres up the road opposite the pub and switches off the engine and lights. There is no one around; the street is dead. Light edges the windows of front rooms covered by thick curtains. Bins are out on the pavement, some haphazardly abandoned, others like hers, neatly placed in the same position every week so as not to get in people's way. Especially mothers with buggies or people in wheelchairs. There are two kinds of people in this world. Ones who only think of themselves and ones who think of others. Selfish people like the ones who've taken Shay, don't understand how good it can feel to be kind to another person without seeking personal gain.

She can't see anyone and there's no vehicle parked nearby, but they must be watching from somewhere, ready to swoop in and take their bounty. It might be a set up. They could kidnap her too. She takes a few deep breaths to control her racing pulse. It's six minutes to nine. Perhaps they should have told the police. Too late now. She grabs the rucksack in one hand, phone and torch in the other and quietly gets out of the car.

The trees and criss-crossing branches form a high wall of impenetrable darkness. The ghostly hoot of an owl rings out from deep in the woods. She shivers, cold air biting into her face. She tries to imagine groups of teenagers spilling into the clearing, unaware of the dangers around them. No fear of the morals told in childhood fairy tales.

She spots the large tree stump and props the rucksack up against the foot of it. Then she checks her phone. No new messages. No other instructions. She texts the word 'dropped' to David. Switching on her torch, she strides into the woods towards the clearing to collect her son. Images of him in a beaten-up state push into her mind on repeat, his broken glasses twisted and cracked on his face, blood and snot smeared into his hair. She bats them away. Twigs snap beneath her tread and the air is even cooler and quite still under the canopy of branches and leaves, as though every living thing is holding its breath waiting for her to pass by. The damp earthy and woody smell fills her nostrils and her breathing becomes heavier.

A bang like a door slamming startles her. She spins around, her heart pounding up to her throat. Is someone following her? She waves the torch wildly but can't see anyone. As she swings round to carry on towards the clearing, she is suddenly disorientated. Is this the right direction? Everywhere looks the same; there is nothing to mark her position. Did she turn 180 degrees or a full three-sixty? She stumbles forwards, almost tripping over an exposed root of an oak tree. In the distance, a dog's mournful howl fills the crisp air. She tries to walk faster. Someone is behind her, she's sure she can hear their breath and heavy footfall, crunching through twigs. She breaks into a run, the white cloud of her breathing billowing in front of her, but there's no clear path ahead. She climbs through bracken and over piles of rotting fern branches, then her face is trapped in a sticky web and she screams, pawing at her skin to get it off. The smell of burning wood tingles her nose and at last she spots a bright gem of red light glowing up ahead. She is almost there.

'Shay!' she calls, cupping her hands around her mouth. Her

voice sounds strange in the night air. Someone has been here to light the fire; he must be here. They promised he would be waiting. Joy floods through her and she can't reach Shay quick enough. She keeps calling to him but there's no reply. Can't he hear her? She steps into the clearing. The fire is crackling and spitting and the brightness and heat is welcoming. Her eyes dart around for Shay, but there's no one there. Perhaps the person she thinks she heard is bringing him to her now. She sits on a felled log near the fire and warms her hands then takes her phone out for any further instructions. Shit, she has no signal. She raises it up then stands again. When are they bringing him? How long will she have to wait? If they're trying to contact her, they won't be able to. It's almost ten past nine.

She paces up and down, calling Shay's name then waits quietly for a reply, cupping her ear for his voice or a noise she can attribute to him. He could be anywhere in here, it's so vast. Maybe he's tied to a tree, and she's expected to find him. She walks the perimeter of the clearing, shining her torch into the woods as far as she can see, but there is no one there, no sign of Shay or anyone. If only her mobile had the tiniest bit of signal. They could be trying to call her to give instructions about where they've left him. Maybe he's been gagged so he can hear her but can't respond.

'I'm here Shay, Mum is here, where are you? Please try and make a noise so I can find you.' A mist is slowly descending a couple of metres from the ground, blurring her view. She blinks as though it will clear it. Something must have gone wrong. He should be here. They *said* he'd be here. What if she's being watched and this is a trap? She swings round, checking behind her and to the sides. Her breaths become short and fast and the cold air burns through her lungs. She rubs a fist to her breastbone to ease the pain. Holding the phone in the air, she waves it one way then the other but there's not even one bar of signal. She lets out a sob and continues to check everywhere possible, calling Shay's name. Eventually she trudges back the way she came. If the bag of money is still there, then they're late and she'll go back to the clearing and wait again for Shay to arrive.

It seems to take longer to walk back through the woods. The mist deceives her and she veers off in the wrong direction, coming out to the road further up. She runs along the pavement to get back to the stump. The rucksack has gone. There's no one around, no vehicles or people walking by. Where's Shay? A sick feeling rises in her throat. She's been cheated. Perhaps they never intended to exchange Shay for the money. They only said that to make her pay and now she's lost fifty thousand pounds of David's money. And more importantly, she doesn't have her son back.

Her phone beeps several times in her pocket. At last, a signal. She takes it out and rows of messages light up the screen. She unlocks it. There are a few from David and Mick. She goes straight to one from the kidnappers.

YOU GAVE US FAKE MONEY! SO NOW YOU OWE US DOUBLE. PAY IT IN THE NEXT TWENTY-FOUR HOURS OR YOU'LL NEVER SEE YOUR SON AGAIN.

'What?' she cries. The cash can't be fake. David wouldn't do that to her.

Would he?

34

Rachel runs back to her car, debating whether to text Mick and David straight away or get home as soon as possible to tell them what has happened. Who are these people who have Shay and where could they be keeping him? She can't believe she is going home without him. What will she say to Josh? Her heart aches. She'll have to tell the police now; they need their help, even if she is charged for withholding information but hopefully DS Groom will understand.

She stops by the side of her car out of breath and the tears come hot and fast.

Across the road a group of men spill out of the pub and call something she doesn't quite hear. The others laugh and make animal noises. One of them is crossing the road towards her, holding something in his hand. She fumbles with her key fob, trying to unlock the door before he reaches her. It beeps open and she climbs in, slamming the door and clicking the central locking. The man bangs on the window and holds up his cigarette. She shakes her head and starts the engine. He thumps again and swears angrily, his spit spraying the window. He steps back and waves his fist at the jeering men who raise their fists in solidarity. Her hands are shaking, barely gripping the wheel as she accelerates away.

All the way home the tears stream down her face. Her phone keeps pinging. She wishes she'd put it on silent. She doesn't want to go back and face David. Has he really given them fake notes or are they lying? Once again, she feels like she's let a stranger into her home. Maybe he's trying to scupper her chances of getting Shay back. But it doesn't make any sense for him to do that. Perhaps he still has the same stance as the other parents and doesn't believe she should pay the ransom. She has to admit they were right about one thing: the kidnapper is asking for more money. One hundred thousand pounds. That's an extortionate amount. It's possible David didn't have fifty thousand to give her and was too embarrassed to admit it. But if so, why mislead her? And where does this leave them now? There's no chance they'll be able to raise double the ransom. Oh God, now she has no idea when she will see Shay again.

As she pulls into her road, she slows the car down, scanning the windows on either side where her neighbours are tucked up warm and snug in their comfortable houses. They'd never believe what is happening to the family at number ninety-five. It's a quiet leafy road where almost nothing happens except an ambulance occasionally taking one of the older residents to hospital. As she reaches the end of the cul-de-sac, a grey Nissan speeds past in the opposite direction. The driver is wearing a baseball cap, head down as she looks across at him. He seems small in the seat, almost the size of a petite woman or child, except it's definitely a man with stubble. It's not a car she's seen before. He could have been visiting one of her neighbours although he didn't look like the usual type of visitor and why go so fast? It's a cul-de-sac not a through road.

She parks behind David's car on the drive and looks up. Her bedroom light is on. She's steeling herself for a confrontation with

David, but she can't face it tonight, she's completely drained. Shay should be here with her, by her side. She needs to call Mick and tell him what happened and speak to Josh, if he even wants to talk to her after she's broken her promise to bring his brother home. She dials Mick's number. He picks up before the second ring.

'How'd it go?' he asks, breathless. 'Is Shay there, is he okay?'

In the second of hesitation before she replies, he lets out a breath and surely senses what's coming.

'He wasn't there.' Her voice is flat, hollow. She stares at her bedroom window. The curtain moves.

'Why not?' His voice is loaded with anxiety and emotion from waiting for good news and now being told there is none. He may even be crying.

'Is Josh awake?' she asks, both wanting and not wanting to speak to him.

'He's fallen asleep next to me, poor kid. Exhausted. He tried to stay awake. Thinks it's all his fault for not speaking up sooner. So, tell me what happened.'

'I did everything they asked. I dropped the money and waited in the clearing. The bonfire was lit but there was no one there. I called and searched for Shay but there was no sign of him or anyone.'

'Do you think they ever intended to give him back?'

'I'm beginning to wonder. I lost signal in there and when I came out, they'd messaged to say the money wasn't real, but they'd taken it anyway.'

'What do you mean not real? David went to the bank. They must be lying.'

'I don't know.' She combs through her hair with her hand and her fingertips touch some cobweb. She screeches and shakes her hand but it won't come off, so she wipes it on the side of her seat.

'Jesus, what's wrong?'

'Everything, everything is wrong,' she cries.

'David wouldn't do that.'

'I don't think so either, but he wasn't keen on us paying the ransom.'

'It could have put you in danger.'

'I need to ask him.' Her bedroom light goes off. She imagines David walking downstairs. She's not sure why but she's suddenly uneasy about him being alone in her house.

'Well done for going, Rach. I bet it was scary out there in the dark, not knowing who might be around.'

'I was terrified, I won't lie.' Oh God. That's something Shay always says: 'I won't lie'. She sighs, aching that he's not here next to her, safe. 'There was something else in the kidnapper's last message and I honestly don't know what we're going to do about it.'

Mick coughs nervously.

'They've doubled the ransom.'

'Oh no.' He goes quiet. All she can hear is his breathing.

'Where are we going to find a hundred thousand pounds?' she sobs, unable to give herself a moment to finish. 'They said if we don't pay it in twenty-four hours, we'll never see Shay again.'

She breaks down into heaving cries. Speaking the words aloud makes it all so painfully real.

Mick is talking to her, but she can't take in a word. She believed she'd be bringing her son home tonight, but instead she doesn't know if she'll ever see him again.

35

Rachel finds a tissue from a packet she keeps near the gear stick and wipes her eyes and blows her nose.

'What are we going to do?' she asks.

'I think it's time we told the police.'

'I do too. Look, I'm parked on the drive. I'd better go in.' She gets out of the car and locks it. As she approaches her front door, she spots a small box on her doorstep. 'Oh no, not again.'

'What is it?' Mick's voice is panicky. 'Are you okay?'

'There's another parcel.'

'Shit, what's in it?'

'I'm going to take it inside and open it there. A car sped down this road right past me a few minutes ago. I wonder if they were delivering it.'

'Did you get their number plate?'

'No but it was an old car, a Nissan Almera I think, and the driver was short, a bit like a boy racer.' She flicks her torch on and shines it at the doorbell camera. 'I'll call you back.' Surprise, surprise there's another sticker over the lens. She unlocks the door, picks up the package and goes in.

David is standing in the living room doorway, half in shadow. He's wearing his dressing gown and slippers. Rachel shuts the front door and they face each other.

'No Shay then?' He doesn't sound surprised.

'He wasn't there. They messaged to tell me the money was fake. Can you tell me why?' She's trying hard to stay calm and not sound accusing.

'I'm sorry, I thought they'd fall for it.' His face is pale and drawn. He rubs his eyes.

Rachel raises her eyebrows in utter disbelief, her pulse hammering so hard in her head, it hurts. 'What and me too? You could have told me.'

'I'm sorry, I should have but I thought it would put you in danger and it was safer you not knowing.'

'Clearly not.'

'I hoped we'd get away with it. Buy Shay back but not give them real money.'

'That's my son's life you're playing with,' she shouts. 'I can't believe you did that. I could have Shay home with me now. Don't you understand how important that is to me?'

'I know, I'm sorry. Did you think they were going to hand him back so easily? What's to stop them keeping him longer and asking for more money?'

'They said he'd be there, in the clearing.'

'I didn't believe them.'

'Well, I did! This is my son, not yours. It's not up to you to decide.'

David nods and stares down at his slippers.

'How did you even know where to get fake money from?'

'You can get anything on the internet if you look hard enough. Everything's available on the dark web.'

She blinks at him, wondering what sort of person he is to know this. Is he including the photos of Shay in that summary?

'Whoever these people are, they're serious and you've put his life in even more danger. I can't understand why you would take a risk, especially without telling me.'

'It could be any chancer doing this, like one of the thugs he's been hanging out with. I didn't want to hand over a large sum of cash and be made a fool of.'

Rachel is speechless. Is that what this is about? Losing face? So many questions are swirling around in her head, anger bursting out of every pore. How well does she know this man in front of her? She's let him into her house, into her life, but she barely knows him really. He is not the man she's constructed in her head. Money is more important to him than children. Again, she wonders who set fire to his house. What if it's the same people who have taken Shay?

'Now they want double, or I won't see Shay again. Is that serious enough for you?' She slams her hand down.

'I'm so sorry, but this is exactly what I was worried about. They could keep coming back for more; when will it end?'

'This is my son, my flesh and blood.'

'I know, I know. I'll get you the money if that's what you want.'

'Will you though? Can I trust you this time?'

'I promise.' He holds up his fingers in scout's honour. She's not sure if he's serious or mocking her.

'Can you get that kind of money at such short notice?'

'I've got various accounts. I'll talk to my accountant first thing, move some cash around. When do they want it by?'

'We've got less than twenty-four hours. We can't afford to fuck this up.'

'We won't. I'll get it sorted out in the morning.'

'What about the others?'

He pulls his phone out of his dressing gown pocket and scrolls through his messages. 'They've all got the update. One hundred each now.'

'Are they going to pay it?'

'I don't know.'

'Did you tell them about Shay's trainers? Did they receive anything similar?'

'Yes, they all received their child's shoes.'

'Jesus. Have they told the police? Because I'm going to have to tell them this time.'

'I believe they have.'

'I'm too tired to do anything now. I've just found another package on the doorstep.' She holds up the small box. 'Did you see or hear who left it?'

'I heard a car speeding up and down the road, but I assumed it was kids.'

'You didn't look out of the window?'

'I had a quick look, but I didn't recognise the car.'

The package is addressed to Rachel again, on a plain label like last time. She turns it over and shakes it. Something rattles inside. Carefully she slips her nail under the fold of parcel paper and rips it open.

Inside is a white cardboard jewellery box. She takes off the lid and lifts up the cushion of tissue paper and sucks in a breath, covering her mouth with her fingers. Inside is Shay's thumb ring engraved with the letters SG. The ring is threaded through his silver chain.

The two things he never takes off.

36

'Oh my God, what have they done to him? His shoes and now these? I have to call the police.'

'Why not wait until morning?' David turns to go upstairs.

'Seriously, David?' she swallows down the rage building in her chest. 'I need to phone Mick *now*; I promised I'd call him back.' She dials his number and he picks up straight away. David nods at her and climbs the stairs. She sits in the living room and tells Mick what was in the package.

'I don't know what to think. Someone is playing with us,' Mick says.

'Who though and why Shay? Why the others?'

'I don't know if they've been picked by random playing that game.'

'That's what I keep mulling over and over.' Rachel opens a window and lets in the cool breeze. 'What if Shay was never going to be at the woods tonight because he's already been trafficked?'

'How, without his passport?'

'I'm not sure.'

'So what do we do now?'

'Do we go ahead and pay a hundred thousand pounds not knowing if we're going to get Shay back?'

'We have to try. Is David going to stump up real cash this time?'

'He says he will.' Rachel shuts the window again. The air has an icy feel.

'But look what he did.'

'What other choice do we have, except to go to the police?'

'I don't know. Maybe we should wait a bit longer. If the kidnappers get wind of the police being in on it, it could blow the whole thing and prevent us getting Shay back.'

'Mick...' Rachel pauses and checks in the hall and up the stairs before going back in the living room. She shuts the door behind her. Confiding in her ex is not something she planned to do but he's the only one who cares about Shay as much as she does. '...I'm not sure how much I can trust David,' she whispers.

'I'm not sure if I can either. I think I should check him out online.'

'What I mean is, I found a couple of draft emails on Shay's laptop that he'd started writing to me but didn't send.'

'What did they say?'

'He was warning me not to trust David.'

'Do you have any idea why?'

'No. I can't stop thinking about what he was trying to tell me. Why didn't he finish it and send it to me?'

37

DAY THREE

Rachel wakes early the next morning. It says ten past five on the digital clock by her bed. David is still asleep. Recalling her conversation with Mick last night, she feels as if she's been unfaithful. But she trusted David with her son's life, and he gave her a bag of fake money.

She climbs out of bed, slips on her dressing gown and pads along to David's office. His desk is always so neat with everything in its place. The in-tray and out-tray have various papers and envelopes stacked up and it doesn't take long before she finds one stamped with the insurer's name. She takes it to the bathroom with her and locks the door.

There's a wad of paper inside which she slides out and flicks through pages of a long report. She scans it and catches the main points. *Suspected arson. Evidence of accelerant used. Bundle of fire-lighters dropped through the letterbox bound in fuse wire which had already been lit. Homeowner out at the time. Came home to house on fire and fire brigade in attendance. Ground floor and part first floor gutted. CCTV camera above door smashed. Doorbell camera covered with a round black sticker.*

Shit.

She takes a couple of photos of the pages to show Mick. Could this prove that it's the same person who's taken Shay or is this putting stickers on doorbell cameras some sort of prank people do? She flips through some more pages but there's nothing else that tells her that the insurance company or the police know who could have set fire to David's house.

She flushes the toilet and takes the envelope back to David's office, leaving it exactly where she found it. Scanning round, she looks more closely at the few things of his that were untouched by the fire, rescued from his upstairs office. A ceramic model of a human head, a deadly black widow spider captured in resin and several framed photographs of when he was a medical student. One is of a line of friends, arms across each other's shoulders. David has shoulder length hair and is wearing jeans and a Nirvana T-shirt. She recognises Ethan's dad Simon. She doesn't know the others. One man is taller and maybe a little older than all the rest; perhaps he's their tutor. He is next to a woman with long black hair who was looking up at him when the camera clicked because her face has turned away. Something about her is familiar but she can't pinpoint why. In another photo, David is at a garden party with Simon and the taller man. They're older, the soft boyish features now defined with stubble and hair cut sensibly short. In another it's the four of them again but with children. Ethan is a little boy and there's another boy with short black hair, several years older, holding the hand of a younger girl with black hair tied on her head in plaits. Presumably they're the children of the taller man and the woman. It hits her hard that there's still so much she doesn't know about David.

She turns back to his desk. Facing his seat is a photo of David at about Josh's age with his parents and little sister, Fiona. He told her on their first date that she'd died of leukaemia when she was ten years old and that's what drove him to become a surgeon. This is the small, unexpected detail which made her fall in love with him. In that moment she'd believed she understood him from the inside out. His pain and vulnerability laid bare. He'd bowed his head, wringing his fingers round and round and when he'd looked up at her, she'd laid her hand on his to still them, and his red watery eyes had met hers. His genuine desire to help people in need, in pain, fix them so they didn't die like Fiona, made her love him more deeply. She'd understood then why he hadn't married or had children. He was married to his job. He'd told her it was only his friends nagging him that had made him come out that night they met.

But maybe she's been too impulsive, too sure of herself. People are more complex than that. There's always another side hidden from view. There's so much more to him that he's choosing not to show her. He must have his suspicions about who would set fire to his house. Someone other than Shay. Did someone want him dead?

The traffic on the road beyond hers rumbles with the increasing early morning lorries and buses. She pulls back the curtains and wonders if any of her neighbours' security cameras caught an image of the speeding car last night. She makes a mental note to go and ask them.

Downstairs, she puts the coffee on and checks her phone. Still no answer from Alice Kirby about postponing her appointment at midday. If she turns up, she'll just have to explain that it's really not a good time right now. According to the calendar, David has a doctor's appointment at 11.45 a.m.

Mick sends her a text saying he'll bring Josh home in an hour. He's going to call the school and tell them he's too stressed to come in today. She doesn't argue. It's a relief for someone else to make the decisions. She makes a small coffee, drinks it and then goes upstairs for a shower. David is still asleep. She slips into the en-suite and locks the door.

By the time she comes out wrapped in a towel, David isn't in bed. He must have smelt the coffee and gone downstairs. She dresses quickly, not wanting him to burst in and see her naked. She might ask him to sleep in the spare room or move into Simon's house. He did offer on the night of the fire, but she wanted to help, she wanted to be the one to save him.

She goes downstairs, straight to the kitchen. David is slumped over the breakfast bar and straightens up when he sees her.

'I'm so sorry, for everything.' His voice is heavy with sleep. Or is it guilt? He takes a slug of coffee and refills his cup. 'I've texted my accountant. He'll get the money ready for me to collect from the bank. You can come with me to check it this time.'

Rachel nods and pours herself a fresh cup. 'I will, thanks. Don't forget your doctor's appointment at 11.45.'

David nods, but doesn't quite meet her eyes.

'Everything okay?' she asks. It's a stupid question but it seems the only polite way in.

'It's time to review my meds, that's all.'

He told her once that he's on Sertraline for anxiety and depression, but he's never told her why. She's always assumed it's because of what happened to his sister, but now she wonders if she should find out more. It feels like prying though, especially now they've fallen out.

'You think you still need them?'

He nods and drags his hand through his messy hair. The bald patch on his crown seems bigger.

'You've never said why you're on them, what exactly triggered your anxiety.'

'It's something I can't really talk about.' His voice is small and tight. He draws in a sharp breath as though even the mention of it is too painful.

'That's okay, you don't have to tell me.' She could kick herself; she shouldn't have pushed him. How insensitive of her.

'I wish I could. One day, maybe I can.' He does some long slow breaths, palm to his chest. His hand is trembling. Is he about to have a panic attack?

'Are you okay?' Part of her doesn't believe he deserves her sympathy but he looks so wrung out. Maybe she's been too hard on him.

He nods and slowly lifts his coffee mug and takes a sip.

They eat breakfast together in silence. Then he goes up for a shower. If she's being honest, the spark between them began to dim as soon as he moved in. The kids were always around so the loud spontaneous sex they'd enjoyed at his house in those first few months, vanished overnight. They slipped into a comfortable existence as if they'd been married for thirty years.

Except she's not known him anywhere near that long, and she's not sure what he's capable of.

38

Mick arrives with Josh while David is still in the shower. Josh runs into her arms, tears in his eyes.

'It's all right darling, we'll find him, I promise.' Rachel breathes in the warm unwashed aroma of her son, grateful to have him back.

'Do you really think so?' Josh's voice is like a small child's, seeking reassurance. She'll do anything to protect him. Did she do enough to protect Shay? Part of her wishes both her boys were small again and under her control, but part of being a mother is learning how to give them space to develop, become independent, let them go. But not like this. Shay wasn't ready. He's still so naïve. And Josh has such a long way to go.

'I'm sure of it.' She squeezes him tighter and pulls a pained face of hope at Mick over the top of Josh's head. 'Why don't you put the TV on in the other room, Josh? I'll make you a nice hot chocolate with marshmallows and bring it in for you.'

'Okay.' He slopes off, head down and they hear the blast of music from the surround sound as he switches the television on.

'I've been going over it half the night and I think we should hold off getting the police involved, Rach,' Mick says.

'I think so too. If David can get the money, do the drop, we could have Shay back by the end of the day.'

'I'm not sure I want to rely on David again though.' They look each other in the eyes. 'You said yourself, you don't know if you can trust him,' Mick whispers.

'I know, but he's genuinely sorry, and I want to trust him. What choice do we have? Did you look him up online?'

'Yeah. Got to admit there was nothing unusual there. All I found was that he used to run his business with another surgeon; it seems they went their separate ways a couple of years ago.'

'Was it amicable?'

'Didn't say it wasn't.'

'Is there a way of finding out if he had any patients who made complaints against him? You hear about these things, don't you?'

'Then why target the parents of the other children?'

'Like the police said, it might just be that the kids know each other through this game.'

'I don't think so. There must be more to it.'

They both look up at the sound of a creak in the floorboard indicating David coming out of her bedroom. Rachel turns the coffee maker on, and Mick grabs a magazine and pretends to be reading it.

'Morning Mick,' David says as he walks in a few moments later.

'Hi.' Mick nods at him.

'I'm really sorry about yesterday.' David is dressed casually, navy V-neck jumper and beige Chinos, one hand in his pocket. 'I was trying to be clever thinking they wouldn't check to see if the money was real or not.'

'Seems like they know exactly what they're doing,' Mick replies, his tone solemn. 'I just hope our boy is still okay.'

'I know, I do too.' David turns to Rachel. 'The other parents are still saying they won't pay up and Julie can't afford to anyway. None of them have heard from their kids and they've received weird packages too. Let's get this money to the kidnappers today and pray Shay is there because if he's not, we're going back to the police. I'm going to put a tracking device at the bottom of the bag this time, so the police have something concrete to go on.'

'Sounds like a good idea.' Mick nods, impressed.

'No it is not. I'm not going to risk it.' Rachel raises her voice, unable to believe they think that. 'What if the kidnapper detects it before they give Shay back to me?' She pours them both coffee, sloshing it into the mugs, and puts the glass pot down on the cork mat with a bump.

'They won't do, unless they empty the bag right there.' David drinks his coffee straight down.

'I don't care, you're not doing it.'

'Okay, okay. I'm off to work and then the doctors, and then when I get back, we'll go and collect the money.'

'See you later.' Normally she'd kiss him on the cheek, but instead they glance at each other before he leaves. Will they ever get back to where they were before Shay went missing or are they going to carry on being semi-polite until one of them acknowledges that it's over?

Mick takes his coffee into the living room and sits with Josh. He's having time off work too and she appreciates it. This would be so much harder to cope with on her own. She checks her phone. At last Alice has seen her message but she still hasn't replied. Hopefully that means she won't turn up. She takes a glass of water upstairs and lies down on the bed. The little sleep she's had over the past few days is catching up with her. She closes her eyes, but just as she's drifting off, she jolts awake, a younger Shay's voice filling her head: *Where are you, Mummy? I want to come home now.*

She shuts her eyes again, trying to block it out, but she must have drifted off because she wakes a few moments later in a sweat.

Shay was tied up and cowering in the corner of a bright white room crying. She sits upright and rubs her head, groggy with sleep.

The doorbell rings. She glances at the clock. Midday. How has she slept over three hours? Oh no, it must be Alice. She's too zoned out to rush down and answer it. Perhaps she'll go away. But a moment later, the front door rattles open and Mick's voice drifts up the stairs. She forgot he was still here. She wills him to turn her away. The front door shuts and Rachel lets out a breath of relief and shuts her eyes again to give herself time to wake up properly.

'Rachel, are you there?' A familiar voice calls from the landing and the floorboards creak.

Rachel's eyes ping open. She sits up in bed, holding her head. This cannot be happening. Alice Kirby is waving and walking towards her.

39

'Hello Alice, what are you doing here? Didn't you get my message?' Rachel swings her legs off the bed. Alice comes in and sits next to her.

'I did, but I knew something must be terribly wrong and wanted to come and offer my support.'

'Thank you, but I'm okay. I have my family to help me.' Rachel smooths down her hair, certain she must look a mess. She needs to get this woman out of her bedroom and out of her house.

'Is it about your boy? Is he still missing?' Alice raises her hand as if to touch Rachel's arm, but Rachel leans back. 'I thought the police would have tracked him down by now.'

'No... they haven't yet.'

'Oh, that is awful for you.' She frowns, taking it in. 'Do you think he's left home for good then? Gone off with a girl perhaps?'

'No, no. He's not like that.'

'Have you tried calling him?'

'Of course I have.' Rachel doesn't mean to snap but she feels uncomfortable having this woman in her bedroom. Doesn't she have boundaries? 'I'm so sorry.' She looks Alice square on and the hint of a smile is on her glossy red lips, as if she's enjoying someone else's misery. Perhaps she is too damaged to move on yet.

'Boys do that, they grow up and move away, become another woman's responsibility, but girls, daughters, they're always yours.' Alice is staring into the distance. There are tears brimming her eyes.

'I'm so sorry you lost your child,' Rachel says without planning to.

Alice's head whips round, the hint of a snarl on her lips as though no one has the right to speak to her about it. 'There is no greater loss in the whole world.'

Rachel is taken aback by her sudden anger. Is this what will become of her if Shay isn't found?

'I'm so sorry, Alice.'

'More than two years but it feels like a day.' Alice folds her hands over and over in a continual loop.

'You're clearly still in a lot of pain. You don't have to tell me about it, that's not my role, but I wonder if you need some further bereavement counselling before we carry on with our sessions.'

Alice nods and looks down at her empty palms.

'Let's go downstairs. Would you like a cup of tea?' Rachel stands up and puts out her hand.

'Just a glass of water, please.' Alice stands too and lets Rachel gently guide her by the elbow as if she's suddenly aged twenty years.

Rachel leads her down to the kitchen and into a chair. She lets the cold tap run before filling a glass.

'I think it's a good idea to put our sessions on hold for a few weeks,' Rachel says, gazing up at the rain clouds. 'Then when you're ready, we'll resume.'

Alice drinks back the water but doesn't reply.

'Thanks for coming over and for your concern for me, and my

son. I'm hopeful that he'll come home very soon.' Rachel walks her to the door and opens it, not wanting to delay her exit any further. Alice gives her a tight little smile and leaves.

'Has your friend gone already?' Mick asks, carrying two mugs out of the living room.

'My friend? Is that what she told you?' Rachel's eyes blaze at him.

'Yeah, she said you were great friends and she promised to come and check you were okay, have a little girly chat.'

'So you sent her upstairs. Since when do I do girly chats?'

'I don't know, maybe you've changed.' He laughs but when Rachel doesn't reply he continues, 'I've done something wrong, haven't I?'

'She was a new client, essentially a stranger who I think is maybe a little unstable. Taking a slightly unhealthy interest in my family.'

'Maybe *she* thought you were friends and was just being kind?'

'I don't think so.' She takes the mugs from him and pads into the kitchen.

'She seemed pretty harmless to me,' he says, following her. 'Asked who I was but knew Josh's name, wanted to know how he was coping, and wondered if David was at home.'

'Did she now.' She crosses her arms, hackles rising. How dare she be so familiar, as though she knows him, and why is she asking after David?

The front door opens and shuts. Rachel leans around Mick to check who it is.

'Who was that woman?' David asks, striding in with a small paper bag from the chemist. His cheeks are ruddy from the cold air and exertion.

'My new client. She came even though I messaged her not to.

Says she wanted to see how I was. Apparently was asking if you were at home.'

'Really? What's her name?'

'Alice Kirby.'

'Mmm. Are you sure?'

'Yes, of course I'm sure, why?'

'She looked familiar, but I don't recognise that name. I thought maybe she was...' He frowns, deep in thought.

'Who?'

'Just the wife of someone I used to know.' He bows his head and leaves the room.

Rachel shrugs at Mick and his eyebrows rise.

'How odd,' she whispers.

'Not really. He must see loads of people at the hospital. Probably an occupational hazard thinking you've seen someone before.'

'I suppose so.' She handwashes the mugs and gazes out at the garden. The junior goal posts either end, the scuffs in the grass from the boys playing football year after year. The skateboards, the old tyre dangling from the tree on thick rope. What if she never sees her Shay ever again? How would she be able to carry on? Life without him. Gone forever. Her mind spaces out at the seismic reality of the loss. The mug drops from her hands into the sink. Her knees weaken and fold beneath her.

40

When Rachel comes to, Mick is holding her up under her arms, manoeuvring her into one of the kitchen chairs.

'What happened?' she asks, her throat croaky.

'You collapsed.'

Once she is sitting still and not in danger of swaying to one side, he grabs her a glass of water and holds it to her lips. She sips, grateful to him for looking after her. David and Josh rush in.

'Mum, are you okay?' Josh reaches out and hugs her around her neck. She nods and kisses his cheek. *Is* she okay? Her body is wobbly, bones soft.

David crouches in front of her, taking her hands in his. 'Tell me what happened.'

'I think I blacked out. I had a horrible thought that I may never see Shay again.'

'You will, I promise.' He gently squeezes her fingers. But he can't know for sure. Shay said not to trust him. She pulls her hands away.

'That woman that was here, Alice, her child died, and I couldn't help thinking what if that happens to me?'

'How did hers die?'

'She didn't say.'

'It could have been anything. It doesn't mean you're going to lose Shay.'

'But she can't get over the loss and I was thinking I don't think I could cope if Shay died.' She tips her head forward into his chest and cries. He strokes her hair and wraps his arms around her.

When she straightens up and wipes her eyes with her fingers, his face is pale, blank, eyes glassed over in a trance. He becomes aware of her watching him and snaps out of it.

'Do you think you need to go to the hospital?' he asks.

'No, I'm all right now, thanks, but I don't feel up to going to the bank.'

'That's fine, don't worry.' David smooths his hands down her arms.

'Could Mick go with you instead?' She nods once to where he is standing silently in the corner, and he nods back.

'Of course.' David glances at him over his shoulder then stands up.

'I'll look after Mum,' Josh says.

Rachel reaches out to him, and he burrows his hand into hers.

'I'll make us waffles and ice cream and we'll watch *Wallace & Gromit*,' Josh tells her.

'That would be lovely, thank you.' She smiles and kisses the back of his hand. Ever since he had chicken pox a few years ago, *The Curse of the Were-Rabbit* has been his go-to film when he's feeling unwell. This is as much about some TLC for him as it is for her. Josh desperately misses Shay even though he infuriates his older brother sometimes.

Josh dashes off to the living room to dig out the DVD.

Mick turns to Rachel. 'I'll let you know as soon as we've got the cash, then you know you're ready when you hear from the kidnappers about where to drop it off.'

'Okay.' She tries to get up, but her limbs are still weak. David links his arm through hers and walks her into the living room. Josh is grinning, holding the TV remote control and a cosy fleece, ready to snuggle up with her.

'We'll see you later,' David says, pecking her cheek.

'Look after your mum now,' Mick tells Josh and follows David out.

Half an hour later, Josh pauses the film and goes out to the kitchen to assemble toffee waffles and a scoop of double chocolate ice cream into two bowls. He carries it in on a tray with a bottle of raspberry sauce.

A few minutes into eating, Rachel's phone silently pings a message from Mick letting her know they have the cash.

She tucks the phone under the cushion next to her and goes back to watching the film, but she's not taking a word of it in.

Her phone pings again several minutes later.

Woods 9 p.m. tonight. Come alone. No police.

She types a reply, trying not to distract Josh from enjoying the film.

What about my son?

The reply is immediate.

Middle of the woods. Near the fire.

Her finger hovers over the reply button. She wants to ask more, like how Shay is and are they really bringing him because last time she saw no sign of him having been there, unless they bundled him away before she reached the clearing. She forwards the replies to

Mick and David. Josh is lost in the film. Wallace has transformed into a Were-Rabbit and is stalking the neighbourhood at night. Thank goodness Josh can escape into this fantasy world for a while.

Her nerves are jangling. She shifts position for the umpteenth time. Sitting here, sitting still goes against everything her instincts are telling her to do. But once again she's forced to put her son's life in the hands of a stranger.

41

David and Mick arrive with a bag of fish and chips. The smell wafts in as soon as they come in the door. David is holding a rucksack which is straining at the handles, presumably with the weight of cash. He lets it drop to the floor.

'Thought we might have something to eat, then I'll get back to work,' David says.

'Everything go smoothly?' Rachel asks.

'Yes, it's all there in fifties.'

'I think I'd better drive you to the woods this time,' Mick says, following her into the kitchen.

'Drop you off in a street round the corner from the woods.'

'Why?' She looks from Mick to David, wondering if they've been talking about her.

'Because you've not been well today. It's too much stress for you,' David says.

'Is it? So you two have decided what's best for me, have you?' She needs to calm down so she can stay in control of what they do and don't do. It's the only way she can get through this and bring Shay home safely.

'It's only because we care about you,' David mumbles as he rattles open the cutlery drawer.

'What if you collapse again, out there on your own?' Mick takes the stack of plates from her.

'Can I come?' Josh asks, taking the knives and forks from David.

'No way.' Rachel pours him a glass of squash.

'Why not? I'm the one who's been looking after you.'

'He's got a point,' Mick says, winking openly at Josh. 'We promise to keep well out of the way.'

'We *promise*, Mum,' Josh begs, grinning at his dad.

Rachel crosses her arms and rolls her eyes at them. There's no point arguing when they're all ganging up on her.

'As long as you do keep right out of sight. You can't be seen anywhere near the woods, or they'll use that as a reason not to let me have Shay back.' She shivers. It cannot go wrong this time. They have to do everything to the letter. And even then, they could be playing her and ask for more money.

'We know,' Josh says, sounding so grown up she's in danger of bursting into tears. He shouldn't have to deal with things like this at his age. She can't even contemplate how badly it will affect him if his brother doesn't come home.

* * *

Mick drives Rachel to the woods at quarter to nine that evening. Josh is sitting in the back seat ostensibly playing on his phone, but he keeps checking out of the window. David is at home, tracking her movements on his phone in case they kidnap her too.

This time, she has her cagoule on with the hood zipped up as far as it will go so only her face is showing. She hopes to avoid cobwebs and scratchy twigs and anything else that might get in her face. Her phone is on and charged up. She's going to keep it in her gloved hand and use the phone's torch, so she has a free hand to navigate through the trees.

There is no one around when she gets out of Mick's car. A misty rain settles on her face. It gives the street lights a soft focus. She blows a kiss to Josh and hoists the rucksack onto her back. She's not going to forget the weight of £100,000 in a hurry. She clenches her fist until she can feel the bite of her nails through her glove. As long as it brings Shay back to her. That's all that matters.

She checks no one is around. There's not even a lone dog walker in this miserable weather. No one she can see anyway. Although they could be watching her, ready to pounce on the cash. Is she walking into a trap? It's hard to know, but she has to chance it, for Shay's sake. He could be locked up somewhere, starved and beaten. Oh God. Somewhere he doesn't need his trainers. A shiver slides through her.

She hurries along the pavement, her footsteps echoing down the empty street as they pound the tarmac. Around the corner into the next street, she presses on towards the edge of the woods. Once again, she leaves the rucksack by the large tree stump. She scans the area before entering the woods and checks her phone. No new messages, although the signal is weakening already. She switches the phone torch on and moves as fast as she's able towards the clearing, and hopefully towards Shay.

The shrill bark of a fox startles her and echoes around the damp dark air. Her breathing is heavy, expelling a cloud of vapour in front of her face, but she tries to stay focused as she weaves through the trees, as if it's an assault course she's already familiar with. Leaves rustle as she pushes branches out of her way and twigs snap underfoot. She keeps going in as straight a line as she can and it's not long before she can see the distant glow of fire up ahead.

'Shay! Shay!' she calls out and waits for his answer. She pauses and strains to hear beyond the rush of wind through leaves and foxes barking. A large bird, maybe a pigeon, rises from the tree above her, making her flinch at its loud flapping wings as it ascends into the inky sky.

And then she hears a voice. Shay's voice.

Her boy is here!

42

'Shay! Shay!' Rachel runs towards the clearing. As she gets closer, she can hear his voice again.

'Mum... Mum... where are you? Please come and help me...'

'Shay, I'm here, where are you?' She breaks into the grassy clearing and spins this way and that, but she can't see him. 'Where are you, darling? I can't see you.' She can't work out where Shay's voice is coming from. She moves closer to the fire. It crackles and spits and there's a large log at the heart of it, half burnt through so it must have been lit a while ago.

'Mum... Mum... I'm over here. Come and get me please... Take me home.'

'Please, Shay, tell me where you are. Are you hurt?' She charges around, shining the torch into the trees, the bushes and the gaps on all four sides. An owl's haunting hoot sends chills through her.

'I can't see anything, Mum. Please find me. I want to go home.'

'I'm right here darling, why can't you see me? Are you blindfold-ed?' She runs into the wood and out again at different points, shining the torch and calling his name.

'Mum... Mum... where are you? Please come and help me...'

She grits her teeth and pushes back her hood to concentrate harder on where his voice is coming from. It's still distant, as if he's in or under something. But where? Stupid of her to think he'd just be standing here waiting for her. He must be tied up and blindfolded somewhere. How will she ever find him?

'Mum... Mum... I'm over here. Come and get me please... Take me home.' Shay's voice is child-like, frightened. Why can't she see him? She wishes she'd brought the big torch now for a wider beam. What if he's hurt? Fear trickles through her veins.

'I'm right here, Shay. Can you see my light?' Her voice wavers. She can't let him hear how scared she is, so she inhales deeply to steady her breath. 'I've come to take you home. Can you tell me where you think you are? Can you describe it to me? Are you tied down somewhere?' She says it loudly into the night sky, shining the light in every direction, hoping to catch a glimpse of him.

'I can't see anything, Mum. Please find me. I want to go home.'

She shivers. The exact same words, same tone. Why is he repeating what he's already said? His voice sounds as if it could be coming from the pile of logs near the fire. She pictures a row of teenagers sitting there toasting marshmallows at the party he wasn't supposed to go to. She shines her torch over every inch of the logs. Something metal shines back.

There, wedged in a gap between two logs is a black and silver box. She pulls at one of the logs and moves it a couple of centimetres so she can dip her hand in. The box feels plastic but solid. She pulls it out and holds the light over it. Jesus. A tape recorder.

'Mum... Mum... where are you? Please...'

She clicks it off. What sick bastards have recorded her son begging? Where are they holding him? He said he couldn't see... and oh God, a stab of pain hits her chest – he thinks she's coming to save him. She gazes up at the night sky and screams with all her might until she has nothing left and drops to her knees sobbing.

Only now can she see they never intended to bring him here. They weren't going to let her take Shay home. Why did she trust them? None of the other parents did. She should have told the police; they could have been here to catch them. Going by his recorded message he must be bound and maybe gagged after they recorded his voice. What have they done to him? She must tell the police straight away. If she gets into trouble for not telling them about the ransom demands sooner, then she'll just have to take her punishment; she'll deserve it for making such a bad judgement, possibly putting her son's life in danger. She checks her phone, hoping for a signal but there is none. She wishes she could text the kidnappers, demand to know where Shay is, but they change the number every time they contact her. So they can't be traced.

Pulling her hood up, she keeps hold of the tape recorder and heads back through the woods. Hopefully this box holds vital evidence to help them find her son.

But first, she must face Mick and Josh.

As soon as she's worked her way back through the tangle of woods, a bar of signal emerges on her mobile.

The rucksack is gone. The bastards have tricked her. What will she say to David about losing all his money? She'll still have to pay him back somehow, probably by selling the house.

The air is cooler now so she puts her gloves back on and hurries in the direction of Mick's car. She checks the time. She's been gone forty minutes. It seems longer, as though she's been to another land.

Her phone beeps as she's about to turn the corner. Her hands are trembling. She swipes the screen hoping it's a message about where Shay is. But it's not. She glances at a news story headline, but can't take it in. She stops and re-reads it, blinking at every word then looks away, holding the phone by her side, telling herself it's a bizarre coincidence. It's not possible it's anything to do with Shay. The police said his phone was found in France, but it doesn't mean he's left the UK. He's supposed to be here with her right now. They must be holding him nearby. Her eyes fill with tears. They probably want more money. That's what it's about. That's why he's not here. The other parents were right. David was right. But she'll give them more if she's forced to. She'll do anything to bring Shay home.

But this is not her son. *It can't be.*

Bringing the screen up to her face again, the blue light bright in the murky darkness, she reads the headline once more and takes a sharp intake of breath.

British teenager found dead on the streets of Morocco

43

Rachel staggers along the pavement, hand to her head, phone by her side. She can barely breathe. Mick's car is up ahead, the headlights on low. He lifts a hand to wave then jumps straight out, walking briskly towards her.

'Hey, are you okay?' He reaches out to her and she falls into his arms. It takes a few moments before she can catch her breath and speak.

'He... he wasn't there. We've been cheated again. I can't believe it. I feel so stupid.' She draws a quick breath between each sentence and tells him about the tape recording and how close she thought she was to seeing Shay.

'It's not your fault,' Mick says, walking her to the car.

'Have you seen this?' She stops and shows him the article on her mobile, watching him taking it in. He swallows hard.

'I doubt if it's anything to do with Shay; it doesn't say if it's a boy or girl.'

'Except his phone was found on a ferry.'

'Shay is probably still in the UK, being held somewhere. Christ.

They've got us dangling on a fucking string. I bet they're going to ask for even more money now.'

'We have to tell the police and show them this.' She holds up the tape recorder. 'We can't go on giving them money, hoping we can trust them.'

From the passenger window, Josh's pale face is staring at her.

'Poor Josh.' She covers her mouth as her eyes brim with fresh tears. She opens the door and leans in to give him a hug. 'I'm so sorry. He wasn't there. These cruel, nasty people tricked me.'

'Aren't we going to see him again?' Josh's voice is small and frightened, his bottom lip wobbling. She pulls him into another hug, afraid if she speaks, she will cry her heart out and not be able to stop.

The journey home is in silence. Rachel holds the tape recorder in her lap, as though it's a precious piece of Shay. His voice is all she has for now. She texts David to briefly tell him what's happened and says she'll fill him in with the details when she gets home. There is still no message from the kidnappers. What if that's it? They're not going to bring Shay back to her... *Why* don't they? What do they want him for? If it's for more money, then when will it stop? They can't keep upping the amount.

Maybe she should have listened to the other parents. What are they doing to get their children back? Perhaps the police have found a lead. David's keeping very quiet about it if they have.

Mick turns into her road and slowly drives down to the bottom. There are no pavements so they're always careful, especially at night. A dog walker with a Boxer is striding towards them. They look like a boy wearing a baseball cap, but their frame is petite so it could be a woman. Whoever it is, there's something about them that seems familiar.

'Stop the car.' Rachel slaps her hand on the dashboard and

Mick slams on the brakes. She jumps out and calls after the person to stop. They glance around, face obscured by the shadow from the cap, but they keep walking.

'You've dropped something,' Rachel shouts.

It's an old trick but it works. The person turns towards her and the face, although without make up, is recognisable.

'What are you doing here, Alice?'

'Oh, hello, I didn't see it was you. I'm walking the dog. Well, I'm supposed to be jogging actually.'

She's wearing all the gear: lycra leggings, zip-up hoodie, neon pink trainers, but Rachel can't honestly imagine her running anywhere. She normally walks so stiffly, as though she's not properly exercised in years.

'Did you call round for something?' She gestures to her house only a few metres away.

'No, no. Just happened to walk past. It's such a nice quiet road, isn't it?'

Strange. This is so out of her way. Nowhere near where Alice lives in fact. Is she spying on them?

'I have a feeling you and David know one another?' The words fall out of Rachel's mouth.

'What makes you say that?'

'He saw you leaving earlier today and thought he recognised you.' Saying it aloud makes it sound ridiculous and childish. But what if it's true? And Alice seemed overly interested in him.

'I think I'd know if I'd met him before.' Her mouth moves into one of her tight smiles, and she leans down to pat the dog's head.

'Did you and David used to date each other, is that what this is about? You can tell me. I'd rather know the truth,' Rachel says, trying to lighten her tone.

'No, I told you I don't know him.'

'But I think you do. I think there's something you're not telling me.'

Alice turns to go, but Rachel grabs her arm.

'Why are you so interested in my family, Alice? Why did you come to my house today even though I asked you not to?'

'Let me go.' Alice's tone is low and menacing. She tries to wriggle out of Rachel's grasp, but Rachel tightens her grip.

'You told my ex-husband you're my friend when you're only my client. You came up to my bedroom. Why would you do that when we hardly know each other?' Rachel screws her face up in disgust, squeezing Alice's arm even harder. 'I don't need this, Alice. Do you understand me? I'm under immense pressure.'

Alice glares at her, a mixture of triumph and fear in her eyes. The Boxer barks and wags his stubby tail.

'Rach, what's going on?' Mick calls out of the car window. Rachel glances at him, and in that moment's distraction she loosens her grip. Alice pulls away and starts to run, the dog trotting in front of her.

Rachel stands there stunned, watching her disappear into the darkness. A moment later a car speeds past, going in the direction they've just come. It's so quick and dark she can't work out if it's the same one as before.

While Mick parks the car on her drive, she explains to him how odd it is to see Alice walk by here, especially at this time of night. It's hardly en route to any parks from where she lives. Could she have been calling on David or is she being paranoid?

She helps Josh out of the back seat and tucks him under her wing, his head down. They stomp together up to the front door and she digs in her jacket pocket for her keys.

'What's that?' Josh asks.

'What?'

'That box.'

Rachel follows his pointing finger and sitting in the shadows in the corner of the porch is a small oblong box.

'It's addressed to you,' Mick says, picking it up.

Rachel shivers and holds a hand to her chest as though she's taken a bullet.

'Oh no, not another one.'

44

Rachel snatches the small package and gently shakes it. Something rattles inside. Mick takes the key from her shaking hand and unlocks the front door. They head straight for the living room. Josh loiters in the doorway, eyeing up the box, but she wants to see what's in it first.

'Go upstairs please.' Her fuse is short and she didn't mean to shout, but Josh's well-being is the only thing she's in control of right now. She puts the tape recorder on the dining table.

'But Mum...'

She crosses her arms. Josh kicks his shoes off and runs upstairs.

David is dozing on the sofa in the dark; the TV is on low, glowing in the corner. Rachel switches the main light on, and David's eyes blink open.

'This was on the doorstep.' She chucks the small package on the coffee table.

'What's that?' David asks, sitting up.

'I'm not sure if I want to know.'

'Shall I open it?' Mick asks, reaching for the parcel.

'Go on then.' She covers her face with her fingers.

Mick rips at the paper and lifts the lid. He takes out another cardboard box. Inside is a plain plastic case. He opens it and stares inside. Then he snaps the case shut and shakes his head. His lips tighten. The whole area around his mouth is trembling.

'What is it? Tell me,' Rachel demands, pawing at his arm. He shakes his head again, pulling away. She snatches at the plastic case and pulls until he lets go.

Opening it slowly, she draws in a sharp breath and carefully takes out Shay's round wire-framed glasses. She shudders. He wears them every day; he can't see without them. She sobs and drops down on the sofa.

'Where's Shay?' David asks.

'He wasn't there,' she cries, turning to him, her hands rising up, 'and they took your money. Left a recording of him in the clearing, can you believe it? I was so convinced he was there, but I couldn't see him. Hearing his voice... he was scared, pleading with me to find him but it was all a trick.'

She slumps into his arms, her face in her hands, sobbing.

'Oh Jesus.'

'I wish I could message them, ask them to bring Shay to me, tell them it's not fair they've taken the money and not given him back. I did everything they asked. Why are they doing this to me?'

David presses his forehead with his palm.

'We have to tell the police,' she says, wiping her tears away with her fingers.

'I've got a horrible feeling they're going to come back for more,' Mick says.

'More? I haven't got more I can easily get my hands on.' David leans his head back on the sofa and stares up at the ceiling. This is what he feared would happen. Rachel's grateful he's not saying so.

'Did you see or hear anyone approach the front door?'

'I dozed off soon after you left.'

She glances at Mick. 'No one came to visit you while we were out?'

'No one. I told you I was asleep. It could have been left there anytime.'

'There was a car speeding away when we arrived,' Mick says.

'I came across Alice Kirby walking her dog past our house, even though she doesn't live anywhere near here.'

'What is she doing down this way then?' David asks.

'I'm not sure, I thought you might know. She said she was passing by, but I think she wanted to see you. She is jealous of my family. Obsessed even.'

'How would I know about that?'

'Because you said you thought you know her, and I think she knows you.'

'She looks a bit like the wife of an old colleague.'

'Who?'

'But it can't be, it's a completely different name.'

'She lied to Mick about who she was. She came up to my bedroom.'

'What?'

'Even though I told her not to come over. She's still grieving but she creeps me out a bit.'

David frowns.

'She said I had a nice family.'

'What happened to her child?' David asks, his face pale.

'She's never said but reading between the lines I think it was sudden and unexpected.'

45

Mick takes the glasses from Rachel and puts them back in the case. He sits her down on the sofa next to David. 'I'm calling the police.' He takes his phone out and goes into the kitchen.

'Who do you think left the parcel?' she says, not looking at David.

Out of the corner of her eye she sees him shaking his head.

Does Alice Kirby have anything to do with it? Strange that she was outside the house. Does she regularly walk down this road at night? She could easily be the one who put round black stickers over the doorbell camera. It is entirely possible that she knows David, or he knows her by a different name and he's lying about it. But why would he lie?

Mick comes back in.

'They've logged my call. Someone will get back to me in the morning. It's late so the DS who saw us before is off shift.'

The story from Morocco comes up on the news.

'You have to listen to this.' Rachel grabs the remote control and turns the volume up.

A female reporter holding a microphone, is standing in front of a colourful bustling street market speaking into a camera. Sweat is dripping from her brow. David sits forward to listen as she speaks.

'The missing teenager, a boy of about seventeen years of age, Caucasian, thought to be British, was found slumped by the side of this road in Tangier during the early hours of this morning. As yet he's not been formally identified, and no further details have been released about the cause of death. The British Embassy in Rabat are working hard to identify and name the boy so his parents can be informed. They will make a statement in due course. This area of Tangier is known as a hot spot for young men looking for drugs and a good time. There is speculation in the local community that the boy was with a crowd of tourists high on drugs. It's believed a small supply has been found in his possession.'

'Oh Jesus.' Rachel springs up from the sofa, hands hovering over her mouth. 'It's Shay, isn't it? I know it is. Oh God, I can't bear it if it's him.'

'Rach, we don't know that. Please don't, it will drive you mad.' Mick stands in front of her, holding her wrists. They exchange pained expressions trying to hang on to the hope that nothing like this could happen to them. He wraps his arms around her tightly, burrowing his head into her shoulder. Not their Shay. Their son. Their baby boy. *Please be alive!*

David pushes himself up, deep in thought. He takes his mobile out of his pocket and leaves the room. Rachel and Mick pull apart. Is David upset because Mick is the one consoling her? He's Shay's dad. What does he expect? They hear David speaking on the phone in the kitchen and exchange a glance with one another.

'He's probably speaking to the other parents,' Rachel says in David's defence. 'This could be our son or one of the other children. Shay's been gone three days now. Someone has him. They've taken his glasses for fuck's sake. He won't be able to do anything without them.'

David comes back in, phone in hand.

'Simon's emailed the British Embassy in London with a list of all the children's names including Shay's. He's given them the times and dates they each went missing and the information about Shay's phone being found in Calais a couple of days ago as well as the ransom demands. He suggests you give him a recent photo of Shay to ping over to them. They're all doing the same, so at least they'll be able to send them to the Embassy in Morocco and hopefully eliminate all your children from their enquiries as soon as possible. Does Shay have any distinguishing marks on him, just in case they need to—'

'Identify his body?' She shudders and holds her arms around herself.

He glances down at the carpet.

'He has a large mole on his back. About five millimetres in diameter and located halfway down near his spine.' Rachel flicks through the photos on her phone. 'Is this photo okay?' She expands the image of Shay in their kitchen, eating a chocolate brownie the day before he went missing.

'That's a good one. Email it to me please.'

She pings it over then zooms in on Shay's face, trying to pinpoint something in his expression or a tiny gesture to indicate that behind his smile he was already planning to lie and deceive her. But there's no hint of it at all.

46

DAY FOUR

Rachel wakes up early and checks the clock by her bed: 5.50 a.m. She taps her phone. No messages. She's barely slept. Dreams of Shay calling her without his glasses on, trying to find her and her chasing around the streets of Morocco have haunted her all night. It usually takes a few minutes of grogginess for her to properly wake up, but this morning her eyes have pinged open wide with a solitary thought:

Shay could be dead.

What if it's his body that's been found in Morocco? She jumps out of bed and goes straight into the shower. Today she must talk to the police. They have to find him. She stands under the powerful jet of water, letting it run into her eyes. If she can hang on to the hope that he is still alive, she'll be able to carry on. Even thinking for a second that he might not be slows and drags her movements. Every breath becomes an effort. The dreadful truth is, if it's not him, it's someone else's son.

After she's showered and dressed, she goes downstairs to make coffee. She checks her phone again then taps open the Google app and searches for any updates on the news story. There don't seem to be any more details yet. If they've found out anything else, they're not necessarily going to report it before they've informed the child's parents. She stares at the house phone, as though it's about to ring any second. No news has to be a good thing, doesn't it? The longer it stays that way, the better. Maybe Simon will find out more from the British Embassy today and keep David updated.

It's not him. Shay is still alive. Picking up his glasses from the kitchen counter, she tries to think where he could be that he's not needing these. How will he be coping not being able to see? Can he really have been taken all the way to Morocco without a passport? If his phone was found in Calais, perhaps it means they travelled by land. Surely someone at the border would have questioned it. She dreads to think what these people want him for. She naively thought it was only girls who were trafficked – for sex and slavery – not that it makes it any better. The thought of it happening to any child let alone her son, disgusts and revolts her. If Shay is made to do those kinds of acts on people for money, he'll be traumatised for the rest of his life.

Mick is asleep on the sofa. Josh didn't want him to go home last night, and he wants to be here this morning for when the police arrive.

He too wakes early.

'Did you sleep?' She opens one curtain and perches on the sofa arm furthest away from him.

'Not much. How about you?' He yawns and stretches an arm up in the air.

'On and off, but my dreams were full of chasing people around the streets of Morocco, so I woke up exhausted.'

'Know what you mean. I feel useless lying here. Feels like we need to be out there searching for him.'

'We'll see what the police say, but I agree, we might need to go over there and try and find him ourselves.'

'It could be dangerous. We don't know how or why this boy died. Or if it's even anything to do with Shay and the others. We should let the police handle it from now on.'

'Maybe you're right. Coffee?' She knows he'll say yes, but she asks anyway. He's the one who got her into drinking it. Before they met, she was a devoted tea drinker. She's pleased they get on better now they're not a couple, but it's sad for their boys. Being the eldest, Shay was affected more by the break-up, and he still hopes they'll get back together.

She opens the other curtain and throws a window wide, letting in the chilled morning air. She tries to imagine where Shay is, what state his feet are in without trainers.

In the kitchen, she measures out the coffee into the filter, adds a pint and a half of water and switches it on. From the cupboard in the downstairs bathroom, she reaches for a fresh towel and takes it into Mick.

'Thanks.' He's sitting up on the edge of the sofa wearing only boxer shorts and raking his fingers through his mop of brown hair. He's still an attractive man. Not let himself go like lots of men seem to in their forties. Excluding David, who does push ups every morning but who, in her opinion, could do with walking more.

She goes into the conservatory as soon as Mick has gone up to the bathroom. It's time to put an end to Alice Kirby's sessions. She cannot work with the woman. There's something disturbing about her and everything about bumping into her outside the house last night seems to confirm her suspicions. Rachel went to self-defence classes a few years ago and the one piece of advice that's stuck in her mind is to listen to your gut instinct. If someone makes you feel uncomfortable, don't ignore it. As far as Alice Kirby goes, she's been ignoring it from day one. Ever since she strolled in here and had a good nosy at her family photos. Some might say Alice was being polite taking an interest, but if that was the case, why did it make

Rachel feel so prickly? In her own home as well. No, she should have nipped it in the bud. Made an excuse as to why she couldn't work with her. It's quite a rarity to get bad vibes from a client. But after Alice ran off last night, she decided she had to listen to herself.

She rummages through the folders in her bookcase. That's strange, the client folder with Alice Kirby's paperwork isn't on the usual shelf. But she doesn't remember taking it out. Perhaps she moved it automatically while she had everything else on her mind. But where would she have put it? She sits down and takes a few deep breaths. This proves she's not ready to go back to work yet. How can she forget doing something so simple? On the table in front of her she stares at a pile of papers. Was she filing these away and got interrupted? She opens her notebook. Her details will be in there from when Alice first made the inquiry. But it still doesn't explain where the folder has gone. She sifts through the stack on the table and finds the file at the bottom. The contents ought to be neatly clipped together but the paperclip has gone and the sheets of paper are spread around. The contact sheet is on top.

Someone has been snooping through her things.

47

Mick comes back dressed and sips his coffee.

'Have you been looking through my papers?' Rachel points to the stack of folders.

'Of course not; why would I do that?'

'I don't know, you tell me.'

'I haven't touched your things. What is it anyway?'

'The folder on Alice Kirby is missing.'

'That woman last night?'

'Yes. The one you sent up to my bedroom.'

'I've said sorry.' He sighs heavily.

'It's okay. You weren't to know she was lying. I can't continue coaching her. She's been acting weirdly from day one. Especially when it comes to David.'

'Ask him then. Maybe he was curious about her.'

'He did say he thought he knew her.'

'Knew who?' David is standing in the doorway.

'Alice Kirby. Have you been going through my papers?'

David stares at her and sighs. 'I was convinced I used to know her by a different name, but I was wrong. I'm sorry; I was looking for information about her.'

'This is confidential.' She gives him a sour look. Of all people, he should understand.

'I know. I'm sorry. I should have asked you first.'

'You said before you thought she was the wife of someone you worked with.' She side-eyes Mick.

'I'm not so sure now,' David says.

'Could it be important?' Is this another of his secrets?

'I don't honestly know.'

'She was asking about you.'

'Was she?' He seems to focus on something on the carpet.

'It's strange that she was passing the house last night and then I found the package with Shay's glasses straight after. It makes me wonder if she's often walked past here and if she has anything to do with the car that whizzed past or the other parcels and stickers on the doorbell camera.'

David nods, still looking at the floor as if in a trance.

The doorbell ringing interrupts them. Mick goes to answer it. A few moments later he shows in DS Groom and her colleague, DI Connor.

'Good morning.' DS Groom stands at ease and seems to examine the scene before her, then each of their faces.

'Have you found out where Shay is yet?' Rachel asks.

'We've been checking all the borders but there's no trace of any British teenagers on the missing list. We can only assume he and the others were smuggled out of the country in a van or a lorry.'

'A bit more information has come in about his phone,' says DI Connor. 'It seems there were a few more messages sent from it, but probably after it fell out of Shay's possession.'

'So you have no idea where he is then? Don't lorries et cetera get checked?' Rachel asks.

'It's not possible to check inside every single lorry or van that comes through the ports.'

'Anything more from his laptop?' Mick asks.

'We're still trying to trace where RED99 has disappeared to, but it seems the account on *Call to Arms* was closed as soon as the children started going missing,' says DI Connor. 'Everything to do with that account: messages, emails, credit card information, has been stripped out as though they were never there. But there are some remnants of messages on the other teenagers' computers and one of them, Ethan I think, has cleverly taken screen shots and saved them on his desktop. All of them met up with RED99 at some point. As with Shay, he made out he was their friend, arranged to meet them at a local park then started threatening them with exposure of private photos taken through their webcams. One of them, Olly, describes RED99 in an email to a cousin as about twenty years old with short spiky black hair, a 'cool' sleeve tattoo down his left arm and a ring through his right eyebrow. We've got nothing else to go on description-wise unfortunately.'

'So what now?' Rachel stands up then sits down again, unable to stay still.

'I understand there's something you wanted to tell me.' DS Groom cocks her head and exaggerates blinking at Rachel. 'About a ransom demand?' She's clearly expecting a swift answer.

'I can explain,' Rachel says, scanning Mick's and David's eyes, hoping they are ready to back her up. She swallows hard and tells DS Groom all about the text messages she received. 'The other parents also received these demands but chose not to pay.'

'I gather you didn't agree with their approach and decided to pay the money?' DS Groom asks as she writes something in her notebook.

Rachel tells her about going to the woods alone, how terrified she was and how Shay not being there was devastating, then finding out the money was fake. Her eyes flit over to David and away again.

'And who obtained this counterfeit money?' DS Groom asks, looking around the room at each of them.

'I did.' David says it so quietly, he can hardly be heard.

'And you got it from where?' She approaches him and looks him in the eye.

'The internet. I asked around. It seems freely available for a reasonable price.'

'Do you know that passing counterfeit currency off as real money is an offence?'

David doesn't reply. He gazes down at the carpet. Then he says, 'I was trying to be clever. I thought I could trick them and get Shay back without having to pay out.' He lets out a deep sigh. 'I agreed with the other parents that we shouldn't dish out money without knowing who we're dealing with.'

Rachel glares at him, wanting to blast him with a whole load of expletives she'd probably regret. 'We tried again yesterday with genuine cash this time.' She rubs her forehead. 'They doubled the money. A hundred thousand pounds. I admit I was desperate and hopeful that if I did everything they asked, I'd get Shay back. And that meant I couldn't risk telling the police; you can understand that can't you?'

'I'm struggling to, to be perfectly honest,' DS Groom says. 'This is the reason why we never recommend paying a ransom – because the perpetrators are likely to increase their demands.'

'I didn't want to tell you and potentially risk his life.'

'You've paid the money and still not got him back,' DS Groom says quietly.

'I wasn't to know that.'

'It was a joint decision,' Mick says.

'I could hear his voice at the woods, pleading with me to find him. I ran around the clearing like a maniac trying to find out where his voice was coming from. He said he couldn't see. I didn't know if he was tied down somewhere and blindfolded or even partially buried. But it was all a trick. His voice was coming from a tape recorder playing in a loop. I kept it as evidence, if that's any help?'

DS Groom nods, though says, 'The kidnappers are bound to have cleaned it of fingerprints.'

Mick picks it up from the sideboard and hands it to her.

'Where would they have recorded him saying those things?' Rachel asks. 'He sounded genuinely frightened. He certainly wasn't acting. I believe he's being kept somewhere blindfolded but now you're saying he might not even be in the UK any more.'

'We believe they've been moved abroad, possibly two days ago, around the time when his phone went missing,' DI Connor says.

DS Groom presses play, and they sit in silence, listening to Shay's stricken voice.

'Mum... Mum... I'm over here. Come and get me please... take me home.'

'I can't see anything Mum, please find me. I want to go home.'

'Mum... Mum... where are you?'

Mick covers his mouth, tears in his eyes. David's face is pale and frozen.

DS Groom switches it off and drops it in an evidence bag DI Connor is holding open. 'We could have assisted you. Caught the perpetrators red-handed. You've no idea who you're dealing with here. This could well be related to the boy found... in Morocco...'

48

David tries to calm Rachel down, clasping her hand inside his, talking to her softly, stroking her face. But she can't bear him touching her and pulls her hand away. DS Groom lets out a sigh.

'We need to do a TV appeal, you and all the other parents together. I firmly believe we're dealing with a highly organised trafficking gang. And I doubt they intended to exchange any money for what they see as one of their commodities, i.e. a live human who can make money for them.'

'Jesus,' Mick says.

Rachel covers her face with her hands.

'Where's Shay?' Josh stands in the doorway. 'I thought I heard his voice.'

Rachel rushes over to him and pulls him into her arms. 'Darling, it was the tape of his voice. Remember I told you about it last night in the car?'

He nods slowly and rests his head on her arm.

'I'm so sorry. We don't know where he is right now, but we will find him,' she whispers in his ear, although the truth is she's never been so unsure of anything in her life.

'How will a TV appeal help if these people aren't going to be responsive to decent behaviour?' David throws a look at DS Groom and DI Connor and sits on the sofa.

'It will serve to alert the general public to look out for white British boys or girls aged around sixteen travelling with people who don't appear to be their family. Children who look nervous or frightened.'

'All the laptops belonging to the other teenagers have been checked over and as I said it was RED99 who groomed them all in the same way as Shay. The one girl in the group, Kim, left a diary under her bed saying they'd all agreed that SC – suicide club – was their only option out of this, what she called their "nightmare" situation. It looks like they'd earmarked a place and a date, made a pledge on the website as a group – for this Saturday night at the woods. If they really were going to go through with it and take their own lives together, in a bizarre and twisted way, being kidnapped has saved their lives.'

'For God's sake.' Mick grabs at his own hair.

'There's something else I need to tell you,' Rachel says. Josh looks up at her and moves closer to his dad.

'We've received parcels with some of Shay's things inside. First his trainers, then his thumb ring threaded through his silver chain and last night' – she swallows down the emotion – 'his glasses.'

She takes in a sharp breath, trying hard not to think of the dead boy in the same second as her son. She needs to believe Shay is still alive.

'I see. And why didn't you tell us about these when you received them?' DS Groom looks disappointed in her.

'They seemed linked to the ransom demands and we were trying so hard not to step out of line in case they didn't keep their end of the bargain.' She sounds so naïve and feels stupid for trusting the kidnappers.

DS Groom follows Rachel into the hall where she points to the boxes under the console table. DI Connor puts on plastic gloves and opens the largest box with the trainers inside.

'Shay would never let them get caked in mud and muck like that. He likes to keep them immaculate,' she tells them.

'I cleaned and buffed them for him before the party,' Josh pipes up. 'He promised to pay me five pounds.'

'These are what he was wearing that night?' DS Groom looks pointedly at her.

'I think so, bearing in mind I thought he'd gone to bed,' Rachel says.

'Yes,' David confirms, reminding her once again that he allowed Shay to go to the party completely against her wishes.

'David went looking for him that night, didn't you?' She stares at him with no emotion, no regret at possibly dropping him in it. 'He chose not to tell me this until we realised Shay was missing.'

David returns her stare and for a moment seems stunned at her betrayal because he doesn't reply. Did he think she was going to cover up for him when her son's life is in danger? As far as she can see, this all began with David lying to her. That could be what Shay's emails were about. She's often said to him if a person lies about one thing how can you trust them about anything else.

'Is this true?' DS Groom narrows her eyes at him.

'Yes, yes, it is.' He looks away from Rachel.

'Why didn't you mention this when we first came here a few days ago?' DS Groom scribbles in her notebook.

'I don't know, it must have slipped my mind.'

'Why did you go looking for Shay? Didn't you think he was coming home? Most people would have waited longer for him to arrive. He might have been a bit late, that's all.'

'Because I told him he could go to the party, but only if he came home by midnight. I left one of his front windows unlocked so he could climb out and back in again. As soon as midnight passed, I had a horrible feeling he'd gone on somewhere else.'

'Why did you say he could go even though he was grounded?'

'I felt sorry for him. He's had a rough time lately: he got beaten up by the people he thought were his friends and I suppose I wanted him to like me. Sad, eh? I wanted him to know I understood that he craved his freedom. I remember being that age, feeling like that.'

'Feeling like what?' Rachel snaps.

'Trapped,' David says, frowning at her, then focusing back on DS Groom. 'I think Rachel is overprotective sometimes but what do I know; I've never really been any good with kids. And now look what's happened.' He sighs.

'What did you do when he didn't come back on time?'

'He wasn't responding to my calls and texts, so I decided to drive to the woods and look for him myself.'

'Without informing his mother?'

'I didn't want to worry her or make her mad. I needed to sort out my own mess before she found out.'

'And what did you find when you got to the woods?' DS Groom jots something in her notepad.

'The bonfire was still going but had died right down. Most of the kids had gone home, a few were camping in tents around the fire. There were food wrappers, rubbish and debris everywhere. I checked in with everyone I came across, asked if they'd seen Shay, scoured the clearing and part of the woods. I don't think I missed anyone, but no one remembered seeing him for maybe half an hour. I called out his name several times and tried his mobile but there was no signal until I got back to my car. There was no sign of him. I guessed he'd left ages before and there I was trying to do the right thing while he was probably sitting in someone's warm house having a good laugh at me. I never imagined something bad might have happened to him. Honestly.' He looks at Rachel pleadingly. She grits her teeth. She wants to shake him and scream at him. He should have called her right then.

'And you didn't come across Bella, the girl who was attacked?'

Rachel sees a look pass between Groom and Connor.

'I wouldn't know what she looks like, but no.' David shakes his head. 'I didn't go that far into the woods.'

'How far is that?' DS Groom pounces on him with her answer. 'How do you know how deep into the woods she was when she was found?'

49

'I don't know. I'm just saying.' David shrugs, palms open.

Rachel examines every inch of his face. She can't tell if he is lying. She doesn't know him well enough. She doesn't know if this man is capable of hitting a girl on the back of the head so hard she lost consciousness. Could he be involved in her son's abduction? That would explain why he was so calm about offering his money for the ransom. It makes perfect sense because he'd get his money back. She lets out the breath she's been holding in.

'Were you concerned for Shay's welfare when you couldn't find him?' DS Groom asks.

'Like I said, my first thought was being annoyed at him having a pop at me. Not coming home when we agreed. He begged me to let him go to the party and to promise not to tell his mum. I didn't want to go behind her back, but he wore me down and I stupidly thought it meant he was beginning to accept me, that maybe we were becoming friends, which I knew would please Rachel. But when I couldn't find him, I was angry that he was deliberately trying to get me into trouble with her.'

'So you didn't think to call the police at that point, or indeed let the boy's mother know you thought her son might have gone missing?'

'No.' He pauses. 'I honestly thought he was fooling me around and had never intended to come back on time. I'm well aware he doesn't really like me, and like I said, I thought this was his way of getting me in trouble with his mum. I guessed he'd deliberately crashed out at a mate's house and let his mobile battery die. He's a sixteen-year-old boy. He's streetwise. I didn't feel like he was in any danger, or that he'd get in any kind of trouble. I certainly didn't want to treat him like a child, because I'd have hated that at his age too.'

DS Groom looks across at DI Connor, purses her lips and writes something down.

'So tell me about these other items, the thumb ring and the chain.'

'Shay always wears them. He only takes them off when he has a shower,' Rachel says.

'And the last item?' She takes the glasses out of the box.

'Shay's glasses. He needs to wear them all the time. Everything will be too blurry without them, and he'll get headaches. He looks good in them too. Kids want to wear glasses nowadays, don't they?'

'These are all very personal items, probably the things he needs the most, that define him, would you say?'

'Definitely. I'm really struggling to picture where he can be without them, how he can be functioning not being able to see.'

'They want you to feel this fear. They're manipulating your emotions by sending you these. Do we know if the other parents have received similar items, their kids' possessions?' DS Groom looks to DI Connor then to David.

'I think so, but I don't know exact details,' David says.

This strikes Rachel as odd. She thought he was discussing everything with them.

'Another strange thing happened last night. I bumped into a client of mine outside here when we returned from the woods. I've only just started life coaching her, but she's been acting a bit weirdly. Asking about my family and David in particular. In fact, he saw her yesterday and thought she looked like someone he used to know.'

'What time was this?'

'About 10 p.m.'

'But I don't know her. I don't know anyone called Alice,' David protests.

'She doesn't live anywhere near here,' Rachel continues, 'and it seemed implausible that she would be in this part of town at that time of night to walk her dog. And then we found the parcel on my doorstep. I've been wondering if she has anything to do with leaving it there or at least if she saw who left it. She tried to make out she walks past here with her dog quite often, but I think she might be stalking me.'

'That's a big claim. Why would you think that?'

'Because she came over when I'd messaged her not to. Then she didn't tell Mick she was my client, she told him we were friends, so he let her come up to my bedroom. It was a shock waking up to her standing there, I can tell you. There's just something about her that doesn't sit right with me.'

'Can you give me her name and contact details? We'll pay her a little visit, see if she's got any involvement in dropping this parcel off or if she saw who left it there. Anything else?'

'Someone has been putting stickers over the doorbell camera and now I'm wondering if that's her too. Conveniently, she's been here every day this week so she could quite easily have done it.'

'Okay, if you can give us access to your cloud, we'll take a look at everything that's been captured over the last couple of weeks.'

'We don't pay for the cloud because David thought we didn't

need it, so it doesn't store any footage. We can only see live activity each day.'

'Ah, that's a shame. And David, who did you think this woman might be?'

'No one important, just the wife of someone I used to work with.'

'And her name is?' DS Groom's pen is poised above her notebook.

'Linda Mercer.' David's face is pale, eyes unblinking.

She writes it down. 'We'll check her out, see if she's linked to Alice Kirby. Is there any reason you can think of why she would be using a different name?'

'Not at all; seems unlikely it's the same person. I've probably got it wrong.'

'We've been working through the list your secretary gave us, the patients who may have a grudge against you or any of your colleagues.'

'Colleagues?' Rachel asks.

'It's a standard line of enquiry, covering all possible angles,' DS Groom says. 'Is there anyone else who should be on that list?'

David swallows. 'No one who springs to mind.' He shakes his head.

DI Connor bags up the boxes of evidence and seals them. 'We'll run fingerprint and DNA checks on all these items and get back to you later today about the TV appeal.'

'There's just one more thing. Do you know who invited Shay to the party? We can't seem to find out who organised it,' DS Groom asks.

'He never said anything to me.' Rachel slowly shakes her head.

'I don't know but maybe Josh does?' David looks to him.

'It was an online invitation everyone was sharing around,' Josh says. 'Shay showed me. It said something like, "Come to the rave of the year at Bayhurst woods and invite all your friends. Shh, pass it on." I don't know who it came from originally but there was a real buzz about it.'

'Josh, that's very helpful indeed,' DS Groom says. 'We have a strong suspicion that the person who set up the party did so with the intention of taking Shay.'

50

A couple of hours later they meet up with the other parents at a studio in Elstree for the live TV appeal. By the time they arrive, reports are coming in that confirm the dead teenager in Morocco is indeed a British boy aged around seventeen, found in a backstreet barefoot and bleeding. There is no word on what sort of injury was sustained or the cause of death. He was wearing joggers and a white T-shirt, make unconfirmed, which means it could be Shay, Ethan, Nate or Olly, or someone completely different. But whoever it is, it is someone's son. More details about his identity are to be released in due course.

Seeing the photos of each of the missing teenagers up on the screens behind them, stabs Rachel in the chest. She pauses at the one of Shay, taken just hours before she last saw him. If only he could have said to her, 'Mum, there's something really bothering me.' If she'd been the sort of mum he could open up to, they might all be at home together now, safe and sound.

It's strange seeing the other parents again after that first initial meeting at George's house. They are far more subdued and somehow older looking, probably from the stress and lack of sleep.

They barely acknowledge her, but David makes a point of shaking hands and speaking with of each of them before they take their seats. Every parent has a name plate in front of them.

David stands at the side with Josh. Rachel sits next to Mick, her hand on top of his under the table for moral support. His leg won't stop jigging up and down. There are rows of journalists scrutinising them, probably wondering what sort of parents they are. Have they already been googled? Photos pulled from their Facebook pages, ready to splash all over the newspapers and on social media in the morning? She's satisfied they at least tried to do the right thing by paying the money, even if they haven't got Shay back. Although David losing £100,000 is hardly a small matter. The thought of having to pay it back to him overwhelms her brain. She can't think about it now, she needs to concentrate on finding Shay first.

DS Groom does most of the talking, describing the time and place each teenager was last seen and how many days and hours have passed since. DI Connor goes on to explain how each child has been enticed online via a seemingly innocent photo requested by the perpetrator, which he goes on to list, bringing it home to Rachel how innocent they all are and how easy it was for this person to groom them. Kim sent RED99 a photo of her new kitten, Ethan, his new bike, Nate, his guitar and Olly, his hamster.

Blown up on screens behind them are photographs of all the items belonging to the children which have been sent to the parents in packages. They are what DS Groom calls 'trophies' which makes Rachel shudder, and think of serial killers more than kidnappers. These trophies include Kim's silver violin brooch, Ethan's Seiko watch, Nate's signet ring engraved with his initials and Olly's leather laced friendship bracelet as well as Shay's glasses, and several other items. On a separate screen is an enlarged photo of the tape recorder Rachel found in the woods. She and Mick have given permission for it to be played to the press, but now, as DS

Groom introduces the recording, a stab of panic courses through Rachel as she questions her rash decision.

She braces herself as the whole room falls silent and Shay's haunting and echoey child-like pleas ring out across the studio. Tears track silently down her face. She squeezes Mick's hand hard, out of sight under the table, holding her composure as best she can. Mick sniffs and blows his nose into a hanky.

'We have distributed photos of all the missing children to our counterparts across Europe and we're checking CCTV at all the ports out of the UK and surrounding areas. One white transit van is of particular interest and is under further investigation. CCTV near the back end of Bayhurst woods near the housing estate and the Cock and Bull pub on the corner has been checked, and a white transit van has been captured on a camera going past the pub car park at 12.08 a.m. on the night of the party, and passing again later going in the opposite direction at 1.19 a.m. On closer inspection, there is a significant amount of mud on its tyres in the second clip, giving us a clear indication that this transit van drove into the woods and may well be the vehicle in which Shay Gulliver was abducted.'

Rachel presses her balled-up fist to her lips. She glances at Josh's pale and frightened face.

DS Groom points to a still of the van in a blown-up photo behind her. 'As you can see, although it is a little blurred, the number plate is visible. It's an old private number currently for sale on a dealer's website, so someone has had a counterfeit set of these plates made up and stuck them on, which means they are more than likely changing the plates illegally along their journey, wherever that's to, to prevent them being tracked. But there is one detail they may have overlooked.' She stands up and holds up her finger which she then plants onto the screen. 'See here? There's a distinctive dent on the left-hand side of the rear bumper.' Another photo comes up, showing a close up of the back of the van. 'Just a small one, but enough for us to distinguish it, despite the number plate it is currently wearing.'

A few agreeable murmurs circulate the room.

'If any member of the public has any information relating to sightings of any of these children or anything else to do with the van we've described in the area around Bayhurst woods on Sunday, Tuesday or Wednesday evening, please contact Operation Indigo on this number.' DS Groom reads out a telephone number, pointing to it on the screen behind her. Then she invites questions from the press. Hands shoot up and she points to a woman on the front row wearing a trouser suit, hair up in a bun.

'Is there any truth in the speculation that these teenagers may have already been trafficked abroad, possibly into the sex trade? And if so, are you able to give any assurance to these parents here today that they will see their children again?'

'We have no concrete evidence that any of these children have been trafficked into the sex trade overseas. As I said, we're working closely with our colleagues across Europe to find these children as quickly as possible and bring them home safely. The parents here are being kept up to date with all the latest information as we receive it. We are doing everything we possibly can to bring these children home.'

'Are you saying you believe they have been taken to Europe?'

'We are working with that possibility. Shay's mobile was found on a ferry in Calais, which doesn't mean he was there too but it's certainly widened our search area, which I'm sure you can appreciate is already large and quite an undertaking.'

'Should parents watching at home stop their children playing this *Call to Arms* game? And what safety information can you give any worried parents?'

DI Connor replies to this. 'There is nothing wrong with children playing this game, but we'd advise children not to engage in conversations via the chatroom, unless they absolutely know for sure who they are speaking to. Do not share any personal information about yourself or anyone else including your location. As we've illustrated, even sharing what may seem an innocent photograph, like that of a pet, could be giving away your location to a stranger who will be able to pinpoint where that image was taken. I say to all parents, be vigilant, keep a check on who your child is interacting with online. Question who they are and if you're not sure, delete or block the contact and report any suspicious behaviour. There is a safety information pack for parents, carers and schools on our website. I urge everyone working with or caring for young people to read it.'

'Do you think the British boy who's been found dead in Morocco is the child of one of these parents here today?' shouts a bald skinny journalist sitting near the back of the room. A collective intake of breath followed by murmurs circulates in the airless space. Simon's wife Lucy bursts into tears. Everyone turns to look at who asked the question, which is surely one that they are all thinking but too afraid to ask. The parents look across at Lucy then shoot daggers at the journalist. Simon puts his arm around his wife's tiny shoulders and Rachel passes her a tissue. The journalist is stretching up in his seat, eyebrows raised expectantly for an answer. He pushes his specs higher on his nose.

DS Groom clears her throat, light pink circles appearing on her cheeks and up from her neck. 'I'm not prepared to speculate, and I think your question is highly insensitive.' She turns to the other side of the audience and with an outstretched arm, points to another journalist. 'Yes.'

'But you've not been taking the case of these missing teenagers seriously, have you?' the journalist with the specs persists in his loud grating voice. 'Five teenagers who knew each other in an online game, who have met in real life, went missing over the space of twenty-four hours, and it's only now when a child of a similar age has been found dead in the backstreet of a foreign country that you're linking these abductions. Isn't that correct, DS Groom?'

'Your speculation is without all the facts and is not relevant here,' DS Groom says to shut him down. 'No more questions. We're done here. Thank you.' DS Groom waves a hand in the air at the flashing cameras, then she walks off. Rachel and Mick stand up, followed by the other parents, and silently follow her out.

51

Rachel waits with Mick for David and Josh in the green room. Simon is still consoling Lucy and the rest of the parents are huddled around them, talking amongst themselves.

'Are you okay?' David asks, his hands on Rachel's shoulders. His gaze strays over to the other parents. 'Give me a minute,' he says and goes over to them. He's more concerned about their welfare than hers.

'Charming.' Rachel turns back to Mick. David could include her in their discussions a bit more. He's always leaving her out.

'The police still don't seem to know much at all, do they?' Mick says.

'I think they know more than they're letting on, otherwise why go through with this fiasco? Like the journalist in there said, why are they only really taking this seriously now that one of our children could be dead?'

'I don't think it's just because of that. It's been four days now. They're not just runaway teenagers any more, plus they have proof that they were all being groomed by the same person.'

'What about the van with false plates? Do you think the children have been taken abroad?'

'I don't know, but I still can't believe they were seriously considering taking their own lives. I wish Shay could have talked to us.'

'Me too.' They stand together for a few moments in silence then Rachel nudges Mick to look at Lucy who is emerging from the group of parents around her, wiping her eyes with a tissue. 'I think we should go and say something before we go.'

'Yeah, you're right.'

Before they can move, DS Groom stands in the middle of the room, hand up. 'I'm really grateful to you all for coming today and as soon as we have more information we'll be in touch. In the meantime, please call me immediately if you receive any more messages or packages from the kidnappers. Any contact from them now could lead us to finding your children quicker. So please stay vigilant.'

As soon as DS Groom stops speaking, Rachel and Mick join the group re-forming around Simon and Lucy. It's upsetting for all of them, but Rachel understands from her work that some people are naturally more sensitive than others, and she wants to show the rest of them she cares, despite their differences.

The more she ponders on it, the more unlikely she thinks the dead boy is one of their sons. He sounds as if he's at least a year older for a start. He could have been there on holiday with friends. Doing drugs or drink or both. It's probably his first independent holiday and he's gone over the top with everything on offer. Some poor parents somewhere are going to get that life-altering call to say it's their boy who has been found. And how can the police be so sure he's British? Maybe he had his passport on him. In which case it can't be one of theirs because none of their passports were taken.

Back at home, David trudges straight upstairs, head down while Rachel wanders into the kitchen and puts the kettle on. She takes out a large Spanish onion and starts chopping it, not sure what to make for dinner. Her eyes smart and sting so much she can hardly see through the mist. She doesn't try to stop the tears that follow.

Mick switches on the TV and when the news comes up, Rachel is standing in the doorway drying her hands on a towel, watching the edited clip of their appeal. It's hard to believe she is standing here watching herself on television, sitting there with the other parents. It doesn't seem real. Half of her expects Shay to come up behind her and tap her on the shoulder like he always does. He'd duck away so when she turned round, he wasn't there, but standing right in front of her. That was before he became so serious all those months ago. For some reason she didn't notice when he changed. He just became unhappy and grumpy, angry at everything, every-one, snappy and aggressive, hitting walls and banging doors, hurting his knuckles, because he couldn't control his emotions. She supposes she put it down to him becoming a stroppy teenager but all the time he was being blackmailed for thousands of pounds and he couldn't ask her for help. He probably thought she'd tell him off or blame him for playing that game. Whatever the reason, she wasn't there for him. He couldn't count on her.

Her knees weaken at the truth of it. Her abject failure as a mother. She puts a hand out to the door frame to stop herself sink-ing. Hopefully some good will come of this appeal but she can't help dwelling on the journalist's question. Will another child be next?

52

'Are you staying for dinner?' Rachel asks Mick. She's not spent this much time with him since their disastrous holiday in Cornwall before they split up. Funny how they get on better now there's no sex involved. When all of this is over, she'll suggest to David that he moves out. It's not working any more. He's not the person she thought he was and that's not necessarily his fault. She took the good stuff she knew about him and constructed who he was in her mind; except he's not really that person at all, only the one she wanted him to be. Hard to admit but she hardly knows him. It's clear his loyalties are not with her and her children. It's hardly surprising. He barely knows her either.

'I'll stay, if that's okay, although I ought to get home later, see if I still have a girlfriend.' He laughs nervously and glances down at his phone. Andie's probably tolerating his situation but spending so long with his ex-wife will be pissing her off by now for sure.

'Actually, Andie's texted to say I may as well stay another night as she's going out with her friends. Is that okay with you?'

'Of course,' Rachel says.

Josh nudges his dad in the ribs and Mick tickles him under both arms. They tumble across the sofa giggling. She's glad Mick's here. He's helped Josh cope so much.

Back in the kitchen, Rachel stares out of the window. Images of where Shay could be flash in her mind. She forces herself to carry on when all her body wants to do is curl up on the floor and cry. She fries the onions, peppers and garlic and adds slices of cold potatoes from yesterday. Then she beats six eggs and pours the liquid on top, followed by a sprinkle of grated cheddar from a packet. When it's half done, she turns off the heat, puts the pan into the oven on low and drags herself upstairs.

David is lying on the bed, arms by his sides, staring at the ceiling. Has he forgotten to take one of his tablets? It's possible he missed one a couple of weeks ago when he was ill with a bug. It normally takes that long for the dip in his mood to show.

'Are you okay?' she asks, standing at the door.

'Not really,' he says, still staring upwards. 'How about you?'

'I'm exhausted.' She flops down on the bed.

'I feel like this is all my fault.' He continues to stare at the ceiling.

'Why?'

'It has to be something to do with me.'

'How?'

'Like you said, it could be linked to whoever started the fire at my house.'

'There's no point beating yourself up. You're not the one who's kidnapped them.'

'I suppose you're right.' He turns his head to look at her.

'Come down and eat. I've cooked frittata.' She forces herself to sit up.

David doesn't say much over dinner. They watch the news again, hoping for more information from Morocco but there's nothing and she tells herself that has to be a good thing. She keeps her phone by her side, breaking her own rules about no gadgets at the table. There are no more updates, so they all decide on an early night.

* * *

Rachel is woken by the muffled sound of a mobile beeping. She opens one eye and reaches out for her phone, but it's not hers making the noise, it's David's. The clock by her bed says 12.17 a.m. He sits up and the mattress shifts.

She tucks her phone under her pillow and shuts her eyes. He must be on call. By the time she's rolled over, he's quietly shutting the door to the bathroom. She tries not to listen to him go to the toilet. She turns back over and attempts to go to sleep but then he's splashing water, presumably on his face, and the gush from the tap is so loud it's hard to block out. Then he's brushing his teeth. The water is still running.

Moments later the bathroom door opens, and he switches off the light. There's a rustling sound of him putting his clothes on, the creak of springs as he sits on the bed. Normally he'd come round to her side and whisper goodbye in her ear, kiss her cheek, but she made a point of telling him how exhausted she was last night and didn't want to be disturbed. He leaves the room, shutting the door quietly behind him.

Damn. Now she is wide awake. She sits bolt upright, hearing every sound he makes downstairs. But something isn't right. His work suit is still hanging on the wardrobe door. His jeans and sweatshirt from the chair by his bedside have gone.

She grabs her phone, checks the screen and jumps out of bed. In another few moments she has pulled on socks and trousers from yesterday and a jumper from the back of the armchair in the corner. She layers it over the long T-shirt she wears to bed. Leaning over the banister, she strains to hear David go out, shutting the front door quietly with his key. She glances at him out of the front window. His car is electric so it is completely silent when it starts up and pulls away. No wonder she didn't hear him when he went out looking for Shay that night.

Josh is sound asleep in his room. She creeps downstairs. Mick is asleep on the sofa. She grabs her car keys and slips out of the front door. Wherever David is going, if it's to do with Shay and the other children, she is going to find out.

She tries to make as little noise as possible when she starts the engine, hoping she doesn't wake Josh or Mick. She puts her foot down and is quick to catch up with David but tries to keep some distance, so he doesn't notice her following.

When he turns onto the main road, she tries to guess where he's going; it's definitely not to the hospital. What is so urgent at this time of night? Who was calling him? If it was news on one of the children, he'd have woken her, wouldn't he? He suddenly speeds up and for a while she's not sure if he's seen her or if she can keep up with him. He seems to be heading in the direction of the woods, down all those unlit winding lanes which terrify her even in daylight. She keeps her beam low and stays back so her lights don't shine in his rear-view mirror and make him wonder who might be behind him. Low branches and twigs sweep past her windows, etching and scratching the paint and glass. She passes remote houses with eerie green and red lights in their front gardens and mirrors on corners reflecting her car back at her, making her jumpy, but she clenches her teeth and carries on.

Where can he be going? Dark thoughts crowd in on her. David may not be so innocent after all. He's lied to her before. He could be the link between her family and these other children. Without him none of this would have happened. Is it possible David is the one who abducted them? Oh God, no. Why? And where would he be keeping them? He could have sent those messages from another phone. And easily have put a sticker over the camera. Did David go to the woods for another reason that night? Her breathing becomes sharp and shallow as panic crawls up her throat. Is he going to them now? They could be locked up somewhere. He couldn't have done it alone. Who's doing this with him? Is it to get money out of the parents? But no, he didn't even want to pay the ransom.

Stop, stop, stop!

She takes some slow deep breaths, her hands shaking. This is insane. David is a good man, a surgeon. He saves people.

53

DAY FIVE

Rachel follows David back onto a main road lit with white streetlights. They turn into a familiar tree-lined lane of large individually designed houses set back from the road. David's car has slowed right down. Rachel slows her car to a crawl, leaning forward to see exactly where he pulls in. A house on the left with high hedges, large sweeping drive, a double fronted detached property. Simon and Lucy's house.

Rachel sighs, crazy with relief. As if David would abduct five children. How utterly ridiculous. Still, she wants to know what he's up to. Why he's got out of his bed in the middle of the night to come here.

She finds a space and parks on the street then walks quickly up to the driveway of number 125, which is displayed in swirly gold letters on the fence post. A clipped hedge surrounds the front garden. David is standing on the stone doorstep, staring down at his phone. She wonders what he'd say if she called him right now, asked him where he was, if he'd lie to her again.

He must have rung the bell or tapped on the door already because moments later it opens and of all people, Julie answers.

David says something and puts his hand on her arm and goes in. It seems intimate. What is she doing at Simon and Lucy's house, answering the door as if she lives there?

Rachel creeps up the drive. The light is on in the front room, curtains open. Someone is standing with their back to the window. She hides behind a magnolia in the middle of the front lawn and tries to stretch up to see. It's not David, it's another man, darker hair, wider shoulders. He turns slightly to the side, a whisky glass in his hand, and says something she wishes she could hear. It is George, Nate's dad.

This is confusing. Are all the parents here? Why hasn't she been invited? What are they doing meeting up at this time of night? She stays watching them, Julie and David standing close together, bending down to someone sitting on the sofa. She hears David's voice rise, arms rising too. She reads his lips telling everyone to *just calm down*. This has gone far enough. She needs to know what's going on in there.

She presses her finger hard on the doorbell and watches them all look at each other and fall silent. Standing close to the door at the ready, as soon as Julie opens it a crack, Rachel shoves it with her fist and her foot at the same time, forcing the door out of Julie's hand.

'David,' Julie shouts over her shoulder, but Rachel storms in. Julie makes a grab for her but gets a handful of coat instead. Rachel bursts into the front room as David is poised to come out.

'What are you doing here?' he asks, swilling a drop of whisky in his glass as he steps back.

'Same goes for you. What are you doing getting up in the night and sneaking out?' She takes in his astonished face and those of the other parents in the room. 'What's going on?' Her gaze lands on Simon and Lucy huddled together on the sofa, their faces gaunt and etched with anxiety.

'I was called over to help.' David's voice is calm, steady and in control.

'Help with what?'

They all glance at each other, then at David, as if waiting for permission to speak. A shared secret she's not in on.

'I'm not being funny, but if this is a party it's a bit maudlin for my taste.' Her attempt to lighten the mood, get someone to speak, doesn't work. 'Why are you all here?' They're lounging on sofas and chairs, and it dawns on her how comfortable they are in each other's company. Simon, Julie, Suki and George are wearing the same navy polo shirt David wears, with the clinic logo embroidered on it.

'We're all here to help,' Julie says with a defiant edge to her tone, her eyes flicking at David as if they've rehearsed what to say.

'Help who? Why wasn't I invited?' Rachel searches their faces, but they are closed off from questions. 'What are you not telling me?'

'It didn't seem important when our kids already know each other.' Julie steps closer to David and Rachel has the urge to shove her smug face into next week.

'It never came up.'

'What never came up?' Rachel tries to catch the look passing between Julie and David. 'That you already know each other? All of you.'

For a moment, neither of them speaks.

'You're right. These are my colleagues,' David says.

'Why didn't you tell me?' she bellows at him.

'We didn't think it was an important factor,' he says in his calm, practiced voice.

'What? Who's the royal we?' Rachel scans round their blank faces. 'Not one of you considered telling me you all work together? It could be why our children have been taken.' All the time they've been discussing this behind her back, leaving her out. She's not sure what she finds more distressing: David lying to her again or the other parents keeping her out of their little group.

Still no one speaks.

'It's my fault you weren't kept in the loop. I didn't want to worry you more than you already were.' David reaches for her hand, but she pulls away, frowning at him. Does he think he can sweet talk her in front of everyone? Who is this man who crawls out of her bed at night and lies about where he's going, what he's up to?

'You didn't think I needed to know? You didn't think it was important?' she shouts at him.

'Not straight away, no.'

'Because it's not your child who's missing, is it? You don't care about Shay, do you? In fact, it was you who helped him go out that night. So, have you got something to do with him being abducted? Seems mighty convenient that the night he went missing, you went to the woods.' Rachel stabs her finger into his chest. She turns away from him, shaking her head in disbelief. The other parents stay silent. Julie has moved away from David and is perched on a chair on the other side of the room.

'So are you going to tell me why you're all here in the middle of the night?'

'I was going to wait until the morning,' David says. 'I thought you needed to sleep after the evening you've had.' Is this the tone he uses when he speaks to patients to reassure them before an operation? If it is, she finds it condescending. She doesn't need nannying.

'Has something happened?' She casts her eye around all the guilty faces, as though she's the enemy. They are all silent, watching her.

'We've had news, about the boy they found,' David says, his voice cracking slightly.

'In Morocco?' Rachel's pulse spikes.

He nods and tries to hold her hand again, but she yanks her arm away as if he's trying to hurt her. She holds her arms around her body, not sure she wants to hear what he's going to say. Everyone is staring at her with pitying, pained expressions. She couldn't have got this more wrong. She suddenly feels bone cold, and the colour must surely have drained from her skin. David glances over at Simon who returns the slightest nod.

'We're here because the police believe the boy they found dead in Morocco is one of ours.'

'No!' Rachel cries out and cups her face with her hands. She leans forward, her stomach and chest aching. Her head fills with the horror that it could be her boy. David wraps his arms around her, and she has no energy to push him away.

'It's not Shay,' he says quietly. Rachel sobs into his shoulder but stops herself and pulls back, searching his face.

'It's Ethan.'

54

Rachel's eyes immediately dart over to Lucy and Simon. 'Oh my God, I'm so, so sorry.' She reaches out to them. They look up briefly then clasp each other's hands tighter and bow their heads together.

'How? What on earth happened?' She blinks at David, wanting answers, but there are none.

'Too soon to say.' He shakes his head. 'They're flying out tomorrow to identify Ethan's body.'

Rachel's heart breaks for them. Part of her wants to scream: *Where is my son?* An image of his glasses flashes up in her mind. Is he still alive or could he be next?

'I'm going to go with them,' David says.

'To Morocco?' Rachel asks, still trying to absorb that they all lied to her. 'Why?' There must still be things they're not telling her, like why the children might have been taken to Morocco in the first place.

'To try and find the other children.'

'You think they're all there?' She examines David's face. What is he not saying?

'We all do,' George says, and the others murmur and nod. How can she believe a word of what any of them say?

'We think they were kidnapped and smuggled over the border,' David says, finishing his whisky.

'How?' This is crazy. They can't know that. This doesn't feel real. Yet they seem to know more than they're letting on.

'We're not sure exactly but it could have been in the transit van the police spotted near the woods. We're guessing Shay was the first one, then Ethan, then the other three. We think they were hidden somehow in the van, more than likely drugged.'

'So we still don't know if the others are okay, if they're alive?' Rachel presses her sternum as a pocket of air or bile threatens to come up. How could they be working all this out and not tell her any of it?

'We have to hope they're all right, but we need to get to them quickly because I have a nasty feeling that time is running out.'

'Then I'm coming with you too,' Rachel says.

'It's too dangerous.'

'Why? What are you not telling me?'

'Whatever happened to Ethan, it's given the kidnappers publicity they won't want, and they'll know the police are closing in. We don't know yet how Ethan died. These people could be capable of anything. Whoever is holding him might be armed.' David's eyes are small from lack of sleep. It's the first time in all this that Rachel has seen him look so stressed and concerned. He hides his feelings well.

'Who is doing this? Is it a trafficking gang like the police are saying?' Rachel regards each of their faces. 'Why are you only telling me what you want me to know?'

She holds her arms around her body to stop herself shaking from cold or fear, or both. The not knowing if Shay is alive is sapping the life out of her.

David looks to Julie, but neither of them speaks.

'You need to tell me everything you know, right now,' Rachel yells at them.

'We have a theory about who might be behind all this,' Julie says and wraps a curl of hair behind her ear.

'Which is?'

'An old colleague of ours who we think holds a grudge against us. He left the hospital under a dark cloud, and we've not seen or heard from him since,' David says.

'Why, what happened? Was he struck off for malpractice?' She's read about them, doctors making an incorrect diagnosis or failing to diagnose a problem that exists. The consequences can be devastating for the patient.

'We can't really say. Patient confidentiality,' Julie says, glancing sideways at David.

'But he did do something to a patient?' She clenches her teeth to stop herself shouting at them. Something else they all know but are keeping her out of. 'Why can't you just tell me? My son's life is at stake here. You don't need to name the patient.'

None of them answer her. Julie tips her head to the side as if to say, I've given you the only answer I can. The official line. They were like this the first time she met them, so she wasn't imagining it when they closed ranks. She wonders what secrets they're holding for each other. The mistakes they've made while treating patients in their care. It's not necessarily their fault. Everyone knows they work long hours, often without a break.

'Then why haven't you told the police?' Rachel pushes them.

'We have told the police, but they didn't find anything unusual.'

'Why don't I know about this?' Rachel can't believe they've left her out of this too.

'They couldn't mention it in front of you because of our need to keep confidentiality,' David says. 'The police say our ex-colleague has an alibi, so we could be wrong; it's just a hunch. I can't tell you any more at the moment, except I've been researching where he's working, what he's up to. You have to trust me.'

'Seriously?' Rachel raises her voice. The one thing she's struggling with right now. Trust. How can she trust David after all his lies? 'I have a right to know what's going on, do you understand? I need to find my son.'

David nods.

Looking at Lucy and Simon, what choice does she have? She'd like to scream at all of them but if David thinks he knows where Shay and the others are being kept in Morocco, she needs to believe him so she can find her son and bring him home.

'I have to come with you,' she says. 'If there's any chance that something might happen to Shay, I can't stay here and hope that it doesn't.'

David exchanges a look with Simon and George.

'I'm sorry, it's not possible. All the flight arrangements have been made. Besides, you need to stay at home. Josh needs you.'

'I want to come. I need to see for myself what's happened to Shay.'

David walks away from her, shaking his head.

'What if he's hurt? He's just a boy. It'll be me he wants by his side, not you,' she says, trying not to shout at him.

David pauses and turns back to face her. 'Fine, I'll try and get you a ticket on the same flight as me, but I can't promise anything.'

'Thank you.'

'Simon and Lucy are flying out in the morning from Heathrow with a police escort. They need to get there as soon as possible to identify Ethan's body. If I can get you a ticket, you and I will go on a different flight from Luton. We don't want to alert the police to us going too. We'll stay somewhere different, and Simon will communicate any information to us about where they think Ethan was being held before he was found, see if it ties in with our research.'

Rachel nods. They have it all worked out. They've made these arrangements behind her back as though it's got nothing to do with her. 'And where is it you're planning to look?'

'We have a couple of places in mind we want to check out.'

'What sort of places?' If they'd been more open from the beginning, she wouldn't have to query every little thing.

'Hospitals and clinics. There are several in the district of Tangier. It looks like he's worked in a couple of them, but one in particular according to their website.'

'Why has he gone to Morocco if he used to work with you here?'

'He worked over there years ago. He has connections and often talked about setting up his own clinic in Morocco.'

'And you're just going to bowl in there and ask him a few questions?'

'Not exactly.' He pours himself a glass of water from a jug on the table and drinks it straight down.

'What are you going to do then? Who is he? Are you telling me he's dangerous?'

'He could be. If he's the person behind abducting our children, who knows what he's got planned because one is already dead.'

'Can't you send the police in if you think it could be dangerous?'

'They don't think he's guilty. Anyway, we fucked up handing the money over for the ransom, having the police involved at this stage could mess up our chances again.'

'I don't understand, what's it all about?'

'There's no time to explain now. I'll tell you when we get there.' David pauses. 'We should go now. We've got a long day ahead and we need some sleep.' The others nod and Julie, George and Suki make a move to leave too.

Rachel says goodnight to everyone, and her eyes linger on Lucy who barely seems to acknowledge they're going. She can't imagine how much pain she must be in or if she'll get a wink of sleep.

55

Back at home, Rachel sits on the bed while David climbs in and within minutes he's asleep. It's almost 2 a.m. and Rachel is exhausted but at the same time wide awake, manically going over and over every detail of the whole evening. Every moment, every glance, every conversation. From before she arrived, suspecting David of being the one behind abducting Shay and the other children, to later, taking in the distraught faces of Lucy and Simon and then the bombshell: finding out about Ethan. Dead. He always had a smile and a joke the few times she saw him. He could be cheeky, leading Shay astray smoking pot and staying out too late, but he didn't deserve to die, for fuck's sake. How can it possibly be true? He and Shay were such happy-go-lucky boys, friends who swapped clothes and listened to music and mucked about together.

She just can't take it in. Shay will be devastated. Does he even know? Were they being kept together? The police said Ethan's body was dumped in a backstreet. Did someone attack him as he walked along the road? Was he shot or stabbed? She doesn't know much about Morocco, but it sounds like it could be a violent place, especially for a white British boy who's never been further from home than Europe. If they've been locked up somewhere since they were taken, how can Ethan have been found dead in the open with people milling around doing their shopping only a few feet away?

David is snoring, sleeping peacefully. He doesn't truly know what it's like to fear for your own child's safety. She lies down on top of the duvet, not bothering to take her clothes off, and reaches for the throw from the bottom of the bed. She drags it over herself, up to her chin. The soft velvet is comforting and warm. It's all she needs right now.

* * *

She wakes at seven to the sound of David in the shower. The memory of last night leaps back into her head. She sits up, eyes wide. They're going to find Shay. There's a horrible twisting feeling in her gut that if they don't hurry, any one of their kids could be next.

Downstairs, she puts the coffee on and goes to wake Mick, who is still asleep on the sofa. He frowns at being woken up, then grins at her still dressed in yesterday's clothes. She explains everything that happened last night and asks if he will stay and look after Josh while she goes to Morocco.

'Maybe I should go instead of you?' he says, sitting up and pulling on his trousers.

'Why?' Rachel asks, leaving his coffee on the table.

'Josh needs you. What if there's some mafia-type gang behind these ransom demands?'

'And you're going to fight them off, are you?' She sips her coffee, hands wrapped around the warmth of the mug.

'Yeah, all right, very funny, but it could be dangerous being a woman in a place like that.' He was like this when they were married. Always trying to clip her wings in case she became too ambitious or more successful than him.

'I'll be with David. Simon and Lucy will be there too.'

'And you're sure you can trust him? I really think I should come too,' Mick says, his voice lowering to a whisper.

'I have to trust him. And who would look after Josh?' Rachel whispers back. 'The police over here don't seem to be any closer to finding out who took our children or where they are. David and the other parents think there's one man behind it. Someone they know.'

'Doesn't seem like lone wolf behaviour to me. Whoever it is more than likely has a gang. You could be walking into all kinds of trouble. Whatever reason they've taken our kids, they're not going to just hand them back, are they?'

'They think it's an old colleague of theirs who was dismissed or struck off for malpractice or something. Whatever it is, they wouldn't tell me.' She takes a moment to calm the fury bubbling inside her. 'All this time they've lied to me about working together. This ex-colleague must have a grudge against all of them. It's nothing to do with me. David has brought this danger on our family.'

'They think? Where's their evidence?'

'David's been searching for him on the internet, but I need to go out there and see for myself what's going on.'

'And what do I say if the police come over asking to speak to you?' He sips his coffee.

'They've got you. You're Shay's dad. Anyway, you'll think of something.'

'I hope you've thought this through Rach, 'cause I'm really not sure this is a good idea.'

'I am not going sit around here for one more day just hoping the police get their shit together and find our son. I have to do whatever it takes.'

'Okay, okay.' Mick nods, avoiding her eye in that way he does because he's worried for her and trying not to show it. Then he comes over and pulls her into a big bear hug.

'It's okay, I'll be fine,' she whispers in his hair, 'although I admit I'm scared.'

She goes up for her shower as David is coming down.

'We need to leave at nine thirty,' he says as they pass each other on the stairs. She knocks lightly on Josh's bedroom door and goes in to make sure he's awake for school and to explain to him about Ethan and their plan to find Shay and the others. She kisses his musty morning hair and hugs him tightly when he starts to cry.

'Why did they have to kill him?' Josh asks. Ethan was always kind to him and often stuck up for him at school.

'We don't know if he was killed. It could have been an accident.' She hopes she sounds convincing because she's not sure of anything herself, and doesn't want Josh thinking it's inevitable that Shay will die too. Just having that thought takes her breath away. Jesus Christ. How did they get to this point? She kisses Josh's hair and discreetly wipes her tears away with her knuckles.

'Do you think Shay's going to be okay?' Josh asks.

'I wish I knew. But I hope so with every shred of me, I really do.'

'Do I have to go to school today?'

'I think it will help you take your mind off things for a while. Dad will be there to pick you up and when he receives any news from us, I'll make sure he tells you straight away. He'll come into school to let you know if necessary.'

'Okay.' Josh bows his head and rests his face on her arm. She ruffles his hair.

'Right, I'm going to shower and pack. You get ready please.'

He gives her a one-armed hug.

'I'll bring your brother back this time, I promise,' she says and kisses his cheek.

56

As soon as Rachel gets Josh off to school with Mick, she goes back upstairs to finish packing.

She's given Mick a door key and as it's Friday, he said he'll probably take Josh over to his place for a pizza later then go to the cinema, make sure he stays occupied.

David drives them to Luton airport, and they catch a plane at midday.

When they touch down in Tangier it's gone four in the afternoon, being an hour ahead. The bright sunshine blasts through the windows of the plane and when the plane doors are opened the heat pushes in on them. As they reach the terminal, David receives a text from Simon to say they've arrived at their hotel.

'They're going to the hospital to identify Ethan's body in an hour,' David says.

Rachel shivers despite the heat. They grab a taxi and make their way to their hotel, which is a short drive from the airport. The aroma of diesel mixed with spices in thirty-degree heat fills the air. Vibrant coloured clothes and silks billow gently in the breeze all around them, together with noise and dust from cars and trucks, beeps from horns and buzzing mopeds like giant bees. In any other circumstances, Rachel would be basking in the heat, soaking up the chaotic array of sounds and colours and scents, but today it's all too much to take in and she can't wait for some peace and quiet, and to lie down on cool cotton sheets.

Their taxi is hardly moving in the heavy afternoon traffic and despite all four windows being open, Rachel is sweating through her clothes. The bustle and noise from outside scrambles her brain so she can't even think. David is sour-faced and barely spoke to her during the three-hour flight. They could hardly discuss the purpose of their journey, near to so many ears. She wasn't in the mood for chatting either, but she's still disappointed they seem to have so little to say to each other.

The smell of rotting food wafts in through the window. Rachel covers her mouth and nose, not caring what it is, she just doesn't want to inhale it again in case she retches. Meat crawling with blow-flies springs to mind.

They pull up outside a hotel and the driver says something she doesn't understand. David hands him a couple of crisp dirham notes and holds his palm up to say keep the change.

Inside the hotel the floor is a mosaic of stone slabs and the walls are covered in blue and white tiles with an intricate Moorish pattern. The foyer is as cool as an English September morning and she's grateful for the relief from the heat. David checks them in and they are taken up in a lift by the bell boy. Their double with an en-suite is surprisingly plain, but it's hardly the time to crave enjoyment or luxury. Lucy and Simon will be shown a dead boy in less than twenty minutes. They will still be hoping it is not their son. If it's not Ethan, then who is it? She can't even go there.

She forfeits a soak in the bath for a speedy refreshing shower. David lies on the bed reading a newspaper he picked up at the airport. He shows her a piece about Simon and Lucy flying to

Morocco to identify the body. The article says Ethan's clothes had name tags ironed on the underside of the labels. Both his trousers and T-shirt identified him, thanks to a skiing trip with the school in February. Ethan also has a mole that can identify him and of course there are always dental records. Did Shay's clothes have labels in too? She doesn't know what he was wearing. Tears prick her eyes. Lucy and Simon will be going in now. She's seen enough crime dramas to know the procedure. Behind glass sometimes. The body under a sheet. But maybe it's a bit different over here.

Not long after, David's mobile beeps. It's a message from Simon.

David stares at his phone for some time. Rachel waits for him to speak, glancing from the phone to his face and back again. Tears are rolling down his cheeks. He drags his hand across his mouth, and she moves closer, wrapping her arms around him. They stay holding each other in silence.

Eventually he pulls away and texts back.

I'm so, so sorry.

'I need to go out, get some air,' he says, reaching for the hotel key.

'I'm coming with you. Where are we going?'

'To find the person who did this.' He swats the rolled-up newspaper on the side of the table.

'Who is he?' She holds his eyes with hers.

'His name is Ralph Mercer. A surgeon, a brilliant one. We went to med school together, became friends and opened the clinic as business partners, but we fell out over a patient whose operation didn't go according to plan. We disagreed about lots of things, but this was... too much. Him leaving was a huge loss to the business. He always wanted to come back here. Help ordinary people. Bring them the sort of health care we take for granted in the UK.'

'Why don't we go to the local police, let them deal with it?'

'You think it's that easy? Why would they believe me?' He shakes his head, disappointed.

'Because you're a well-respected surgeon from the UK.' She's never seen him so angry and agitated.

'So is he. They might go and question him on my say-so if we're lucky, but he'll deny it, laugh it off knowing him, then they've got to look into it, investigate, and that will give him a chance to get away and who knows where he'll operate from next, maybe India or China. No. He's got to be stopped.' David reaches for the door.

'Did Simon say how they think Ethan died?' Rachel's voice is low and small. It feels an intrusion to ask, but she needs to know.

David stops dead, spins back round to face her. 'Ethan was found with a large wound in his side.'

A shiver runs through her.

'Stabbed?' The word catches in her throat.

'No, he'd been cut open and neatly sewn up.' For a second she thinks he's being sarcastic, his surgeon's black humour lost on her, but his face doesn't change and it would be so inappropriate to joke about it.

'What? I don't understand, what do you mean?'

'His left kidney had been removed.'

57

'What?' Rachel jolts at David's answer. 'Presumably taken against his will?'

'Without a doubt.' David opens the hotel room door and shuts it behind them. He crosses the landing and calls the lift.

'And is that how he would have died?' Rachel keeps her voice down so no one can hear them. Maybe it's a stupid question, but she needs to ask. When the lift arrives, they step inside and she presses the button.

'I don't know. It could have been from cardiac arrest on the operating table or a reaction afterwards to the drugs. We'll have to wait for the autopsy report.'

The lift lands on the ground floor and pings to announce its arrival. David strides across the foyer, and she trots after him to keep up. The heat wallops them as soon as they leave the coolness of the hotel. She sticks by his side all the way out to the street, holding her handbag close to her body, having read on the internet about pickpockets and conmen, especially in densely crowded areas of Tangier.

'So they've transplanted Ethan's kidney to someone sick?'

David walks ahead again and she's not sure if he heard her.

'Yes, but without the donor's consent it's known as organ harvesting.'

'Oh God, that's horrific.'

'It happens all over the world. Ethan shouldn't have died from it. Something must have gone wrong.'

'And you think this surgeon you used to work with did this to him?'

'I've got an idea it could be him. Come on,' he says over his shoulder.

'Why would he do this to the son of someone he worked with?' If this man killed Simon's son, what's stopping him killing Shay or any of the others?

David doesn't answer and seems to be walking faster, pulling further and further away from her. She hurries after him and tries to reach out and grab his arm.

'You must know. Tell me what happened between you? You said there was a mistake, and you didn't agree about it. Did someone die? Talk to me, David.' She catches up with him again and links her arm through his, so as not to lose sight of him. The bustle of people and noise on the streets is overwhelming. They push ahead through the crowds around the market. The aroma of fresh fish, ripe fruit and spices fills the air. Vendors try to entice them to buy their vast array of wares, from silks to hand-made trinkets, but they politely hold up a hand or shake their heads and move on.

Further down the street, they reach a small private hospital, a stark white building with classic Moroccan style arched windows among all the bright colours of the other buildings around it. According to the internet and from what David told her, there are lots of hospitals in this district. He's been researching them night after night, trying to track this one man down. It seems after he left

David's practice, none of them knew where he'd gone. They heard he'd moved abroad and wondered if he'd gone back to Morocco.

Outside the hospital entrance is a man with no legs pushing himself along on a low makeshift trolley made from a plank of wood. He holds out his dirty baseball cap with a few coins in the bottom and says something to them in Arabic. His teeth are black to the gums, and it doesn't look like he's changed his clothes in months. She digs around in her pocket and pulls out a handful of dirham coins which she drops into the hat. David tuts at her.

'He'll pester you again when we come out.'

'I don't mind. He clearly needs help. He looks starving and possibly in need of medical attention.'

'It's not that straightforward.' David steers her by the elbow in through the main door, bypassing a haphazard queue in the reception area.

'What do you mean? Don't you agree with helping people less fortunate than you?' She bites her tongue as soon as the words have left her lips.

'Oh no, I never try to save people's lives, do I?'

'I'm sorry, that came out wrong. But what do you mean by it not being straightforward? You always seem to expect me to know things that I haven't got a clue about.'

Using an app on his phone, David is able to translate Arabic to English by taking photos of the signs. She hopes it means he knows where he's going. They turn down a long corridor and up some stairs through a waiting area which is full of patients. It's not as busy as it first seems but everyone is talking at once.

'What I mean is, he may be working for someone else, someone who isn't disabled but is making the poor bastard sit there begging all day for about a tenth of the money he brings in.'

'Do people really do that?'

'Yes, if they can get away with it. So next time buy him something to eat if you want to help him, then at least you know all the benefit is going to him.'

Rachel nods, feeling dumb for not knowing that. It's becoming a theme of their relationship: him finding her unbelievably naïve then telling her off as if he's the adult and she's the child.

'Why hasn't he got prosthetic legs?'

'I doubt very much that's an option for the poor bloke. The health service here is dire and people don't have the same level of confidence in the care patients receive.'

David pauses at a wall of signs in Arabic, not sure which direction to go in.

A woman in a white medical uniform and hair net catches Rachel's eye, making her do a double take. The nurse slips silently out of a door halfway along the corridor, furtively checking around then scurrying away.

'Shit! Did you see that?' Rachel pulls on David's arm. 'That nurse.' She points and starts hurrying after her. 'Come on.'

'What nurse?' He slows down but she waves at him to hurry.

'I'm sure it was her.' She follows the nurse through a side door and down a quiet corridor to what looks like a service lift. They watch the lit-up numbers flash by as it goes down to the lower ground floor. Rachel calls the lift back up.

'Can you please tell me who we're following? We haven't got much time.' David taps his watch.

'Alice Kirby. Except she was dressed in a nurse's uniform. So maybe it couldn't have been her. But her face, those eyes... I'm sure I'm not mistaken.'

David doesn't say anything. Maybe he thinks she's going crazy. The lift arrives and there's no one inside.

'Actually, I don't think we're supposed to use this are we?' Rachel points to the thick red outline which probably means it's for emergencies only. She's half expecting him to doubt her judgement, but suddenly he's the one pulling her to get in with him and hurry up.

When the lift doors open again there is only one person around: a cleaner with a trolley. They get out and look both ways but there's no sign of Alice. The ceiling is much lower and lined with large vent pipes. A sharp smell of disinfectant in the air hits the back of her throat. It's clearly a part of the hospital where medical staff bring things like human and medical waste. There's a symbol of fire on one door ahead, which could be the incinerator. On another closed door is a cross which is either the morgue or chapel of rest.

The door with the cross opens. Startled, they quickly shuffle backwards out of sight and the nurse comes out, followed by a couple huddled together.

'There she is,' Rachel whispers and David follows her line of sight.

Alice looks over her shoulder and down the corridor in their direction as she shuts the door quietly and leads the couple away in the opposite direction. They hear a different lift being called, with a softer whirring sound, probably the one for patients.

'Shit,' David whispers.

58

'Alice Kirby told me she was an actress, and I guess it turns out she was one of sorts,' Rachel says, hurrying after him towards the lift.

'She fed you a pack of lies, that's for sure. The woman I saw back there is definitely Linda Mercer, and if she's here, her husband must be too.' The lift goes up.

'Did she work at your clinic too?'

'For a few years. She was a GP but gave it up when they had kids,' David says. 'You know her coming to be coached by you wasn't real, don't you?'

'But she was grieving. They did lose a child.'

The lift doors open.

'She must have been the one who was leaving parcels on my doorstep.'

'I'd say so.'

They come out of the lift in another part of the hospital. There's no sign of Linda Mercer. Rachel spots the couple that were with her earlier, and Linda is standing by the side of them, partially hidden. Rachel pulls David behind a screen.

'She's with the couple at the check-in desk. Let's see where she goes.'

Linda appears to hand the couple over to someone at the desk, then she digs her hands in her pockets and continues down the corridor away from them. Rachel and David follow, watching her go through a set of sliding doors at the end. David peers through the square of glass.

'The double doors with a red sign above could lead to the theatre. This might be it. Let's get some scrubs on and go in.' David gently pushes open the door and they find a cupboard with new sets of scrubs which they quickly put on over their own clothes. They both finish with hair nets, face masks and gloves.

'Right, follow my lead, head down. Grab a tray to collect medical instruments and let's go in.'

Rachel doesn't have much of a stomach for blood and gore but she's not sure this is the right time to tell David. She stays close behind him as they enter the brightly lit room, fully gowned up.

There's a patient on the operating table covered in blue drapes and surrounded by a medical team. A couple of the theatre staff glance up at them, but David turns toward the bench with purpose. She copies him so they look like they're busy clearing the surgical instruments away. She sneaks another look behind them. A huge bulk of a man in full scrubs has his back to them, standing over the patient while he's being passed instruments by a colleague next to him.

'Right, that's it. Let's sew him up.'

Rachel wasn't expecting such a clear-cut English accent. David pauses, seeming to bristle next to her. He picks up a scalpel and holds it tightly in his fist, the sharp end pointing outwards. Rachel shoots him a look of alarm.

'We're all done here,' the surgeon says a few minutes later. 'Let's get these two into recovery.'

Two? Rachel's mind goes into a spin. She didn't see another patient. Has he just finished another transplant? A shiver runs through her.

'Is that him?' she whispers. David nods.

Ralph Mercer goes off to an adjoining room to clean his hands. As he comes back in, David swings round and faces him, holding the scalpel by his side.

'Whose child have you got on the table this time, Mercer?'

Ralph Mercer's astonishment is slow to register on his face.

'You!' he booms. 'Who let him in here?' He spins around, frantically waving his hands at his team who all shake their heads, bewildered. One of the other doctors hurriedly pushes the first bed towards the double doors. The patient is a girl, a teenager. The second bed is pushed after it by another doctor. Linda Mercer holds up a sheet around the patient as they pass, but Rachel lunges at it, unveiling the pale face of an unconscious boy.

'That's my son!' Rachel shouts and tries to push the nurse out of the way, but she grabs Rachel's wrist and holds it tight. Rachel pulls Linda's mask off. 'How dare you,' she hisses at her.

'Jesus. What have you done to him?' David scuffles with Ralph to try to get closer.

Rachel reaches for Shay's hand, but the doctor is too quick and pushes his bed out of the theatre doors.

'Leave him alone,' Rachel cries, but Linda's hold tightens.

David dodges Ralph and charges towards the exit, grabbing the side of the bed to stop them leaving. He lifts the sheet covering Shay and his face screws up in horror. 'You bastard.'

'No!' Rachel screams and struggles in Linda's hold.

David raises his fist holding the scalpel and lunges at Ralph, but Ralph moves away, leaving him flailing.

'Watch out!' Rachel shouts but it's too late, Ralph shoves David from behind and he drops the scalpel with a clang on the tiled floor, falling flat onto his face.

'Get them to ICU,' Ralph orders and the girl and Shay are wheeled out of the door in their hospital beds. Rachel lets out a small cry as she watches her son go. 'Everyone else out.' The rest of the staff scuttle off, looking over their shoulders in concern.

'Know what if feels like now, don't you?' Linda says and spits at David on the floor.

'What does she mean?' Rachel demands, looking down at David trying to get up. 'What is this really about?' She eyes up the door ready to bolt out of there. Linda squeezes and twists her wrist.

Whatever David's got her mixed up in, all she cares about right now is saving Shay. She stamps as hard as she can on Linda's foot, making her howl in pain. Linda reaches down to pull off her shoe, releasing Rachel.

Ralph stalks towards her. Rachel runs for the door.

'Your boyfriend is responsible for killing our daughter,' Ralph says, blocking her exit.

59

'I'm so sorry for what happened, but it wasn't my fault.' David looks up at Ralph pleadingly, his nose bleeding. Linda stands over him, hand on her hip. Rachel doesn't know who to believe.

'I trusted you,' Ralph bellows at David as he reaches out and clasps Rachel's arms, securing them behind her back in his big hands. Hands which have removed her son's kidney without his consent. Was Shay aware of what they were going to do to him? Nausea hits her throat. She needs to find where the ICU is and make sure Shay is okay. The police need to be called and oh God, she promised to let Mick and Josh know the moment she found him... She falters as her emotions threaten to take over. She grits her teeth and pulls hard against Ralph, but he won't let go of her. She must hold her nerve; she cannot fall apart. She needs to get out of here and take Shay home.

'I did everything I could to save her, you know that.' David pushes himself up, but his nose is dripping blood. He cups his hand around it and groans as Linda pushes him back down.

'It should never have happened,' Ralph says.

'Like Ethan? What did you do to that boy?'

'Simon's boy ran away. He left the hospital and we couldn't find him. He needed to take his drugs and pain relief, but he'd gone. He'd been out of surgery less than twenty-four hours. With the heat and dirt out there on the streets and lack of food and water...'

'Why are you doing this to our children?' Rachel tries to pull her arm out of Ralph's hold. 'Grooming them online, taking intimate photos of them, threatening them with exposure if they didn't pay up. What kind of sick bastards are you?'

'That was our son's clever idea,' Linda says. 'A way of ensuring the children complied with our rules: gain their trust and let them know they owed us.'

'They hadn't done anything wrong. They were scared stiff. Do you know they contemplated taking their own lives? And you, coming into my house, pretending you needed my help when all the time you were spying on me, leaving me packages, covering up the camera, enjoying watching me suffer. What did I or my son ever do to either of you?'

'You got caught up with the wrong man. Burning his house down failed, so we worked out how to make money while getting him back for what he did to our family. He doesn't have children of his own, so your son was the next best thing.'

'Where's my money?' David shouts, trying to sit up.

'Is that what's more important to you?' Rachel asks, pulling to get away from Ralph and his hot sour breath.

'No, of course not. And I'm so sorry you got caught up in this,' David says to her, but she won't look at him.

'You're sorry? I have a son who's been violated. Left with only one kidney.' She knees Ralph in his leg but he holds her tighter. 'I hope you're going to destroy the images you have of him and the other children.'

'We didn't keep them. What do you think we are? Anyway, the recipient of your son's generous donation is a local girl who has been on dialysis for three years. Shay has gifted her a new life. You should be pleased. You should be thanking me.' Ralph raises one hand in triumph.

'Her parents paid you good money for Shay's kidney? And now they're in debt?' David asks. He explained to Rachel on the flight over how private clinics like this charge the earth for medical procedures. It's unlikely to be available through the public healthcare system because of how poorly funded it is.

'You've always had so little faith in me, David.' Ralph's warm breath envelopes Rachel as he turns to her. 'He's always been envious of me, from right back at med school. When Linda chose me, he was heartbroken.'

'You always have to go too far don't you, Ralph? The class show-off.'

'You flatter me, David. I was merely striving for bigger things. You should come out here and join me. As you can see, business is booming. People are crying out for donors, and we've sourced a steady stream of them.'

'Not only did you kidnap Shay and the other children to be donors, you've been preying on the poorest people around here. Am I right? Paying them a pittance for their kidneys then charging the richest patients for a brand-new organ?'

'We're performing a service. They don't have a culture of donation here but we're striving to change that.'

'I think you'll find that's illegal. I thought you wanted to come here to help people.'

'And I am. We're a private enterprise; all medical procedures have to be paid for. We pay a fair price to the local donors for the gift they are passing on. Money which helps their families thrive.'

'What about the price our children have paid? You took Shay's kidney against his will. You kidnapped him. You attacked a girl and left her for dead.'

Ralph smiles down at Rachel's face, his dull blue eyes pitying her.

'How did you get him to Morocco without the police finding any trace?' she asks.

'In the back of a transit van. Quite easy when they're sleeping.' Linda smirks.

'You mean you drugged them?'

'Drove down to Spain, hopped over to Gibraltar then took the ferry to Tangier; only an hour crossing.'

'How were they not found?'

'We made a cosy little area hidden behind the driver and passenger seats. Perfect for sleeping children and don't worry, there was plenty of air circulating. Once we were back on the road, we could pass water and food to them, make sure they were comfortable.'

'You're sick!' Rachel pulls again to try to release her arms from him. His hands touching her makes her skin crawl.

'He hasn't told you anything about what happened, has he?' Ralph's laugh is hollow and sends a chill through her. 'The children needed to pay for what their parents did to my Daisy. Taking a kidney from each of them is nothing compared to what she went through. They still get to live normal lives and enjoy themselves.'

'Except Ethan,' David says, pushing himself up, past Linda.

'That was his own doing,' Linda says, scowling at him.

'The whole medical team failed our daughter, especially him.' Ralph points at David who shakes his head slowly. He wets a paper towel and holds it to his nose, leaning over the sink.

'I don't understand what he could have done to warrant you treating our children like this?' Rachel's voice rises.

'He carried out a transplant on our daughter, who had kidney failure from a very young age. I gave one of my kidneys to save her. We were a perfect match. It was meant to be, and I trusted him above everyone to do the operation. I trusted him with her life, but he and his medical team messed it up and our darling girl died on the operating table.'

A whimper escapes from Linda's lips.

'I'm so sorry,' Rachel whispers, not wanting to look at David but at the same time wishing he could have confided in her. The guilt he must carry with him at a little girl dying under his care, even if it was out of his control. It must have triggered memories of losing his sister and be the reason why he's on anti-depressants.

The large beast of a man finally lets go of her arms and sits down in a chair, slumping backwards into it heavily. He drags his palm across his face and Linda goes to him, where she wraps her arms around his head, rocking them both gently back and forth.

60

Rachel darts out of the theatre doors and runs along the corridor, asking anyone who might understand English where the Intensive Care Unit is. A couple of people point towards another set of double doors. She goes straight through them, not caring if she's allowed to or not.

'Shay, Shay!' she calls, even though he's probably still unconscious. A male nurse comes towards her, and she expects him to escort her out, but he indicates to the bed by the door. Shay is lying there still and pale, eyes shut. She takes his hand in hers and kisses it. It seems so fragile. 'Mummy's here now, sweetheart.' Her heart fills up being with him at last. She gently hugs him, tears in her eyes. She wants to shout out: he's alive, he's alive!

She steps outside and quickly texts Mick to say she's found Shay. Mick texts back straight away.

Can we speak to him?

He must have been carrying the phone everywhere with him waiting for her call.

Not just yet.

She doesn't want to explain what's happened over text.

I'll call you when I get back to the hotel later.

She goes back into ICU and kisses Shay's forehead then rests her cheek on his bed, not letting go of his hand.

A commotion outside rouses her from briefly shutting her eyes: loud voices speaking Arabic and the sound of heavy boots running past. She hopes it's the police coming for Ralph and Linda. Several minutes later, David opens the door and looks round. She turns away, unable to look at his face or speak to him. It's his fault that her son has ended up here in hospital, his kidney stolen from him. There's not a cell in her body that will be able to forgive David. She flicks a momentary glance his way but he's not getting the message to leave her alone, so she drags herself away from Shay's bed, telling herself he may have important news.

'They tried to make a run for it, but security have managed to catch up with them and the police are on their way.'

She nods, not trusting herself to speak to him in a measured way. Her boy has been cut open. She's not sure how she'll ever get past the moment of horror at realising it was him on the operating table. The deep suffocating hurt and upset bubbling in her chest right now wants to spill out into a cascade of words she won't be able to take back. And there are so many questions she needs answers to, but they will have to wait until another day. David's face is drained and troubled when she leaves him standing there and returns to Shay's bedside.

It is some hours later, after she's spoken to the police, when David comes back again to let her know Simon has arrived.

She follows David out to the corridor. He says he's going off to find a drink.

Simon's face is haggard. He looks so diminished now from the confident person she first met that she automatically opens her arms and hugs him. He hugs her back tightly and asks how Shay is. He tells her that Ethan's body will be brought home in a few days once the British Embassy have sorted out the paperwork. Lucy is exhausted, sleeping at the hotel.

'I'm so glad you found Shay, but sorry for what Ralph has done to him,' he says, pain etched on his face, no doubt thinking of Ethan going through the same operation.

'It's okay, it's not your fault.'

'But I'm sorry we didn't tell you we all worked together, that we suspected Ralph might be something to do with it. Don't take it out on David. It wasn't his fault Daisy died. She had a rare reaction to the anaesthetic. We were all so devastated when it happened but never thought Ralph and Linda would turn on us. I guess it was impossible to come to terms with. It was easier for them to blame us.'

Rachel thanks him and gives her best wishes for Lucy. His head is down as he walks away and her heart aches for his terrible loss. She's not sure she can forgive David for not being honest with her from the beginning. She's not naïve enough to think that nothing ever goes wrong in operations, but he chose not to confide in her and that's because they never had a close enough relationship. She shouldn't have asked him to move in.

David approaches from the other end of the corridor.

'Can we talk?' He's holding two polystyrene cups.

She nods and takes a herbal tea from him and follows him to a quiet seated area along the corridor. The minty aroma is refreshing after the chemical smell of intensive care.

'Olly, Nate and Kim have been found in hospital beds on a

ward,' he tells her. 'They've been having tests and checks to see if they are a match for any of the patients waiting for a transplant, so they were lined up ready to be donors too. The Embassy are contacting their parents to fly them over and take them home.'

'I'm pleased. They're the lucky ones,' she says.

'Are you coming back to the hotel?' His nose is red and swollen from where he landed on it. 'You look like you could do with a rest and something to eat.'

'I don't think so. You go. I want to stay with Shay until he's well enough to travel home.'

'Can you forgive me?' he blurts out, his eyes pleading with her.

'Simon says not to blame you, but how can I not? You've deliberately lied to me. If you'd told me about letting Shay go to the party straight away, I might have been able to stop him being kidnapped.'

'I know, and I'm sorry, it was my bad judgement. I had no idea he would come to any harm.'

'No parent knows if or when their child might come to harm, but we try to minimise it by putting sensible rules in place, teaching our children not to lie to us.'

'I'm sorry. I undermined you. I thought I was letting him spread his wings.'

His words wash over her. She stares at him in disbelief.

'It's the going behind my back. Thinking you could become best friends with him by giving in to him, working against me by keeping secrets. And then not telling me all the other parents were your colleagues? I don't understand. Why couldn't you trust me?' Her voice rises in a fresh wave of incredulity. Nothing he says will dampen her burning rage.

'Because we didn't know if there was a link, and I admit I didn't want you to know about Daisy. I didn't cope well when she died. I blamed myself.' His eyes fix on the floor.

'You couldn't confide in me.' He was on anti-depressants and she didn't know why. All this time she thought they were good together, special. This is her failing too. Rushing in, constructing a fairy tale relationship in her head, assuming he felt the same. Her eyes shut for a moment. She's already sure. Her words are cold and calm. 'It's over, David.'

He nods once at her dismissal as though he was waiting for it. He stands up, knocks back his drink and walks away.

Rachel strides straight back into ICU, and as though he knows, Shay's eyes flutter open.

'Shay, it's Mum. How are you feeling?' He doesn't seem to focus, and his eyes shut again. Is he aware of what they've done to him?

He makes a small sound like an injured animal. His eyes open wide.

'Are you okay, are you in pain?'

He shakes his head.

'It's so good to have you back.' Her eyes fill with tears. Does he know Ethan is dead? Did they discuss the idea of him running away from the hospital to try to get help? If he hadn't, the story wouldn't have made the international news. They may never have found them.

Shay blinks at her and tears form in his eyes. She leans over and hugs him, trying not to knock the wires and tubes plugged into his body. Whatever happens now, at least she has her son back, and thank goodness he's alive.

EPILOGUE

FOUR MONTHS LATER

Rachel's got a new client coming in an hour. Just enough time to prep the slow cooked lamb for dinner. Mick's coming over this evening. They're in a better place now and are properly co-parenting. None of the bickering of the old days. Sometimes she fantasises about them getting back together. She still loves him. But for now, it's working like this, so why spoil it? He stays over occasionally. The boys don't have to know; she doesn't want to get their hopes up. It suits them. They're both single again so they can do what they like.

David moved out as soon as he got back to the UK. She didn't even have to ask him. By the time she returned with Shay a few days later, he'd gone. Taken all his stuff. The police are recovering his money so at least she doesn't have to worry about paying it back. They talk occasionally, but she has the feeling it will peter out eventually. Maybe if she'd known about the guilt he was carrying around with him, and the reason why he was on medication for depression, she could have supported him, got to know him better, empathised with him.

Simon and Lucy weren't sure about contacting the recipient of Ethan's kidney to start with. They found out a bit about Larah, a mother of two small children, and now they receive updates on her progress. It's going a long way to helping them come to terms with their loss.

'Mum, I'm going now, see you later.'

Rachel rushes out to the hall where Shay is standing in his uniform and new coat. His first full day back at school.

'I've made you a sandwich.' She hands him a small plastic bag of wrapped food. He opens his mouth, probably about to complain, but shuts it again and she hugs him. Always tighter and for a bit longer than they used to.

He's become a bit of a local celebrity since he came back from Morocco. Aidan and Finlay joke that he's had a personality transplant because his outlook is so positive after his experience. His therapist says it's the elation stage of survivor syndrome. At first, when he found out about Ethan, he sank into a deep depression, wondered why his friend had died instead of him, but the therapist helped him reframe it by thinking of Ethan as his hero because he knew he was putting his life at risk for his friends. It was their duty to have a good and happy life. Ethan wouldn't want any of them to be moping about. After that, it was like a switch had flicked in Shay's head.

'Mind the road, won't you?' She unlocks the door and waves him off. The postman is whistling along the road and says hello to Shay as he walks up their path. He hands her a bundle of letters, and she spots the one from Maya straight away by the butterfly patterned envelope. She's tempted to run after Shay so he can take it with him and read it during his lunch break. But it can wait. It'll be a nice treat for when he comes home. He and Maya have become great friends since she was given his kidney. She's learning English and writes to him every week on fancy paper he sent to her, and she always reminds him that her life is back to normal thanks to him. It's the most wonderful outcome from this otherwise dark situation.

It's helped them all to heal knowing that her life has been saved because of what happened to Shay.

She stands on the doorstep on tiptoes until he turns the corner in the distance out of sight. He's as grateful to be home as she is to have him there, knowing he's safe. She doubts that feeling will ever wear off.

ACKNOWLEDGMENTS

I wrote this novel primarily for myself and for my readers. It's a little different from my previous novels, but still very much hardwired to the domestic suspense genre – an ordinary family plunged into a desperate situation. I needed to tell this story whether anyone was going to publish it or not! Elements of it are personal to me and my family, as well as to my husband's family.

I was absolutely delighted when I heard that Emily Yau and the team at Boldwood Books wanted to publish, *Gone*. Thank you so much for bringing it to the reading world. I'm eternally grateful. Emily's astute and thoughtful editing has ensured *Gone* is the thrilling story I hoped it would be.

Huge thanks too, to Candida Bradford for her thorough copy-edit. Her little comments of enjoyment were so encouraging. Thank you too to my proofreader, Rachel Sargeant. Your enthusiasm for this story gave me a real boost!

Thank you to the cover designer, Aaron Munday, for coming up with such an atmospheric design, and thank you to the Boldwood marketing team: Amanda Ridout CEO, Nia Beynon, Claire Fenby, Sue Lamprell and Jenna Houston for all your hard work on my book.

Thank you as always to my fabulous agent, Jo Bell for her support, and thank you to the team at Bell Lomax Moreton.

Special thanks to my early reader friends, Susan Elliot-Wright and Rose McGinty, for believing in the story I was determined to tell. Thank you, Susan, for reading my manuscript almost as quickly as I was writing it (towards the end anyway!) and giving vital early feedback and reaction. Thank you, Rose, for your kindness and encouragement through our various difficult times while writing this book, and for your medical and geographic advice. Thank you to the many other supportive friends online and in real life, including: Mandy Byatt, Sally Harris, Lucille Grant, Sophie Flynn, Charly Cox, Alex Chaudhuri, Helga Jensen, Sara N. Cox, Jude Brown and Caroline Priestly.

Without the constant support and encouragement of my husband Richard, I could not write as much as I do. Thank you as always to my children, Charlie, Edward and Sophie, who inspire me every day in their different ways. I've changed some of the location details to fit the story, but Bayhurst woods is a real place in Harefield, Uxbridge. Thank you to my parents for being the constant rocks in my life, and for feeding my imagination from my earliest years. I owe you both everything.

Finally, in memory of our dear family friend, Lloyd Ridgwell. He was one of my oldest and dearest readers, who died unexpectedly as I was completing the edits for this book. He told me he'd rediscovered the love of reading through my novels and each time one was published, he would buy a copy and post it to me to sign and send back. He will be sadly missed.

Also, in memory of Richard's Auntie Val, who was taken from us too soon.

MORE FROM RUBY SPEECHLEY

We hope you enjoyed reading *Gone*. If you did, please leave a review.

If you'd like to gift a copy, this book is also available as an ebook, large print, hardback, digital audio download and audiobook CD.

Sign up to the Ruby Speechley mailing list for news, competitions and updates on future books:

https://bit.ly/RubySpeechleyNews

ABOUT THE AUTHOR

Ruby Speechley is a bestselling psychological thriller writer, whose titles include *Someone Else's Baby*. Previously published by Hera, she has been a journalist and worked in PR and lives in Cheshire.

Visit Ruby's website: www.rubyspeechley.com

Follow Ruby on social media:

facebook.com/Ruby-Speechley-Author-100063999185095

twitter.com/rubyspeechley

instagram.com/rubyjtspeechley

THE

Murder

LIST

THE MURDER LIST IS A NEWSLETTER DEDICATED TO SPINE-CHILLING FICTION AND GRIPPING PAGE-TURNERS!

SIGN UP TO MAKE SURE YOU'RE ON OUR HIT LIST FOR EXCLUSIVE DEALS, AUTHOR CONTENT, AND COMPETITIONS.

SIGN UP TO OUR NEWSLETTER

BIT.LY/THEMURDERLISTNEWS

Boldwood

Boldwood Books is an award-winning fiction
publishing company seeking out the best
stories from around the world.

Find out more at www.boldwoodbooks.com

Join our reader community for brilliant books,
competitions and offers!

Follow us
@BoldwoodBooks
@BookandTonic

**Sign up to our weekly
deals newsletter**

https://bit.ly/BoldwoodBNewsletter